William Trevor was born in Mitchelstown, Co Cork, in 1928, and spent his childhood in provincial Ireland. He attended a number of Irish schools and later Trinity College, Dublin. He is a member of the Irish Academy of Letters.

Among his books are *The Old Boys* (1964), winner of the Hawthornden Prize, *The Boarding House* (1965), *The Love Department* (1966), *Mrs Eckdorf in O'Neill's Hotel* (1969), *Miss Gomez and the Brethren* (1971), *Elizabeth Alone* (1973), *The Children of Dynmouth* (1976), winner of the Whitbread Award, *The Distant Past* (1979), *Other People's Worlds* (1980), *Fools of Fortune* (1983), winner of the Whitbread Award, *A Writer's Ireland* (1984), *The Silence in the Garden* (1988), winner of the *Yorkshire Post* Book of the Year Award, and *Two Lives* (1991), which was shortlisted for the *Sunday Express* Book of the Year Award and includes the Booker-shortlisted novella *Reading Turgenev*. Many of his books are published by Penguin. His collections of short stories are *The Day We Got Drunk on Cake* (1967), *The Ballroom of Romance* (1972), *Angels at the Ritz* (1975), winner of the Royal Society of Literature Award, *Lovers of Their Time* (1978), *Beyond the Pale* (1981), *The News from Ireland* (1986) and *Family Sins* (1989), all of which are published by Penguin in *Collected Stories*, together with four stories not included in previous collections. He has published a collection of autobiographical essays, *Excursions in the Real World* (1993) and is the editor of *The Oxford Book of Irish Short Stories* (1989). He has also written plays for the stage and for radio and television. Several of his television plays have been based on his short stories. In 1976 William Trevor received the Allied Irish Banks' Prize, and in 1977 was awarded an honorary CBE in recognition of his valuable services to literature. In 1992 he received the *Sunday Times* Award for Literary Excellence.

WILLIAM TREVOR

Other People's Worlds

PENGUIN BOOKS

PENGUIN BOOKS

Published by the Penguin Group
Penguin Books Ltd, 27 Wrights Lane, London W8 5TZ, England
Penguin Books USA Inc., 375 Hudson Street, New York, New York 10014, USA
Penguin Books Australia Ltd, Ringwood, Victoria, Australia
Penguin Books Canada Ltd, 10 Alcorn Avenue, Toronto, Ontario, Canada M4V 3B2
Penguin Books (NZ) Ltd, 182–190 Wairau Road, Auckland 10, New Zealand

Penguin Books Ltd, Registered Offices: Harmondsworth, Middlesex, England

First published in Great Britain by The Bodley Head 1980
First published in the United States of America by The Viking Press 1981
Published in Penguin Books 1982
5 7 9 10 8 6

Printed in England by Clays Ltd, St Ives plc
Photoset in 10/12 pt Plantin

To Jane

Contents

· I ·
Julia's

All over the Gloucestershire countryside the poppies that summer were delicate on sunny banks, cowparsley and campion profuse. The japonica bloomed as it hadn't for years in the garden of Swan House, as if already celebrating the wedding there was to be. It was not Henrietta Ferndale of that house, nor her sister Katherine, who intended to marry, although both had reached marrying age: it was their mother Julia, an army officer's widow for almost exactly nine years. But Henrietta and Katherine, both of whom had left the small town of Stone St Martin for the greater excitements of London, were delighted about the coming event; so was Mrs Anstey, Julia's mother, who lived with her in Swan House; and Mrs Spanners, who came to clean it once a week.

Most delighted of all was Julia herself, who on a warm Wednesday afternoon was one of four women pinkly draped in Stone St Martin's Crowning Glory Salon. Simon, who ran the place – the best friend of Arthur, who had the flower-shop next door – spared a moment for all the ladies, while attending himself to old, deaf Mrs Anstruther, who never missed her Wednesday appointment in the Crowning Glory. There was another salon in Stone St Martin, cheaper by quite a bit, but reputed to be dirty.

'Such weather, Mrs Ferndale!' Diane remarked, and when Julia murmured a reply the girl went on to speak about her parents' opinion of her boyfriend, Nevil Clapp. 'I mean,' she finished up eventually, 'they're not being fair.'

The hair that Diane snipped at was short and brown, with quite some grey in it. Faint little lines had begun to blink around Julia's eyes, coming or going with changes of expression or mood; a few faint freckles had always been just visible on her forehead. At forty-seven her round face was not yet empty of the beauty that had once distinguished it: now and again it echoed in her smile, or in the depths of her blue-green eyes. Her mother had once said that Julia had a look of a Filippo Lippi madonna, a similar delicacy in profile, the same reddish tinge in her hair. But there was plumpness now as well: Julia's daughters had stolen the madonna look.

'I'm sorry,' she said in reply to Diane's protest about the unfairness of her parents, and yet felt sympathy for them. Parental doubt was understandable, since Nevil Clapp was currently on probation after the thieving of a car battery and other items from the Red Robin filling station. He was now working in the Orchard Motel on the Cheltenham road, having sworn to a bench of magistrates that he had turned over a new leaf.

'First thing my dad said was Nevil's a criminal. And Mum: was I pregnant?'

Julia tried to nod. She knew a lot about Diane's life, being by nature a listener, but this afternoon she found it hard to concentrate.

'I'd never get pregnant, Mrs Ferndale. I didn't know where to look when Mum said it.'

'Parents do worry,' Julia said, hoping she wasn't sounding vague.

It still seemed extraordinary to her that she was to marry again, that she had fallen so completely and so passionately in love with a man who was fourteen years younger than she was. It seemed extraordinary that she no longer belonged in the shadows cast by her daughters and her mother, for since Roger Ferndale's death she had become used to occupying the background, though not unhappily. In the yard of a barracks near Berlin he had fallen from his horse and was later discovered to be dead. There had been no history of heart trouble, but a heart attack had appeared to be the cause of death. 'Some kind of blackout, Mrs Ferndale,' a military doctor had informed her, bewildered himself and unwilling to be more precise. The funeral had been grimmer than it might have been because of the military honours, and the return to England had collected an extra note of finality because it was the end of army life, of all the trekking about there had been, married quarters in Germany and Malaya, in Africa and Singapore. Coming home, Julia had settled into Swan House and the doziness of Stone St Martin. It was the house her mother had moved to when years ago she had sold Anstey's Mill, a grander residence, outside the town; it was where Henrietta and Katherine had often spent their school holidays when their parents were abroad; and it seemed the natural place for Julia in her unexpected widowhood. Reduced in circumstances, she had set about making ends meet by typing legal documents for a firm of solicitors in the town, Warboys, Smith and Toogood. She did so still, working at home on an antiquated Remington, in the kitchen or the drawing-room, whenever she had a moment. Over the years the payments she received had enabled her to employ Mrs Spanners and, until his retirement a month ago, to have old Mr Pocock on Saturday mornings to help with the heavy work in the garden. In spite of the loneliness which had replaced a contented marriage, she considered that good fortune had not deserted her.

'You know what I mean, Mrs Ferndale?'

'Yes, of course.'

The conversation had changed. Julia was told about the plans of Diane's sister to become a physiotherapist, but again she found concentration difficult. 'I thought you might be a Catholic,' Francis Tyte had said, early in their relationship, delighting her when he confessed that he was one himself. For many generations the Ansteys had been a Catholic family; Julia had been sent to St Mildred's Convent near Stratford-upon-Avon and had later carried the family tradition on. She was not devout, but had never been able to think of life without God, without the sacraments and the mass. Her daughters had gone to St Mildred's also, though they had afterwards abandoned religion with an ease that had distressed her at the time. Roger Ferndale had not shared her faith, nor did her mother: it seemed like a treat, plucked out of nowhere, when Francis made his revelation.

'I just want to try this,' Diane murmured, fiddling at the back of Julia's head and bringing her down to earth by causing her to feel nervous. She was well aware of Diane's opinion that much more could be done with her hair, but had no wish to feel like mutton dressed as lamb, as her mother would have said. 'Bouffant would suit you, you know,' Diane had once suggested, and with greater daring had even mentioned rinses.

Unable quite to see what was happening at the back, Julia issued a slight protesting noise. She had made this appointment at the Crowning Glory because of the handful of people who were coming to Swan House that evening for drinks. Father Lavin, who had already met Francis several times, would be present, but there would be others who did not yet know him, including Father Lavin's curate, Father Dawne. The two priests would be urged to stay to dinner, as usually they were on such occasions. In a cream-coloured house on the outskirts of the town they did their own catering, and because Julia assumed they didn't feed themselves properly priestly meals at Swan House now and again took place. During the one tonight she had no wish to have the back of her head looking funny.

'Just a little spring,' Diane assured. 'Nothing you'd notice, Mrs Ferndale, only it needs a touch of lift. Mrs Anstey keeping well, is she?'

'Yes, thank you.'

'And Mr Tyte?'

'He's very well too. You're not doing anything too elaborate, are you, Diane?'

'Heavens, no. Finished in a sec. I see Mr Tyte's in that ad again. With the pipe.'

'Yes, he is.'

Since it had become known that she was to remarry, the identity of her fiancé had been of interest in Stone St Martin and its neighbourhood. 'A famous actor,' people had said at first, and so he had remained, though the parts Francis were offered were never large. In the realm of television advertisements he had established himself as a figure with a particular English charm and a smile that stayed in the mind. He was currently on show in a series which promoted a brand of tobacco.

'Anything new to watch out for, is there?' Diane inquired, holding up a glass so that Julia could see the back of her head.

'Oh, that's quite nice. Thank you, Diane.' Rehearsals were about to begin, she added: the reconstruction of a famous Victorian murder.

'Sounds exciting, Mrs Ferndale.'

'Yes, it probably may be.'

The pink wrap was lifted from Julia's shoulders. 'I hope your parents come to see your point of view,' she said, giving Diane her tip.

Diane made a face, and Julia said goodbye. She had to shop in the town, which she intended to do in a leisurely way because of the heat. 'Goodbye, Mrs Ferndale,' Simon called after her, looking up from the grey, scant hair of old Mrs Anstruther. Julia paused to smile at him before she left the salon.

Geographically, Stone St Martin was simple, comprising for the most part a street on a hill called Highhill Street. Lesser streets ran off to the left and right, rows of houses rather than shops, residential tributaries that further from the town's centre blossomed into modest suburbs. The green sign of Lloyd's Bank hung at the corner of a Cotswold stone building, the Lloyd's architecture as familiar as the black horse that danced on the sign itself. The same yellow-grey stone was ubiquitous elsewhere: the gaunt King's Head was built of it, so was the Anglican church at the top of Highhill Street, and the Courtesy Cleaners and the old wool bank, now the co-op. The Bay Tree Café was different, all black timber beams and white stucco, a style reflected in the building which contained the Crowning Glory, a bread shop, and Moate & Greenly, estate agents. But the sub-offices of insurance companies and building societies were of the local stone, as were grocers' shops and newsagents', the Post Office, Baxter's the Butcher's, Super Cycles, the Midland Bank, and two schools. There wasn't a great deal more to Stone St Martin except a set of traffic-lights, and the offices of Warboys, Smith and Toogood, Solicitors and Commissioners for Oaths.

Beyond the town, on another hill, there was Julia's church:

dating from 1451 but tidily renovated in 1923, the Church of St Martin was named after St Martin of Braga for reasons which remained obscure. It was the centre of a far-flung parish, Father Lavin and his curate being responsible for several other churches in the area, as the priests of Stone St Martin had been since the Reformation. In her childhood Julia had often visited the cream-coloured priests' house to unburden to an elderly confessor her many worries about her own inadequacy.

It was in childhood, also, that she had begun to keep the diaries which nobody except herself had ever read. *When I was seven*, she had written, long after the event, *I stole Melissa's pencil-sharpener. For weeks I hadn't been able to resist it because it was a globe of the world as well.* Melissa afterwards became her best friend, occupying the bed next to hers in the Green Dormitory at St Mildred's. But Julia had never told her about the pencil-sharpener. *Sister Burkardt doesn't like me*, she'd written also. *She looks at me and I can feel her thinking that but for the accident to her face her features would be quite like mine. We have the same arrangement in our faces, the same bones, eyes of the same colour, a mouth that's quite alike. Yet Sister Burkardt is ugly and I am not. I feel she has picked me out as the pupil most to resent, though she tries never to let it show and always smiles. She takes it out on others, and on girls who aren't pretty either. I feel so sorry for her, and pray for her.*

In Julia's diaries there remained her childhood vision of the God she still addressed: greyly bearded and venerable in a tropical garden, mistily depicted, as if viewed through gauze or cloud. Only the eyes were startling: among jungly foliage, where birds with coloured plumage flew and where fruit, not quite identified, was richly vivid, her God was a watching presence. *You know He is there*, she wrote, *as people sense a ghost.* She had wept over the betrayal and the crown of thorns, and the story of Mary Magdalene. *Sister Murray considers the English an agnostic people*, she wrote while still at St Mildred's. *She asked for questions after she had said so in her provocative way, but no one had any. No one inquired if it would be stifling for Catholics such as we are to live among the naturally religious, the Spanish or the Italians for instance. Sister*

Murray passed on to something else, a definition of piety I think. Years afterwards Julia considered these observations silly and tore the page from her diary. *I am going to be a nun,* she had declared when she was ten, and had torn that out as well.

Her engagement to an army officer was in a diary also, a long résumé of her friendship with him, her searching for guidance through the entanglements of romance. She had known Roger Ferndale for as long as she could remember. They had played together as children, he was the first man to kiss her. After that she had developed an interest in military matters, in his regiment and his career, in tennis, at which he was good. She had supposed she was in love with him and apparently had been right. There was a honeymoon in Wales, and then the years abroad, the birth of Henrietta and Katherine, and finally the death that broke everything apart. The death itself – and being a mother and a widow – was recorded in lines that revealed a certain stoicism, for Julia's tendency was to find herself haunted by plights that were not her own. Her own she could somehow cope with, but long after she had left St Mildred's, even after her husband's death, she was uneasily concerned whenever she thought of the unhappy nun.

Perhaps the trouble with Sister Burkardt was that the contemplation of so many girls growing up was too much for her. When I think of her I see her as a girl with a looking-glass, making the decision to take the veil so that she could hide away instead of feeling rejected. But she couldn't lose her longing to be beautiful, reminded of it cruelly by the faces all around, my own perhaps in particular. She left the convent and later left the order. Was it Sally Fryer who came across her working in a shop that sold sacred objects?

Julia's mother, whose opinion Julia did not lightly dismiss, considered this kind of concern misplaced; and so, privately, did Julia's daughters. 'You have an innocence I don't possess,' Mrs Anstey used to say when Julia was a girl. 'There's a sense of guilt which comes from that.' But Julia preferred to accept whatever facts there were: her mother was a different kind of person, her view of people sharper, her charity differently disposed, it wasn't something to argue about. And because relationships within the family had always been tinged with this old-fashioned politeness, the emerging of Francis Tyte as a possible bridegroom had at first been a signal for tact rather than a display of even the faintest doubt. Conversations had taken place – Julia's mother and her daughters equally contributing – and in the end it was quite naturally accepted that an actor could be an army officer's successor without undue courting of folly. The difference in age of course didn't matter, Mrs Anstey had set the mood by proclaiming.

We'd been shopping in Cheltenham, Julia wrote a week after she'd first met Francis. *In the lounge of the Queen's Hotel there was a man whose face seemed just familiar, though we'd never heard of him when he told us his name and that he was an actor. Fair-haired and rather elegant, a look of Leslie Howard. One day, he promised, he'll come and see us in Stone St Martin, for time is sometimes on his hands in Cheltenham. He doesn't live there. In Folkestone, I think he said. Francis Tyte he's called.*

'Boursin,' she said in Dobie's Stores. 'The one with garlic if you have it, please.' She smiled at the ageing assistant who had served her since she was a child, but who now apologetically replied that today he could offer her no Boursin with garlic in it. 'Edam, Mr Humphreys? About six ounces, please.'

'Oh yes, there's Edam, ma'am.' He cut with his cheese-wire into a new scarlet ball of it while telling her about his ailing father. Again she found the necessary concentration difficult. Three weeks had to pass before the wedding and the honeymoon in Italy; after that the plan was that Francis should continue his theatrical career, while living in Swan House. Longing for the time to go by made Julia feel like a schoolgirl again, a pleasant, reckless feeling, part of being in love. She nodded at Mr Humphreys, not hearing or caring what he said.

A single pool of shade was cast by the tulip tree beneath which Julia's mother sat in a high-backed wicker chair, her two walking-sticks crooked over each of its arms. The tulip tree was at the bottom of the narrow garden, on a lawn that ran to the edge of the river. Swans had once congregated here, picking the spot out and giving Swan House its name. It was a favourite place of Mrs Anstey's also.

She had been reading the first pages of *Martin Chuzzlewit*, but no longer did so. In the distance, near to the house, the man who was soon to be her son-in-law continued to weed a flowerbed: idly she watched him. Since old Mr Pocock had had to give up his work in the garden Julia had been trying to find someone else, but on her engagement to Francis Tyte this search had seemed less urgent. 'I think I'll quite like gardening,' Francis had said and ever since, whenever he came to stay for a few days at Swan House, he had been content to do whatever jobs he was allocated.

Mrs Anstey was a small woman with sharp blue eyes that in certain lights appeared to be black. Her face was tight, like a knob, her white hair hidden away now beneath a brimmed white hat. Her body, twisted out of shape with arthritis, retained a certain compactness, though its affliction meant that she could not move without the assistance of her walking-sticks. In her wicker chair she wore a green dress with small white dots on it, which she did not intend to change when people later came to drinks.

She had placed *Martin Chuzzlewit* on a beech-wood table beside her chair. She picked it up again, then hesitated because she noticed that Francis had stood up from his task and was approaching her, dawdling down the narrow garden. On either side of him were high stone walls with plum- and pear-trees on them, and flowerbeds lively with daisy bushes and aubretia. She observed his advance, wondering if she could tell from his walk what part he was passing the time by playing. Of average height, lean and fair-haired, he was dressed in a grey-striped shirt and matching trousers. Too distant for her yet to discern, his features registered in Mrs Anstey's imagination: eyes dimly blue, mouth not quite thin, his smile the element that made him handsome, reminding television viewers – as it had reminded Julia – of the late Leslie Howard. He strolled past quince and broom, through arches of trailing clematis, across the rose garden. When he was close to her she saw he carried, limply in his left hand, a leaf from a hosta.

'No, not a weed,' she said.

'Well, I haven't pulled it up.' He smiled, causing the angularities of his face to soften. The way he'd held the hosta leaf towards her had reminded her of another, or a continued, theatrical interpretation, as if greater significance should be attached to the gesture than the gesture itself implied. From being casually borne, the leaf had abruptly become precious, proffered on the palms of both his hands, a talisman or a dagger. Had he been a royal personage as he passed among the circular rose-beds, or a disaffected duke lost in melancholy and plotting? He couldn't help it, it wasn't affectation. Nor could she help her gossipy speculations.

'I'll bring us tea,' he said, caressing the hosta leaf with a fingernail. He smiled again and turned to make his way back to the house. His manner invariably inspired pleasantries. He might easily have stayed beside her, listening to her talk about hostas for another ten minutes or so, his weight on one leg and then imperceptibly shifted to the other. He had a way of leaning against the Rayburn stove in the kitchen, no trace of boredom affecting his features, while he absorbed Mrs Spanners's chatter about Princess Margaret. On one of his first visits to the house he'd revealed that his parents had died when he was still a child, both of them in the same railway crash. In his pensive moods there seemed to Mrs Anstey to be, just now and again, traces of that loss lurking in his light-blue eyes.

Lucky in her first marriage, Julia might as easily have ended up a second time with someone awful. There'd been, for instance, Mrs Enright's elderly brother-in-law, and weekend men at Sunday cocktail parties, all of them in Mrs Anstey's view unsuitable. There'd been a restorer of pictures, a man with an unkempt beard who'd settled briefly in the neighbourhood, whose name was foreign and difficult. 'Professor Doings' he was familiarly called and to her mother's horror Julia had taken exception to this, claiming that the man was being denigrated, which of course wasn't in the least the case. He was a lone and untidy individual, his ties stained with food droppings, his suits a mass of creases. He and

Julia began to have coffee together in the Bay Tree Café, which mildly became a talking point in the town. It wasn't apparent at the time that he was just another of her lame ducks, of whom there was quite a collection.

Thankfully dismissing the memory of this man, Mrs Anstey watched the slow progress of the river. Philadelphus blossom floated by, and then a tattered red rose. Such delicate remains might not reach the house called Anstey's Mill, eight miles from the town, which for so long had been her home; but more robust debris would safely make the journey, through the mill-race empty of a wheel, through the mill-yard and the meadows beyond. Sixty years ago she had been brought to Anstey's Mill as a bride, to a house she had adored, different in every way from the one she lived in now. She turned her head to examine the grey stuccoed back of Swan House, its narrow tallness and the semi-circular conservatory that jutted into the garden beneath an arrangement of windows set in pairs, the top two almost reaching a slated roof. She envisaged features she could not see: the bow windows of the house's façade, the gateless pillars standing high between a cobbled courtyard and the street, the white swan in a niche above the hall door, wistaria in profusion. It had been called the plainest house in Stone St Martin, built without the assistance of an architect in 1871.

The other house was a field centre now, devoted to the study of geography, but externally it hadn't changed. A long avenue of beech trees, branches interweaving overhead, led to its two storeys of Cotswold stone, set among lawns. Its roof was prettily tiled, its garden full of little corners. Behind it, close to where the river flowed, a railway line – used once upon a time to convey grain from the mill-yard to Cheltenham – had been removed, leaving behind a long straight path of grass on which Julia as a child had trotted a pony called Dandy. In 1954 Mrs Anstey's husband – whose portrait hung above the mantelpiece of the drawing-room in Swan House – had succumbed to bankruptcy due to his own mismanagement, and had died a year later.

Not wishing to think about any of that, Mrs Anstey tried to read but found that the past she had stirred still nagged a little: her husband had had stubborn ideas about the Anstey family, she herself should have firmly spoken out, the bankruptcy had been ridiculous and avoidable. Her role in the end had been to hold grimly on to her jewellery, refusing to admit to the bailiffs that it even existed. She was proud that she had done so, that what she had salvaged was now occasionally worn by Julia and would eventually pass to Henrietta and Katherine. There weren't many pieces for them to share, and they weren't even particularly valuable, but at least they constituted something: almost all that remained of a marriage and a house, and the life that had gone with both. That they were also a reminder of a family down on its luck didn't matter, for time had created its perspective and the nagging always ceased when she thought her way through the change in circumstances. She had done so now and picking up her book again, she read with more success. Ten minutes later Francis returned with a tray of tea, and macaroons and coffee cake.

Social occasions at Swan House were not frequent but whenever one occurred Mrs Spanners presented herself, unbidden, in the kitchen. Her henna-shaded hair was always freshly dyed, her sixty-year-old face decorated with eye-shadow and lipstick. She smelt of Love-in-a-Mist, her favourite.

This evening she wore a cherry-coloured dress, precisely matched by cherry-coloured shoes and fingernails, and a cherry-coloured wisp of handkerchief tucked beneath the strap of her watch. In the kitchen, which was high-ceilinged and faintly pink and which easily absorbed a large oak dresser and a table that proportionally matched it, she hummed a dance tune of her youth as she arranged cocktail tit-bits on Wedgwood-patterned plates. The kitchen also contained the Rayburn against which Francis liked to lean, a fridge and a washing machine, and blue-painted cupboards built into the walls, on either side of the sink and draining-boards. After fifteen years' service in the house Mrs Spanners considered this spacious room her very personal domain and if extra work had to be done there, such as that entailed by a party, she liked to have a hand in it. In Mrs Anstey's opinion she held pride of place among Julia's lame but greedy ducks: fifteen years ago Mrs Spanners had been on her uppers, a pathetic coughing woman, in a fix because her husband, Charle, had lost his job as a farm labourer and could not find another. Julia had taken both of them under her wing, offering Mrs Spanners a morning's work every Monday, and helping Charle to a position with the Forestry Commission. Neither had ever looked back.

'Oh lovely, Mrs Spanners,' Julia said, coming into the kitchen with her shopping and noticing at once the arranged tit-bits.

'Are we having the little sausages then? I could easily fry a few up.'

'I'm afraid I haven't bought any. Very few people are coming, actually.'

'I just thought something hot. I could nip back for a half of chipolatas I have in the fridge. Easy as anything.'

'Oh no, no. No, thank you very much, Mrs Spanners.'

'Very nice your hair is. I was saying to Charle dinnertime I must go in for a change of style one of these days. Thought maybe I'd go short again.'

'Oh, I think it suits you the way it is.'

'Charle says it suits. But of course you never know with men, do you? Not where there's money involved.'

Julia laughed since it was expected of her. She put away the things she'd bought. Mrs Spanners stood on a chair to reach down the glasses which she knew from experience were the right ones. She wiped them with a tea-cloth in case they should be dusty, still talking about the shortcomings of men as arbiters where hair and clothes were concerned. 'Like that beige pleated I was after. See right through him you could, the way he said it didn't suit on the hips.'

'I think I'd better change,' Julia said, interrupting this flow. What she meant, and felt shy of saying, was that she must go and find Francis. It was nice, his wanting to garden. It was nice the trouble he took over her mother and Mrs Spanners, so attentively listening to her mother's evocation of the past and Mrs Spanners's speculations about the life of Princess Margaret. It was nice, as well, that he had so enthusiastically fallen in with her own desire to go to Florence for their honeymoon. Henrietta and Katherine had spent some time in Italy, and at one time of her life Mrs Anstey had travelled to the cities of Tuscany and Umbria every autumn, but Julia never had. For as long as she could remember, her mother had been pressing photographs and postcard reproductions on her, memories of well-to-do days in Perugia and Urbino, Florence and Arezzo. Julia had established her own favourites among all the della Robbias, and had become particularly attached to Donatello's summery David and Lorenzo di Credi's Adoration of the Shepherds. *Are they gossiping*, she had wondered in a diary, *those two angels at the back*? She had saved up to make the journey herself, intending to take her mother with her as a guide; that it should be Francis with whom she would wander now, who would stroll with her among the lemon trees of Fiesole and in the cool of Santa Croce, seemed like a luxury she didn't deserve. Yet it was fitting that it should be he, for in spite of Mrs Anstey's appreciation of the Italian Renaissance and the religious faith it honoured, her agnosticism remained. Julia had never revealed to her the original plan she had had for this journey, nor mentioned the savings she had accumulated in order to implement it. She was glad of that now.

Further delayed by Mrs Spanners in the kitchen, she found herself dwelling again on the circumstances of being in love at forty-seven. Was it because her passion more properly belonged to an earlier period of her life that she experienced such impatience? She wondered, but didn't know. All she could say to herself was that even on the very first occasion, eighteen months ago in the lounge of the Queen's Hotel in Cheltenham, Francis Tyte had been different from all other men. She had known that as soon as he'd spoken, as soon as he'd smiled and slightly inclined his head. And weeks afterwards, when he'd visited Swan House, that special quality had been bit by bit confirmed. His life had been shattered by tragedy, but it wasn't from this wounding or from his gentleness that the flickers of excitement emanated. They came mysteriously, from the mystery that made him what he was. And what would have happened, she wondered, if Roger had not died? Would she still, in middle age, have fallen in love again? There was the thought as well – wretched and unwelcome – that her marriage to Francis would have a quality that hers and Roger's hadn't possessed because of the shared Catholicism. She hated all this disloyalty to Roger's memory, and felt she deserved the guilt that pursued it, spoiling the perfection. Roger was like an old brown photograph now, young in his uniform, no longer real, and yet he mattered more than ever.

'You've only got twenty-five minutes,' Mrs Spanners reminded her, nibbling an asparagus canapé, 'if you're thinking of doing your face.'

But Julia postponed attention to her face. She found Francis among the raspberry canes, working with a hoe. He put it down in order to embrace her, to admire the handiwork of Diane, and to tell her he'd quite painfully missed her.

An hour later the guests stood on the river bank beneath the tulip tree. Mrs Spanners bustled about with cocktail food, Francis passed among them with a glass jug full of gin and vermouth, and Julia with a decanter of sherry. Mrs Anstey remained in her high-backed wicker chair.

Hands were raised against the evening sun, backs were turned on it as it came low across the lawn. Voices chattered, faces smiled. There were a dozen people on the lawn, including the inmates of Swan House and Mrs Spanners. Six cars stood on the cobbles in front of the house. In one of them a forgotten radio whispered, relaying to no one the everyday adventures of *The Archers*.

Francis was being a waiter tonight, Mrs Anstey thought: obligingly he had lost himself in the role, sustaining the demands of all these people he hardly knew. 'Cox's,' a man with a tanned face said, going on to praise at length this brand of apple, and then regaled her with Laxton's shortcomings.

Not paying attention, she next watched Mrs Spanners. It was

silly that a cocktail party could not be given without her presence. The only real labour there ever was was the washing of glasses, which due to the woman's surreptitious intake of alcohol tended to end up broken. As well as which, she had a way of engaging the guests in quite lengthy conversations, retailing to them the gossip gleaned by her husband in the Three Swallows or mentioning Princess Margaret. 'Who on earth is that extraordinary woman?' a stranger to the house had once inquired of Mrs Anstey.

Her glance passed from Mrs Spanners's painted face to the undecorated one of Father Lavin. It was a grey face, small and tidy above his clerical attire. The white tip of a handkerchief protruded from the upper pocket of his jacket, his jet-black vest bore not a speck of dust or fluff, his black shoes gleamed. Without straining her eyes to peer at him Mrs Anstey knew all that, for the priest was never different. 'Oh yes, yes,' she heard him murmur, his soft Cork accent easy to pick out among the other voices. 'Yes, I've always rather liked Sweet William.'

A girl in a red dress, who had brought a whippet on a lead, laughed and chatted with a woman whose name Mrs Anstey had once been told but had not managed to retain. Beside them young Father Dawne was tall and long-armed, with a shock of pale hair falling into his eyes. Dr Tameguard was different with his social air turned on.

The voices clashed, fragments of conversations wafting easily to Mrs Anstey, for she had no trouble with deafness. Someone spoke of racing pigeons, inquiring if they were raced for gain, if betting took place. Most certainly they were, another voice replied. Breeding and gambling were an industry, the sums involved sizeable. Birds had been known to race from Estepona to Cheltenham, and there was laughter after a joke about a pigeon was told.

Such gatherings had been familiar to Mrs Anstey ever since she'd come from Anstey's Mill to live in the town. Voices and faces had changed with the years, but the essence that remained was similar. 'No good whatsoever,' was another verdict on another brand of apple, and then she noticed that the whippet had strayed from its owner's side and was rooting in a flowerbed. A long-jawed woman was making a point about money, that nowadays it was in the wrong pockets. It was the Englishness of everything that hadn't changed, Mrs Anstey reflected, the leisurely standing about of the middle classes in evening sunshine, the Gloucestershire landscape that stretched away on the other side of the river. The owner of the whippet called her dog. 'Baloney!' she seemed to cry, her voice almost lost in the hubbub. Mrs Spanners was swaying a little now, Julia was hastening to Dr Tameguard and his fat wife. Accepting more cocktail mixture from Francis, Father Lavin inclined his head in a sideways bow. Young Father Dawne was laughing.

Her long association with the Anstey family had caused Mrs Anstey to become used to priests. Her husband had regularly attended the Church of St Martin, with which the Ansteys had connections that were pecuniary as well as religious. At Anstey's Mill there had been different priests in the past, and at Julia's convent there had been nuns. Mrs Anstey had always managed to get on perfectly well with these spiritual people, respecting their views and their beliefs just as she had respected her husband's and still respected her daughter's desire to keep the Ansteys' Catholic tradition going. It was only that the whole notion of prayer, and of the son of a universal God made man in a miraculous way, seemed more than a little absurd. She thought so now, watching Father Lavin with his cocktail glass, yet conceded that he brought comfort and consolation into lives that needed them. And personally she counted him as a friend.

'Beauty of Bath of course,' the man beside her said, after which the stream of information about apples ceased. The long-jawed woman came to talk to her, and then the owner of the whippet. Others came too, a youngish couple who lived in someone's gate-lodge, the wife of a man who'd retired from a job in Africa, another man who appeared to be drunk. In the end she was left alone in her wicker chair while Julia and Francis saw the guests through the house and into their motor-cars, and Mrs Spanners clattered among the glasses in the kitchen.

Something worried Mrs Anstey quite suddenly then, something

formless, like a fragment from a dream: she couldn't establish what it was. She poked about in her mind, but could only find the same sensation of unease. Had it to do with the gathering on the lawn? Had it been there earlier? Had it possibly to do with the distant sound of Mrs Spanners washing up in the kitchen, an elderly worry about breakages? It made her feel stupid that she couldn't track down its source. She closed her eyes, searching for it in the house she didn't care for.

In spite of its bow-windowed façade, Swan House was always dusky and it seemed to Mrs Anstey as she tried to trace her worry through its rooms that this dimness covered a multitude of sins. The Indian carpet and red-striped wallpaper in the drawing-room were so faded that they needed to be replaced, the springs of a sofa and several armchairs needed attention also. Only a set of Redouté roses, in slender mahogany frames, brought the room to life; like Mrs Anstey's jewellery, they had been filched from the grasp of bailiffs. The dining-room, low-ceilinged and green, was friendly; the hall was almost dark, its pitchpine staircase marching squarely out of it, up to landings that were shadowy also. From the depths of other shadows blurred images appeared in Mrs Anstey's mind: a brown marble paperweight, brass candlesticks from the dining-table, the swan in its niche above the hall door, the portrait of her husband, seeming stern above an ormolu clock on the drawing-room mantelpiece. The swan regularly became discoloured and had to be repainted; her husband had not been stern; appearances were nothing. 'We shall be happy here,' her husband whispered, leading her through the rooms of the other house, the home of his family since 1548.

'Hullo,' Julia said, and Mrs Anstey realized she'd dropped off. It was darker than it had been, sounds no longer carried from the house.

'How silly of me,' she said, struggling to her feet.

'Not silly at all, dear.'

'An extraordinary thing, you know. I thought that dog was called Baloney.'

'I think it was.'

'Well, isn't that rather strange?'

'Yes, it is.'

'Though I suppose it's just as odd to be called Mrs Spanners.'

'You say it suits her.'

'Oh, it does.'

The journey to the house was slow, for after sleeping in the evening air Mrs Anstey had become stiffer than she usually was. Her two sticks paused from time to time while she rested. She could sense Julia resisting an instinct to help her on her way, for Julia knew she disliked it.

'Cheerio then, Mrs Ferndale,' Mrs Spanners called from somewhere in the dusk, causing Mrs Anstey to conclude that she'd decided it inadvisable to present herself for closer examination. 'Cheerio, Mrs Anstey dear.'

'Good night, Mrs Spanners,' Julia replied, but Mrs Anstey said nothing. It was patronizing to be addressed familiarly just because she'd reached a certain age. It was patronizing to be called a senior citizen or an O.A.P., as if elderliness implied a desire for regimentation, the individual's spirit dead already.

In the drawing-room they were waiting for her, the lights not yet lit. Francis poured her a glass of sherry, and a conversation that had been going before her entrance was continued, about a film of the past called *Casablanca*. 'A marvellous scene,' Francis said, 'Paul Henreid conducting the Marseillaise in the café.'

Everyone except Father Dawne remembered the film. Mrs Anstey had seen it in Stratford-upon-Avon, taking Julia and a friend called Topsy Blythe out from the convent one weekend; Father Lavin had seen it in the Savoy in Cork. Julia had said that afterwards Topsy Blythe never ceased to sing *As Time Goes By*, and Mrs Anstey imagined that now: Topsy Blythe, very tall with spectacles, striding between two rows of beds in a dormitory, singing the song from the film. It was at St Mildred's that Julia had begun to collect her lame ducks. 'You should be proud of your daughter, Mrs Anstey,' the Mother Superior had once remarked in a challenging tone of voice.

She listened while Francis told Father Dawne the plot of the film. The other two talked about local events, among them the abandoning of plans for a new road less than half a mile from the town. There was a silence between Julia and the older priest when that subject was exhausted. Then, drawing her mother into the conversation, Julia said:

'Diane has found herself the worst possible boyfriend. Nevil Clapp.'

Mrs Anstey nodded. By all accounts, the little hairdresser had indeed made a preposterous choice and if a marriage took place she would discover her mistake within a week. Yet what girl alive would listen to her parents when they warned her that the boy she loved would one day seek to entice her into the realms of corruption? How could her imagination stretch so that she heard his voice persuading her to take an interest in the handbags that came and went in the Crowning Glory Salon?

'Poor Diane,' Julia said, causing Mrs Anstey to wonder how her daughter would eventually become involved in the disastrous relationship. Inwardly she frowned, although her face revealed no trace of this. Again she had the feeling that she was being touched by a fragment of a dream, that some instinct of her own was failing to communicate with her. Casting her mind back to the gathering beneath the tulip tree, she remembered the dog that appeared to have been oddly named. Was it something as little as that that was upsetting her? From close at hand she heard Francis's voice still retailing the plot of the film. The head of the lanky young priest stood out in silhouette against the dwindling light of the French windows. Now and again it nodded.

Quite a lot had happened in this room she didn't care for. Framed in gilt, the false likeness of the man she'd married was a lie that for more than twenty years had been constantly alive in the room, presiding over everything. Here it was that she had read to Henrietta and Katherine the girls' school stories they had preferred to Hans Andersen and Grimm. Here she had learnt, one Tuesday evening, of the death of Roger Ferndale in Germany. Nine years later, turning to smile at her from the bow windows, Julia had said she was going to marry Francis Tyte.

'I must go and see to things in the kitchen,' Julia said now, and for a moment Mrs Anstey sensed that the unease she felt had to do with the person Julia was and always had been: Julia concerned about the boyfriend of her hairdresser, Julia looking after Topsy Blythe, Julia who couldn't help being charitable.

Father Lavin rose and offered her more sherry, which she accepted since she had drunk nothing on the lawn.

'She's happy now,' she conversationally said. 'Julia.'

'Yes, I believe she is.'

A priest could not help loving a woman: muzzily the thought occurred and she wondered if it could possibly have to do with her elusive worry. During all the years she'd watched Father Lavin hiding from Julia the affection he felt for her, Mrs Anstey had lived quite securely with the knowledge of it: her sudden agitation was as unlikely to have been caused by it as by Mrs Spanners or the dog on the lawn. 'Oh, most remarkable,' the voice of Francis Tyte murmured, and immediately her intuition explained itself. Julia should not be marrying this man.

In Mrs Anstey's mind that statement was repeated, resounding as a simple fact. Yet only a few hours ago Francis had held out the hosta leaf to her in the garden, and she had thought yet again how pleasant he was to talk to. Charmingly, he had helped with their guests on the lawn. Most important of all, Julia loved him.

'Yes, she's happy now,' Father Lavin repeated, when minutes later they were all sitting down to saddle of lamb in the dining-room, while Francis's voice quietly continued, still speaking of the cinema of the past. And there was Julia's voice also, speaking to Father Dawne of something else. An old woman's unfounded fear was of course ridiculous, Mrs Anstey told herself, yet the silly worry continued, appearing to be even sillier when she found herself thinking that Julia was marrying Francis Tyte in much the same way as Diane of the Crowning Glory was contemplating such a union with Nevil Clapp. She didn't know why on earth that suddenly seemed so. Angrily she tried to push it all away from her, bringing up once more the subject of the strangely named whippet and names in general, Mrs Spanners's and

29

Nevil Clapp's. Father Lavin explained that the choice of so bizarre a title for a dog was in keeping with the vagaries of the animal's owner, and after that Father Dawne politely asked her how she would manage when Julia and Francis were in Italy on their honeymoon.

'Mrs Spanners has agreed to sleep here,' she replied, refraining from stating that the presence of the woman in her house for the greater part of every twenty-four hours was something she anticipated with dread. At eighty-one one couldn't say a thing like that, any more than one could suddenly protest that a marriage should not take place.

'Yes, I'll be perfectly all right,' she said instead. 'We're lucky she can come.'

She forced herself to smile around the table and then listened when the talk turned to the Victorian murder case in which Francis was to play a part. He was to be an under-gardener, and while he spoke she endeavoured to fill her mind with the scenes he colourfully described. Someone called Constance Kent it was all about, an adolescent girl who had cut a child's throat.

When the priests left, Julia washed up and Francis tidied the dining-room. Scents from the garden filled the bottom of the house. In the kitchen Julia stacked plates and dishes in a rack on the draining-board; Francis swept crumbs from the mahogany surface of the dining-table and wiped the surface clean. He collected the remaining wine-glasses.

'A few weeks isn't long,' he said when they both had finished.

'Oh, I know, I know.'

They clung together in the hall, his arms around her shoulders, their lips sharing a warmth. For Julia there had been no such embraces since the death of her husband and often she felt it should have been Henrietta or Katherine who stood in Francis's arms, Henrietta's long fingers which stroked his cheek, Katherine's flesh which went on tingling. The madonna face they'd stolen from her complemented his, their slender bodies matched his boyishness.

'You'll bring your dragon brooch?' he said, speaking of their honeymoon. 'And your little sapphires and your seed pearls?'

Surprised, Julia replied that jewellery could be a nuisance when you were travelling.

'I want to show you off.' He smiled at her. One Saturday afternoon all four of them had slowly strolled with her mother near Anstey's Mill, on the grassy path that once had been a railway track. Her mother's feeling for this other place had come to be an affectionate family joke, especially her repeated claim that the past was past and should not be disturbed. While memory and sentiment were indulged, young men with tripods had been measuring something, earnest young geographers from the field centre which the house had become. Like an offering, or a seal of their acceptance, the joke was held out by Henrietta and Katherine, and Francis delicately received it. He laughed when Julia afterwards said so, and laughed again when she hesitantly pointed out that he belonged more to her daughters' generation than her own. 'But it's you I love,' he had replied. 'It's only you I love, Julia.'

'Of course I'll bring my jewellery,' she said.

They went upstairs together and to their different rooms. Julia, in hers, undressed, and washed in the adjoining bathroom, still thinking about him among the della Robbias she had never seen. She gazed at her naked body in the bathroom looking-glass, not fearful of his possessing it. On her other wedding night she had been uncomfortably apprehensive, though trying not to be.

On the inside of Francis's bedroom door there was a key, which he turned. He always did so when he stayed in other people's houses, an involuntary gesture, not because he imagined he'd be disturbed. For a moment he leaned against the door, reflecting that it would be nice when in the evening she wore her dragon brooch and the long loops of her seedpearl necklace, and her sapphires. It would be nice to be seen with her in a piazza, nice if they ran into someone from the past.

He moved from the door and sat on the edge of his bed. Slowly he cleared his lean face of the traces of make-up which he always inconspicuously wore. He worked with a piece of cotton-wool and a little cold cream, no longer thinking about Julia. He wondered about Constance Kent and the nature of her crime. It fascinated him, all that.

·2·
Francis's

When he had met the two women in the lounge of the Queen's Hotel in Cheltenham, Francis had just completed one of the tobacco advertisements for television that people so ubiquitously noticed. He'd had to stand in the Parade with his pipe while various other men, attired and made up to resemble brigadiers and colonels, passed him by and were impressed by the odour of the smoke he was emitting. When all that was over he hadn't returned to London with the others: he didn't like being in their company for longer than he had to be. He'd made some excuse and had set his sights on a later train, inflicting upon himself the chore of killing time in Cheltenham. He'd found it difficult, had wandered into the Queen's Hotel, and when Mrs Anstey and her daughter arrived in the lounge he'd been aware immediately of wishing to charm them. He knew by the look of them that they'd find it interesting, his being an actor, and at once began a conversation while they had their coffee. They demurred when he suggested a drink in the bar, but when he casually said he would be returning to Cheltenham in a week or so the invitation he'd hoped for followed. 'Come over to Stone St Martin,' the old woman suggested, 'if you're ever at a loose end.' Directions were given, which he cut short by saying he did not possess a car. Then he must take a bus, the old woman laid down: the journey would be worth it because the town was pretty and well worth looking at. Something was mentioned about the saint who had apparently given it its name, St Martin of Braga. The younger woman appeared to be a Roman Catholic, and Francis found it easy enough to claim he was one also because, of course, that would be interesting for her too.

It wasn't true that he was obliged to return to Cheltenham in a week or so, but nevertheless he did return. He took the bus to Stone St Martin, having telephoned beforehand the number he'd been given. It was winter then: bitterly cold, fields white with frost for most of the day, the garden of Swan House bleak beneath a misty sky. Darkness had fallen by half-past four when they sat down to tea in the drawing-room, the three of them around a wood fire. 'I'm surprised you don't have a dog,' he laughingly remarked, for a dog stretched out on the hearth-rug would have completed the picture of domestic cheerfulness in the cosy gloom. They had laughed politely also, but he hadn't quite heard the reply of either of them.

Francis had been well dressed that day. Though considerably on his uppers, waiting for the latest tobacco advertisement cheque, he had bought himself a pair of sponge-bag trousers. In his room in Folkestone he had carefully washed a white shirt, gone over his jacket with Thawpit, and borrowed an iron from Denise in the bed-sitter next door. Conversing with Mrs Anstey and her daughter, he transformed this room into a flat, since that seemed called for. 'Quite a pleasant view of the sea,' he reported, although his single window in fact stared straight at the back of another house. Smearing a scone with strawberry jam, he described a flat – all russet brown and white – that had featured in a television drama he'd once taken part in.

Francis had experienced relationships like this before. There were two elderly sisters called Massmith whom he had met by chance almost sixteen years ago on a train in Cheshire. He had been out of work at the time and had taken a temporary job as a milk clerk in the neighbourhood; on the train he'd dropped into conversation with the Massmiths and had later stayed with them in their bungalow. Quite some time later there were a doctor and his wife whom he came to know in Lincolnshire after he'd had to attend the doctor's surgery with a sore finger. 'Well now, that's interesting,' the doctor said when he learnt that Francis – then employed in the offices of a paint factory – was really an actor. The doctor revealed that he and his wife were leading lights in a local amateur group called the Whetton Players. Invited first of all for morning coffee, Francis afterwards returned and stayed for some weeks. After that there were the exceedingly rich Kilvert-Dunnes, with whom he stayed on the Isle of Wight for three months, helping in their glasshouses. A fourth couple took him so warmly under their wing that he remained with them for almost a year, and there were other couples as well.

Francis told Mrs Anstey and her daughter all about himself, as he had told the Massmith sisters and the doctor and his wife, the Kilvert-Dunnes and all the others. After the tragedy of his parents' death when he was eleven he'd spent the remainder of his childhood in Suffolk, with a faded old aunt who had died herself a few years ago. None of that was true. As a child he had developed the fantasy of the train crash; his parents were still alive, the aunt and her cottage figments of his imagination. But in the drawing-room of Swan House he recalled the railway tragedy with suitable regret, and was rewarded with sympathy and another cup of tea. He offered to draw the curtains, on his feet to do so as he spoke. Lights gleamed then on the delicately framed paintings of roses and on various faded, inlaid surfaces. Francis himself put a log on the fire.

'No, I never married,' he revealed, accepting a second buttered scone instead of cake. The women had not asked him if he had, but the statement sounded natural enough in the course of a casual conversation. It wasn't actually true. In 1965, out of work and feeling weary, about to be twenty, Francis had met a widow one afternoon on the sea-front at Folkestone, a town he had taken a train to in an idle moment. She was thirty years older than he was, a

34

Jewish dressmaker who appeared to be well-to-do in a modest way. Over vanilla ice-creams in a café he'd listened to her recital of the emptiness in her life since her husband, a bookmaker, had dropped dead at Brighton races three years ago, leaving her childless. Until she told him she was a dressmaker Francis put her down as a boarding-house keeper or a woman who sold tickets in the kiosk of a cinema. She was overweight and pale, with black dyed hair and dry podgy lips. But she owned a house in a terrace and while speaking of her late husband she revealed that she, too, suffered from a heart condition and might even be living on borrowed time. A month later Francis proposed marriage. He was accepted with alacrity, and looked forward to a brief and peaceful sojourn with a dressmaker who would not expect much of him, whom he would discover one morning dead in her bed. He did all the shopping, going out every day with a basket while she continued to make clothes. He did the washing-up and the cleaning and some of the cooking, but to his consternation the woman he had married showed no sign of handing back her borrowed time and in fact was still alive. No petition for divorce had ever been filed, and Francis often saw his wife on the streets of Folkestone and always endeavoured to have a chat. She'd become even fatter than she'd been when he'd married her, her dyed black hair as black as ever and her lips still podgy in her unhealthy face. Across the width of her workroom she once had thrown a sewing-machine cover at him. It had not hit him, and all he wanted to say when he met her in shops or on the streets of Folkestone was that he forgave her for this violent action. He'd have quite liked to sit with her again over an ice or a cup of tea, listening to her gossip about the women who came to be fitted for the clothes she made them. He had always enjoyed that.

But the marriage itself now belonged in the past, and Francis saw no reason to burden the women of Swan House with it. To have done so would have sounded as out-of-place in their drawing-room as regaling them with the fact that a girl in a department store had once borne a child of his, or with various other facts about himself. He smiled instead on that first visit to Swan House, and accepted a glass of sherry. He held his head a little to one side in a way that drew the best out of his features.

The last bus had already left when it was time for him to return to Cheltenham, and the women laughed when he suggested he should walk the ten miles. They insisted that he should be driven, but when Julia Ferndale's Vauxhall passed over the cobbles in front of the house Francis said he could feel something wrong with one of the front wheels. He got out as soon as Julia brought the car to a halt, and then reported that one of the tyres appeared to have a puncture. A torch was necessary, he said, and by the time Julia had fetched one from the house he had unscrewed the valve and released a quantity of air. 'I'm afraid there's a bit of trouble here,' he said, offering to change the wheel. But in the darkness and the bitter cold the task was not one which the women wished to impose on their guest, so Francis brushed away their apologies and spent the night. Months later all three of them laughed about it, for if the misfortune hadn't occurred he and Julia might never have become friends.

Before finally departing on that occasion Francis had promised to telephone when further filming brought him to Cheltenham in three weeks' time. Although no filming was scheduled and none took place he returned to the city and this time, when the bus dropped him in Stone St Martin, he asked the way to the Catholic church. Already he'd spent a long time reading through the order of Catholic services, and in the church itself he noticed tablets to the memory of several long-dead Ansteys. After that he noticed all sorts of things. Stone St Martin suited the two women as perfectly as their house did, nicely reflecting the lace-work quality of their life. Near-by Cheltenham reflected it too, so architecturally proper, so gracious unless you happened to be in a hurry or a car. He noticed Julia Ferndale's dragon brooch and her seed pearls, and a quickening in her blue-green eyes when he held them with his own.

In the Massmith sisters' bungalow he had noticed details also: the jealousy that had developed because of his presence, the tearstains on their cheeks after a quarrel. They'd vied in fussiness, like two nice little hens petting and patting at him, insisting on Horlicks last thing at night and both of them hurrying away to make it. He could have stayed in the bungalow for ever if only he could have borne the indifferent food, and if they hadn't turned difficult he would certainly have been happy to go on cheering them up for quite a while longer. Unfortunately that was nearly always the trouble, people turning difficult about little things. The sums of money the Massmith sisters had missed could easily have been taken by the TV repair man on both occasions. Francis had explained all that to them, but of course they hadn't wanted to listen, just as the Kilvert-Dunnes hadn't listened about the travelling clock. Nor had it been his fault when the doctor's wife wrote him notes with kisses on them. He hadn't invited the woman's advancing hands; he hadn't relished being asked to perform unpleasant little tasks in the Kilvert-Dunnes' glasshouses; but in both cases he had done his best and hadn't complained. He had tried to explain to the doctor's wife that it went against the grain having to ask her for money because of the notes, that he never would have if he hadn't been so wretchedly short just then. He had tried to explain to Kilvert-Dunne that he'd had every intention of paying back his loans.

Waking in Swan House on the morning after the cocktail party, Francis rose and crossed his bedroom to the window. It was not yet six o'clock. Beyond the garden the river flowed peacefully; cows rested in distant meadows. The garden itself looked cool, its colours softer in the early light than they would later become. On the grass a lone rabbit crouched like a concrete replica of itself, before abruptly darting beneath a pink shrub. What damage the engaging little creature would do! Francis thought, no wonder he'd once suggested there should be a dog about the place. Was the pink shrub deutzia? Or weigela? He'd been told, but couldn't quite remember.

He turned away and again lay down on his bed, allowing his mind to wander. Since childhood he'd conversed with himself, playing different parts, using different voices. 'Oh yes, they're dead all right,' a Northern accent had been saying for more than twenty years, referring to the railway accident that had not taken place. A guard on the train, Francis imagined, bluff and pink-faced, horrified by all that had happened. 'Poor child,' a lady in furs said.

Real people had rarely matched the shadows of this make-belief. As a schoolboy, Francis's greatest pleasure had been to sit alone through an afternoon in a cinema, watching the stories of other people who did not exist: *Bad Day at Black Rock*, *Twelve Angry Men*, *From Here to Eternity*. There was an out-of-the-way Odeon he had favoured, to which entrance might be made through a broken window of the Ladies'. Avoiding long hours of chemistry or mathematics, Francis had slipped into his illicit wonderland, careless of the consequences.

It was a debt-collector, a lodger in his parents' house, who had suggested that he should act himself, in end-of-term entertainments. Francis had done so with some embarrassment at first, taking a part in *Outward Bound*, in sketches and in playlets, as Butters in *Thread o'Scarlet*. 'Good heavens!' his father protested in a startled way. 'An *actor*, Francis?' His mother didn't know what to say. It was the debt-collector who talked them round.

Nowadays it all seemed an age ago. The span of Francis's theatrical life looked like a journey to him, with milestones irregularly placed, indicating moments of achievement or disappointment. There had been the news that a travelling company in Liverpool needed another pair of hands to get it on to the road. There'd been the delivery of the first lines he'd ever been paid for, and the financial problems of the travelling company, and a year spent almost wholly on the dole. There'd been his struggling on, managing as best he could for year after year, and then the tobacco advertisements.

The role of an under-gardener in the story of Constance Kent could hardly be regarded as a milestone, but in the usual way there would be the excitement of performing, and when the rehearsals were over there would be the beginning of a whole new existence. He had said to the two women that he'd like to invite thirty or so guests to the wedding, later explaining that jealousies were so rampant in his profession that it would be difficult to pick out thirty friends without offending three or four times as many – and so in the end had decided to limit himself to his best man. He had already mentioned a boy he'd been at school with, someone called Brian Donsworth who had since made his way in the textile industry. But like the aunt in Suffolk and the guard on the train and the lady in furs, this figure did not exist and at the very last moment Francis intended to bring him low with glandular fever. In real life he had always had trouble cultivating relationships that lasted.

One, though, had: when in London for rehearsals Francis invariably stayed with the woman who had borne his child, a woman who was under the impression that in Folkestone he and the dressmaker still lived together as man and wife. It was convenient that she should imagine so, just as her rather grubby and uncomfortable flat in Fulham was a convenient place to lodge. Occasionally she was a nuisance, so one factor had to be balanced against another, and on this particular visit to London Francis intended to avoid any association with her, and hoped indeed that all association was at an end. He couldn't see himself ever having to make use of the Fulham flat in the future, a fact he'd anticipated by treating himself for the next three weeks to a luxury that seemed in keeping with his change in fortune. He had booked a room with a bath in the Rembrandt Hotel, from which eventually he planned to slip quietly away without attending to his account.

This arrangement pleasurably occupied Francis's mind as he continued to lie awake in the early morning. Such small details in his life were always a source of interest, for above all else his own life was a fascination for him. How he appeared to other people when he entered their different worlds was a constant concern; his destiny was constantly surveyed. He smiled, thinking of the debt-collector who had lodged in his parents' house and of the dressmaker he had married, and of the mother of his child. He found it hard to understand why he had wished, so many years ago, to watch this shop girl becoming pregnant. All he certainly knew was that when the experience of fathering a child had come about it had been only another disappointment. Not that it mattered now:

people helped him or harmed him, yet he had always tried to be nice and not a nuisance, fitting in and forgiving. He hadn't changed his name for the Massmith sisters or for the doctor and his wife, but for the Kilvert-Dunnes it had seemed more suitable to be Adrian Staye, and for other couples to be Edward Osborne. He didn't know why he enjoyed having a different name for a while, any more than he knew why he again began to wonder about Constance Kent, of whom he had never even heard until the television script arrived. Poor violent creature, not to be allowed to remain in the twilight of her death but to end up so trivially on the television screen, neither real nor unreal. In a limbo somewhere she was no doubt a weeping ghost, and out of sympathy, or just for fun, Francis decorated her adolescent nakedness with Julia Ferndale's jewellery. The little sapphires gleamed on her pale white skin, the dragon brooch was miraculously suspended, the seed-pearl necklace fell coolly from her neck. He smiled as he lay there, considering the image extraordinary.

An hour or so later and more than a hundred miles away, in the flat in Fulham which Francis did not again intend to make use of, the mother of his child placed a plate of sausages in front of this child, now aged twelve. Joy, in a green and yellow school uniform, had fluffy fair hair and plastic-rimmed spectacles. She also had a chapped look, as if she'd been left standing in a wind. Her mother, called Doris Smith, was a gaunt woman of forty with an excessively pale and bony face. She was attired in a pink nightdress and was smoking a cigarette.

'Hurry,' she urged. 'Hurry, dear.'

Joy poked at her sausages with a fork. She burst the skin of one and drew her head sharply back. Observing this drama, Doris ignored it.

'I think these sausages is off.'

'There's nothing the matter with the sausages.'

'Smells like vomit, 'smatter of fact. Like someone in the factory –'

'Now, dear, try not to be silly.' Doris spoke sharply. She seized the plate of sausages and applied her thin nose to it. The smell was a perfectly normal one, she declared, and pointed out that sausages were sixty-five a pound and must on no account be wasted.

'I'll be throwing up myself after them. Like Tuesday and that postman – God, I nearly died.'

'That had nothing whatever to do with sausages.'

'Peas and chips all over his letters, and then the curry we had.'

'We're eating a meal, Joy.'

'Poor black bugger didn't know what'd hit him.'

'Joy, will you please stop using that language? And for heaven's sake tell me another time before I've fried your sausages. You've always eaten the things before.'

'I've eaten them evenings. There's a difference between a person's digestion morning and evening.'

'Oh, don't talk nonsense, Joy.'

'Miss Upuku says that. She can't take grease herself first thing.'

'I wish to God Miss Upuku would teach you something, never mind her blooming digestion.'

Joy ate a slice of bread, leaving the sausages on her plate. Having made a fuss, her mother had now gone dreamy and wouldn't notice that they had not been eaten. It was always like that.

Doris smoked and thought about Joy's father, which she did very often. Almost everything in her existence could be traced back to her thirteen-year-old passion for Francis Tyte and to her bearing of his child. That one day they would all three be together was something Frankie was reassuring about every time he came to the flat. Ever since she'd known him Doris had quite accepted the fact that he was married to a dressmaker he couldn't leave because her heart condition mightn't survive the shock. From the word go, fairly and squarely he'd explained all that, but when Doris had gone to a fortune-teller a year ago she had received the news that a future awaited her in which she'd be happy. Without even having to think, she knew what that implied because she could never be happy without Frankie. She knew as well as she knew anything that one red-letter day he'd walk into the flat and quietly say that

41

the dressmaker he'd married in error had passed away in her sleep. Together then they'd watch Joy growing up. There'd be grandchildren to enjoy, and in the end he'd be famous, as he deserved to be. She'd told him about the fortune-teller and he'd said if only it could be. He'd held her hand, the way she loved; no more than a boy he still seemed sometimes.

'Cheers,' Joy said, pushing books and a pencil-case into her briefcase. 'See you.'

Mechanically Doris nodded, wrenching her mind away from her consideration of the future. Mechanically she said, as she did every day:

'You eat your dinner, mind.'

'God, the dinner on a Thursday! Like some dog came into the kitchen –'

'Don't *talk* like that, Joy. And don't go getting into trouble.'

'Which trouble's that?'

'You know as well as I do, Joy.'

'Dump like that, what better's there to do?'

She was gone before her mother could formulate a reply, banging the door of the kitchen and then the door of the flat. Doris lit another cigarette. Just occasionally nowadays it was hard to think of Joy as a child of love, with everything the expression romantically implied. A month ago there'd been a letter from the headmaster of Tite Street Comprehensive which stated that Joy was neither making progress nor choosing her companions wisely. Vandalism, obscenity and thieving were mentioned. The caretaker's car had twice been turned on its side, a student teacher had been gagged and left in a cupboard. When taxed by Doris, Joy spoke of sexual practices in the school's lavatories and Doris had to tell her to be quiet.

All of it was a worry, one which was aggravated by the fact that Joy could apparently not yet read or write. Every day Doris sighed over that in the shoe department of the store where she worked, and often said she didn't know what to do. The girls on the floor were sympathetic, and so was the floor supervisor, a kindly Indian. Irene in Handbags kept urging Doris to complain to Tite Street

Comprehensive and not let the school always get its moaning in first, but Doris felt she couldn't. Sharon, in House Beautiful, was of the opinion that nothing could be done with schools the way they were these days: her sister's kiddy, out Perivale way, couldn't multiply by two even though he'd just turned fourteen. But the Indian floor supervisor refused to permit gloom among his girls on this subject or on any other, and wagged a dark finger at any of them whom he caught promoting it. 'Doris,' he reminded her, 'there are silver linings in that cloudy sky.' Doris was a ready recipient for his cheerfulness, believing enthusiastically in the future he implied. Her faith in this direction was boundless, its vigour alone capable of dissipating her worry about Joy. Nothing mattered when she thought about the future, and with it in mind she had hung the flat with colourful pictures she'd bought in Boots, two of them depicting Negro girls, another of fishing-boats on a sun-gilded sea, others of various jungle animals. The furniture, acquired over the years on hire purchase, was what she could afford. Rugs and carpets reflected that consideration also, but when eventually the future became the present, when at last they were a family, she had plans to make a few replacements with the extra money Frankie would bring with him.

Behind the bread-bin in one of the kitchen cupboards she felt for the half bottle of vodka in which she'd left an inch or two the night before. She raised the bottle to her lips since that was quicker than bothering with a glass. It was ages since he'd been to the flat, ages since all three of them had gone down to Pizzaland for an evening meal, just like a family would. When the bottle was empty she placed it in her handbag, for disposal on her way to work.

Francis's parents, believed by quite a large number of people to have perished on a railway track in the 1950s, lived in the Sundown Home for the elderly in Hampton Wick, and on this particular morning – as on all fine mornings in summer – they made their way after breakfast to the garden. They passed from the dining-room through a hall which had stained-glass panels on either side of the door. This darkened glass, depicting events in the Garden of Eden, reduced the light considerably and at certain times of day cast faintly coloured shadows on the coats and hats that hung in two long rows on either side of a hallstand with a bevelled mirror. At the bottom of a lugubrious chocolate-brown staircase stood an elephant's foot from which the Tytes now lifted their walking-sticks. The rule in the Sundown Home was that the hazards of the garden should never be faced without the assistance of a stick.

'There's no one on the cedar seat,' Mrs Tyte remarked, surveying the suburban garden from the crazy paving outside the hall's side door.

Her husband did not reply. He eyed the sparrows which were busy on the five different bird-tables, pecking at pieces of bacon and toast. Beneath his jacket, folded twice, was the *Daily Telegraph*. He'd taken it from the sun lounge, which was against the rules.

'The chairs by the shed,' he said at length, already moving in the direction of a wooden toolshed. Beyond it, hidden from the windows of the house, was a cinder square with two deck-chairs on it. It was forbidden to move them elsewhere, or to erect them if they had been folded up and placed in the shed.

'It's difficult for me,' she murmured, following him, knowing he would not listen or want to understand. It wasn't easy for her to recline in a deck-chair and the struggle to get up again was sometimes painful. The cedar seat beside the goldfish pond was where she was happiest, looking at the little pots of geraniums and listening to the aeroplanes.

'Ah,' he said with satisfaction, having reached the cinder patch and finding the deck-chairs empty. It was impossible to read the *Daily Telegraph* on a cedar seat, as well she knew. Within two or three minutes the ghastly Purchase female would be bearing down upon them, making smacking noises with her lips. Safe as houses you were behind the shed.

Slowly they eased themselves into the chairs, she taking longer over it than he. The rubber ferrules of their sticks didn't skate

44

about on the gritty surface, which was why the deck-chairs had been placed there. A year ago, when they'd been on the crazy paving outside the back door, old Mrs Love had met her death.

With a continuing air of satisfaction Mr Tyte withdrew the *Daily Telegraph* from beneath his jacket and unfolded it. His eye moved to the top left-hand corner of the front page, to the first word of a headline about peace talks in the Middle East. He read un-hurriedly, passing from the headline to the displayed paragraph beneath and then to the more condensed print which followed it. The news of the peace talks was continued on page five, he was advised, but he did not turn to page five, preferring to arrive there in his own time and in his own way. Instead he involved himself with a car workers' dispute.

His wife, with closed eyes and the sun on her withered cheeks, thought about their only child, who was to her what the *Daily Telegraph* was to her husband. Last night he had been on the television again, smoking the pipe in the advertisement. She'd told the newcomer, Mrs Uprichard. She'd pointed at him, and added that quite often he was on the screen for longer. It was impossible not to feel pleasure, impossible not to say to Mrs Uprichard that the other advertisement, in which he was at a flower-show with his pipe, was better. She'd told Mrs Uprichard that as far as she knew he didn't really smoke a pipe, that it was all an act. In real life she'd never seen Francis smoking anything, not even a cigarette.

Still warmed by the sun, she remembered the moment of his birth, a voice telling her she'd had a boy, and then the child's cry. She remembered holding him for the first time in her arms, cooing into his shrivelled face. Years before that they'd given up hope. She'd had four miscarriages when she was younger and then, to her astonishment and to Henry's too, she'd found herself pregnant again, at forty-four. She'd spent more than seven months just lying down, never believing for a moment that disaster would be avoided, what with the age she was and her past unhappy history. Yet miraculously the child had been born, and 14 Rowena Avenue had immediately become a different kind of house.

But the sadness, she often thought now, was that she and Henry had never been young with their child. Even older than she was, Henry had been fifty-six at the time of the birth, and although they'd naturally done everything they could to make Number 14 a happy home for a growing boy they couldn't change the fact that Francis was a child of middle age. Not that it had seemed a disadvantage at the time. At the time there'd been companionship and affection, Francis learning to make pastry in the kitchen, playing with Meccano in the sitting-room while Henry read *Coral Island* to him. There'd been their Sunday walks on Ealing Common, all three of them together, Francis flying his kite on a windy day. Yet often since, she had wondered if to a boy growing up they'd seemed as old as they were now. He'd come into their lives like a gift, but a boy growing up couldn't be expected to appreciate that.

She opened her eyes and glanced at the portion of bald head that protruded above the newspaper. Henry had not risen high in the Midland Bank. His hope had been that his son might somehow compensate for that, but Francis had entered a world about which they knew nothing, emphasizing the gap that separated them.

Her eyelids drooped again. 'He hasn't been, not for ages,' she had whispered to Miss Purchase in the dining-room a week ago, and Miss Purchase had tightened her lips, which was a habit she had. Henry said it was six years since Francis had been, but Henry might have got it wrong the way he sometimes did these days. Henry didn't care any more; he never wanted to mention Francis; he walked out of the television lounge whenever Francis appeared. Perhaps a father couldn't help feeling disappointment in the circumstances. After all, she wasn't always able to help it herself when the years of childhood kept coming back at her, Rowena Avenue and all it had meant. She hadn't been able to help it when he'd first stopped talking to them, not sharing things any more. But that was so very long ago, as she often, even now, tried to remind Henry. Time altered circumstances and there still was time to come, enough of it for Francis to be the famous actor he'd set out to be. When that happened she knew he would visit them again and

Henry would at last understand how these things were, how a boy could have pride.

Of all that Mrs Tyte was certain, and in the meantime Francis was there on the television for Miss Purchase and everyone else to see: the baby that had so marvellously been born to her, a little thing stumbling across rooms, her most precious possession for year after year. It would be lovely when he came again, when all three of them remembered Rowena Avenue and the walks they'd gone on over Ealing Common, how he'd loved the soggy toast beneath baked beans and had made her a windmill that worked.

'Oh God, let him,' she murmured, mouthing the words softly so that her husband would not hear them. 'Oh God, please.'

He waved as the train crept out of Cheltenham station. Julia waved also, and turned away before the last few coaches began to disappear from sight. Slowly she drove back to Stone St Martin, stopping for petrol at the Red Robin filling station. She called in at Warboys, Smith and Toogood to deliver a batch of typing and to collect some more. 'Thanks, Janet,' she said to the new girl in the outer office, and minutes later she turned into the cobbled courtyard in front of Swan House.

'It's nice, you know,' her mother said on the lawn, referring to *Martin Chuzzlewit*, which Julia carried for her while they made together the slow journey to the wicker chair beneath the tulip tree on the river bank. 'I've never read it before.'

'I think I read it at St Mildred's.'

Mrs Anstey, who had worried in the night over the anxiety that had begun to afflict her, did not mention it because it was so silly. And Julia had no way of knowing that the bedroom occupied by her fiancé had earlier been alive with people she'd never heard of, with the Massmith sisters and the Kilvert-Dunnes, with a doctor and a doctor's wife and a saleswoman of shoes called Doris Smith, with a dressmaker in Folkestone and a debt-collector who had lodged at 14 Rowena Avenue. She had no way of knowing that, just for fun, the jewellery which strictly speaking was still her mother's had that

47

morning adorned an adolescent murderess. Like pieces from a forgotten jigsaw puzzle, the elements of a pattern were scattered, lost in a confusion that Julia wasn't even aware of.

'Shall Francis be back before the wedding?' Mrs Anstey inquired, at last reaching her destination.

Julia shook her head. It wouldn't be worth his while to come for a weekend since rehearsals took place on Saturdays, as on other days. No, they wouldn't see Francis again before the wedding.

She went away to start on her typing, and Mrs Anstey tried to settle down to her book, telling herself yet again not to be so silly.

·3·
Constance Kent's

The drill-hall reflected its primary purpose. Signs of the Territorial Army were everywhere, a wooden horse in a corner, basket-ball stands, charts on the walls depicting guns, a guide to the naming of parts. In another corner there was a beer barrel.

But for the next three weeks the hall was to be put to a use that had nothing to do with the Territorial Army, and signs of that were present also. The floor was marked with lengths of yellow adhesive tape, the ground plan of Road-Hill House, near Bath. On a wall hung a huge blown-up photograph of the house's exterior, four-square in its Victorian splendour, a semi-circle of gravel where the carriages turned, steps rising to a hall door set among pillars. Two trestle-tables had been drawn together and surrounded with chairs. Actors and actresses stood about with plastic cups of tea or coffee. A bearded production assistant bustled, a girl chewed gum.

The director of the piece, a youth in his early twenties, was attired in what appeared to be the garb of a plumber but which closer examination revealed to be a fashionable variation of such workman's clothing: his dungarees were of fawn corduroy, his shirt of red and blue lumberjack checks. He wore boots that were unusual, being silver-coloured; and beneath each arm-pit, in a shade of fawn that matched his dungarees, were sewn-on patches, appearing to symbolize a labourer's excretion of sweat. His hair was profuse, a halo of pale-brown curls that contrasted sharply with the shaven head of the man who had written the script of the Constance Kent story. The director was small, much given to talk and laughter; the scriptwriter was lanky, resembling a length of wire. He wore a black leather jacket and was clipped of speech, a man who did not smile.

Susanna Music, who was to play the part of Constance Kent, knew she didn't look like her. She'd been shown a drawing of the girl, aged sixteen, which was the age she'd been when she'd murdered her infant half-brother; as well, there was a photograph taken five years later, revealing eyes like currants in a square, unpretty face, and hair severely drawn back from a central parting. This hair had been red, Susanna Music's was black and trailed loosely down her back. She was small, and Constance Kent had not been small; Susanna's arms and legs were like a child's, her body narrow. Her eyes were the same deep blue as the plain linen dress she wore.

It was an important day for her. The playing of Constance Kent was the opportunity she had been waiting for ever since she'd left her drama school. Had she had a choice she would have preferred Rosalind or Juliet with whom to be given her chance. Inevitably there was something repellent about a girl who had hacked a baby to death, but there was of course something interesting as well.

'My name's Francis Tyte,' a voice said, and Susanna turned away from her examination of the blown-up photograph of Road-Hill House. She thought at once that Francis Tyte was attractive. He was smiling at her. The grey of his suit matched his

49

shirt and the tweed of his tie. Somewhere before she'd seen that lean face; as she returned his smile she realized it was in a series of television commercials for pipe tobacco.

'Susanna Music,' she said.

'You have quite a part to play, Susanna.' His voice was gentle but what he said caused her to feel nervous all over again, making her even blush.

'She isn't easy,' she agreed, as nonchalantly as she could.

'She's fascinating, Susanna.'

She asked him what his own part was and he replied he was a gardener who hadn't existed, who had been written into the script because in one particular place a voyeur was necessary. 'I don't say much,' he added.

'I've seen you in those ads.'

He smiled again, not commenting on that. 'She'll make you famous, Susanna,' he said, and went away.

An actress, with a man's jacket thrown casually around her shoulders, entered the drill-hall. She caused a lull in various conversations because she was a famous image, a well-known visitor in the nation's sitting-rooms. Her tawny hair was carefully untidy; in a peach-like face a shapely mouth pouted. 'Taxis!' she whispered loudly and with a huskiness. 'My God, the taxis!'

The director buzzed about her like a freshly wound-up toy, gushing and chattering. His bearded assistant hurried everyone to the trestle-tables, including a make-up girl, a wardrobe girl, and the girl chewing gum. When they were all seated, with scripts open in front of them, the director rapidly labelled everyone with a name. The peach-faced actress gave a little sideways bow of her head when hers was mentioned, a special gesture known to television viewers.

'Without being crass,' the director began, with smiles and stabbing gestures, 'we're into a conflict situation where Constance is concerned.' He drew attention to the photographs on the wall and while all the heads in the drill-hall turned towards it he again repeated that they were into a conflict situation.

The eyes of the actors and actresses examined pillars and steps, the mass of windows, the parapet that bounded the roof, with urns at each corner. 'Without being simplistic,' the director hurried on, 'there's a stench of lechery beneath the scent of lovely English roses.' He added that he did not like the colour green and preferred, where possible, not to have it in any of his productions. That might sound extravagant, he pointed out, since the countryside played such a part in the Constance Kent story, but it was surprising what could be done with faded shades of blue and brown, for instance. 'O.K.?' he said.

The girl chewing gum started a stop-watch. Voices began to read the dialogue from the script, and slowly a household flickered into life: the blustering Samuel Kent, inspector of factories, his second wife, the nursemaid Elizabeth Gough, the gardeners and the servants, a crippled groom. The children of the household, with the exception of Constance Kent herself, were silent in this interpretation of the past. They played no part in the scenes of passion, they were asked no questions by policemen. The mother of Constance Kent, reputed to be mad, was replaced in her husband's bed by the household's governess; soon afterwards she miserably died. The governess, hating Constance, became her stepmother, and in her lonely unhappiness Constance wandered the roads of the neighbourhood, her buttoned black shoes endlessly covered with dust. She carried flowers from the hedge-rows back to Road-Hill House and named them for the other children: foxglove, cowslip, mother-of-thyme. The other children loved her for her patience, for her humility and her calmness. She read to them and taught them games.

In the early morning she stood among the pillars, by the hall door. Her hands hung loosely, her eyes fixed on a step that was still damp from its six-o'clock scrubbing. A dog-cart was drawn up on the gravel, the horse's head held by the crippled groom.

'Your mother's been complaining,' her father said. 'You make it difficult for her.'

She didn't reply. The horse was impatient on the gravel, the groom muttered threats and then cajoled it.

'It isn't easy with the servants sometimes,' her father said. 'I would have thought you'd lend support to your mother, Constance.'

She would have hated it, Susanna guessed, when he called his wife her mother. He did it because he didn't care, because it didn't matter to him that her mother was dead. His wife had difficulties with the servants because she was little more than a servant herself. She liked their company and after an hour or two's gossip with them found it hard to change roles, to be peremptory and issue orders.

'Why don't you answer me? Do we ask too much of you, Constance, your mother and I? Please answer me that.'

'You do not ask too much, Father.'

'Then you will kindly obey me when I request you to assist your mother.' He spoke in a low voice so that the groom could not eavesdrop.

'Yes, Father.'

'You're sometimes no comfort to me, Constance.'

He went away. His boots crunched on the gravel, a sound which caused the horse excitedly to throw back its head. Still standing by a pillar, she watched the dog-cart draw away. She listened to the gallop of hooves until she could hear them no longer. She might have stood there longer, for there was nothing she had to do.

'My dear, you're plain today,' her father's wife remarked, hours later that morning. 'You do need rouge, you know.'

In a chilly room Constance's chair was drawn up to a fire that would not blaze. Her needle's progress was slow as she stitched the hem of a bed-cover, the white candlewick spread over her knees. Each stitch was difficult because the thimble was too large. It was the household thimble; her stepmother had thrown away the ones that fitted her, the ones her mother had left behind. 'Pasty,' her stepmother said.

Her stepmother disliked her company because she was different from the maids. She didn't shriek and giggle, she didn't repeat the comments the butcher's man made when he sat for ten minutes in the kitchen, drinking tea. 'You need to colour up,' her stepmother said.

In the orchard she picked plums into a shallow basket and saw her father with Elizabeth Gough. They lay in the long grass, her father's hands lifting off the nursemaid's clothes and then unbuttoning his own. After that they were like animals.

She ran away, hurrying on the dustiest of her roads. The clouds moved beautifully across a pale sky. The flowers looked different in the hedgerows now, their colours brighter, rich with a life she hadn't seen in them before. Somewhere she'd find a life of her own, she'd be a servant in an inn; somewhere she'd find a place to hide.

They locked her in a cellar that smelt of drains. They might forget her. Here she might die, with only the memory of her father like an animal and Elizabeth Gough's hair all wild among the grass, and the white naked limbs of both of them. She could not destroy her father, she could not silence the mockery of her stepmother's tongue, nor exorcize the sin of Elizabeth Gough. Their arms would beat her off, her father would coarsely laugh at her.

'Yes, I am guilty,' she said, and the clergyman inclined his head and said she'd feel the better for saying so. A doctor spoke and there were questions. A magistrate nodded, the butcher's delivery man gave evidence. 'Yes, I am guilty,' she said again.

In the drill-hall there was a silence after Susanna Music repeated those words. 'Great,' the director then exclaimed, jerking his mop of hair interrogatively at the girl chewing gum.

'Twenty-two minutes out,' she reported.

'Sweet Jesus,' said the director.

More tea was produced, with petit beurre biscuits. The actors and actresses remained seated while the wardrobe girl and the make-up girl had a word with those playing parts that required more than the usual attentions. The actor who was Constance Kent's father held Susanna in conversation. He was a heavy man, with broken front teeth in a face that reminded her of meat. A mane of greyish hair hung from a balding dome. He didn't talk about the drama they were all involved in, but about a part he'd just been offered in a film. 'Concerning computers,' he said. 'The world's computers suddenly going wrong. I play Sir Edgar Keane.'

Susanna nodded, trying to be interested. There was something wrong with the script they'd read: it seemed impossible that this

53

unhappy girl possessed the spirit of a murderess. No ordinary person took human life, it wasn't the same as stealing things or telling lies. The script they'd read was facile.

The man who'd written it was muttering to the director through smoke from a slim cigar. The director wasn't listening. 'They're not getting the physical bit across,' the scriptwriter complained in his clipped accents. 'She has to be menstruating at the time of the crime.'

But the director was more concerned about the inordinate length of the drama, and when the scriptwriter again mentioned Constance Kent's menses he smilingly replied that just for the moment he'd prefer not to open that particular can of goods. The scriptwriter did not speak again, and soon afterwards left the drill-hall. 'We'd get a lot more pace,' the director remarked to his assistant, 'if we amalgamated the housekeeper and the cook.' His assistant agreed, and suggested that for the sake of further drama Martha Holley, the daughter of the washerwoman, should be made psychic. 'Fantastic,' cried the toylike director, pacing excitedly up and down in his workman's wear.

Other things were happening in the drill-hall. The man who played Constance's father said that the computers went wrong because of a laser beam. The peach-faced actress was jealous: Susanna could feel the jealousy in the woman's glance, she could feel her trying to control it, trying not to let it show. The glance passed over Susanna's features and her long, loose black hair; it was snatched away but then returned, as if of its own accord. It moved over Susanna's thin legs and over her blue dress. The lips of the actress wanted to curl, but were prevented from doing so. Then very suddenly the director clapped his hands together and asked that the scene in the breakfast-room should be performed. He said he wished everyone to understand this scene since it reflected so well the steaminess in the house. 'Basically, it's the only time Kent's wife accuses him of messing about with the nursemaid, and what she's thinking is that she should know because he messed about with her when his first wife was alive. Greatly given to taking knickers off, was Kent.'

The actors and actresses who were involved took their places and when the scene had been acted the director requested that the whole reconstruction should now be discussed. There was a short silence and then the actor who was playing the part of Constance Kent's judge protested that the pornography in the plum orchard scene had been invented. 'I mean, you'd think the nursemaid was a hooker the fruity way Kent chats her up. I mean, it's not the actual truth we're presenting.'

Another actor complained that in order to reduce the running time most of his lines had been taken away from him. He'd had a name before; now he was just a specialist in mental disorders. Bucknill he'd been called before, he added.

'What sticks out a mile,' an elderly actress said, 'is that there's a lot of incorrect grammar in this script, spoken by people who are meant to be educated. And there's a place where Samuel Kent suddenly says, "No way." I think that's an expression Kojak invented.'

The director did not appear to register these objections. Animatedly addressing his assistant, he continued to stab the air with gestures, enhancing the impression that he was powered by some clockwork mechanism. When he paused for a moment the peach-faced actress made a speech. She stated that in her opinion the facts were in no way represented in the script. The truth was that she herself – in the part of the nursemaid who received the attentions of Samuel Kent in the plum orchard – had caused the death of the child by attempting to stifle its cries. The child, sleeping in her bedroom, had been roused by further love-making between Samuel Kent and herself: she had snatched a pillow in order to quieten it while Kent made his way back to his wife's bedroom. Unfortunately she'd smothered the thing.

'That view,' the peach-faced actress went on, 'was widely held at the time. Charles Dickens believed it to be true. What happened was that Kent afterwards went to work with a knife in order to make the whole thing look like the behaviour of a crazy girl. Then he put the remains down the loo.'

The actor with the broken teeth, approving of this theory since it enriched his part as well as the actress's, pronounced that his stabbing of the cadaver should be shown in detail, that being what excited viewers these days.

The halo of curls danced urgently about as the director shook his head. Words tumbled over one another as he hastened to insist that the person indubitably responsible for the crime was Constance Kent. It was she who had attempted to dispose of a bloodstained nightdress; it was she who had confessed. Swiftly indicating the blown-up photograph, he added that what they were into was an in-depth assessment of a situation that was by no means purely Victorian. He smiled lavishly, a smile of encouragement for his cast, although some of them took it to be one of amusement at the tragedy that had occurred. He didn't wish to sound extravagant, he said, but when you asked how Constance Kent could have butchered a baby you were asking how terrorist girls could blow up the innocent in shops and restaurants and dance-halls. Constance Kent had been a figure of vengeance, today she'd perhaps be a Baader-Meinhof girl. In his opinion, though not wishing to sound crass, human nature hadn't changed since 1860.

Susanna, to whom this interpretation of the facts was primarily directed, endeavoured to visualize a Victorian girl in this contemporary guise. She thought of her in a stranded aeroplane, threatening death, too embittered to care for her victims. She saw her in a department store, with a time-bomb in a carrier-bag. She saw her sitting in a room, watching on television the pictures of another holocaust, proud that she had caused it. 'Yes,' she uncertainly agreed, stepping forward to perform the breakfast-room scene again. Those who were not taking part occupied the chairs that lined the walls, settling down with newspapers or knitting.

'You are totally wrong in this,' Samuel Kent protested, seated, pretending to eat.

'I have the evidence of my eyes,' his wife replied.

'What evidence, may I ask?'

'That you persistently pay attention to Elizabeth Gough.'

'There is nothing amiss between myself and Elizabeth Gough.'

'I warn you, if I discover otherwise I shall not hesitate to act, Samuel.'

'You shall have no cause to. Good morning, Constance.'

'Good morning, Father.'

'Move straight to the sideboard, Susanna,' commanded the director. 'Help yourself to kidneys. Lift the kidneys up so's the camera can catch them. Very, very slowly. Let the silence build. Remember what you're thinking: you're seeing your father in the plum orchard, going to work on the nursemaid. Now, sit down. Very, very slowly. Pick up your knife and fork. Remember, you want to kill someone with that knife. Good. Super. Let's try it from the top again.'

All morning and for part of the afternoon the scenes continued in the drill-hall. At lunchtime the peach-faced actress had a word with the director and after that did not again protest that it was she herself who had committed the atrocity; and she controlled her jealousy of Susanna Music as best she could. No one mentioned pornography again, or unconvincing dialogue; everyone pulled together.

It surprised Susanna that this had happened. Waking that morning in her parents' house in s.w.1, she had gazed about her at the lilac wallpaper of her bedroom, concerned immediately with the part she was to play. The sheets on her bed were a shade of lilac also, but it was the cold white sheets of Constance Kent she had more vividly imagined, and Constance's tortured mind, and her saintliness. What had taken place in the drill-hall seemed nothing in comparison with that simple reality.

'You're right of course,' a voice said, and she turned to find the actor who'd introduced himself as Francis Tyte beside her. He held open a set of swing-doors and walked beside her down the gloomy corridor and out of the drill-hall.

At half-past four that day a lorry full of scrap metal moved slowly through afternoon sunshine, along a street that wasn't far from the drill-hall, and not far either from Tite Street Comprehensive school. As he drove, the driver of the lorry drank milky tea from a bottle, expertly dividing his attention.

On her way to the Rialto Café for chips and a Tizer, Francis's child watched the lorry-driver for a moment and then moved on, past two youths who were loitering in front of a partially demolished house. The youths were naked to the waist, their hair thick with the grime of mortar and plaster, shovels idle in their hands. Another man operated a yellow crane, moving it closer to the house and at the same time swinging through the air a huge pear-shaped weight. As Joy stopped again to watch, this struck a wall and brought the greater part of it crashing down. A fire-place turned in the air. Dust exploded, showering the youths afresh.

All the houses were unoccupied in the street, dingy lace curtains still drooping here and there behind smashed windows. The area where demolition had already taken place was protected by a high fence of corrugated iron, now richly embellished with graffiti and posters advertising rock shows. *Bilo rules OK*, a statement read, sprayed in blue from a paint-gun. Its letters awkward on the wavy surface of the corrugations, a black message asserted that Jesus Christ was alive and well. *Working*, it added, *on a less ambitious project.*

On the other side of the street were the railings of a park that was as empty as the street itself, its grass browned by the sun. Beyond it was a newsagent's shop, beside a café. *Rialto Café* stated a sign that also advertised Coca-Cola.

Joy entered and placed her briefcase on the nearest of half a dozen tables that had green and white oil-cloth on them. Only one was occupied, by a small middle-aged couple who were drinking tea. Displayed on the counter were buns and miniature packets of biscuits beneath a plastic dome.

'What you want?' a woman in an overall demanded.

'Chips,' Joy said, 'and a Tizer.'

'Got the money, have you?'

Joy said she had. By never going on a bus, either to school or on the way home, she managed to save enough for this regular repast. It meant being an hour late at Tite Street Comprehensive every morning, but almost a year ago now Clicky Hines in 3A had done a letter for her, purporting to come from her mother and explaining that due to family problems it was impossible for her to set out for school at the proper time. Arriving home a couple of hours later than she should have didn't matter because the flat was empty then. She liked to linger in the Rialto or the Woo Han, or the Light of India Take-Away. She liked Chik 'n' Chips in Nile Road best of all, but it didn't open until six, which was usually too long to wait.

'Twenty-one,' she said, placing the money on the counter. She felt a little hurt that the woman, who wasn't the usual one in the Rialto, should have distrusted her. The usual one, Sylv, sometimes charged only fifteen for chips and Tizer, saying the chips had been left over from dinnertime. The present woman had been in the café for a week now and didn't seem to like people. Sitting down at one of the tables, Joy resolved not to return to the place without ascertaining first that Sylv had returned also.

The middle-aged couple had begun to argue, which pleased Joy because that was something to listen to. The woman emphasized the points she was making by striking the surface of the table with a ketchup container, a roundish plastic object like a large tomato. 'She come back in a shocking state,' she said. 'Nothing that wasn't torn.' Joy couldn't hear the man's reply, and then the woman said, 'Of course you bloody had the camera going.'

Joy was in 3B at Tite Street Comprehensive, where the current fashion was starting fires. She belonged to a group, the fans of a pop band called The Insane; the other group in the class were supporters of Fulham Football Club. A fire had been started in a French period that morning by one of the Insane fans, and a second one during the lunch-hour by the Fulham supporters. A month ago paint-guns had been all the rage, but everyone was sick of them now.

The woman brought the Tizer and the chips, fewer chips than usual, Joy noticed. 'No bloody way,' the man at the next table protested angrily. 'No way you can call them blue.'

Clicky Hines had a drug. All day he'd been strutting about the place on his high heels, saying what it did to you, how it made you think you were walking on the air. He said he had enough to share out among the Insane fans, fifty pence a go. Clicky Hines was older, being in 3A, and knew the drummer in the group, Bobo Sweat, as he was called. It was Clicky Hines who had begun the fashion for fires, just as he'd begun the fashion for staring, which Joy had found a drag. You had to stare at whatever teacher was in the room, not ever speaking or picking up a ballpoint or opening a book. All the Insane fans in 3A and 3B had kept it up for a term, and the Fulham supporters hadn't been able to retaliate except to shout Front slogans in the middle of whatever the teacher was saying. Even the Abrahams brothers had shouted Front slogans.

The woman at the next table informed her companion that she didn't intend to let any niece of hers take part in activities that involved cameras, no matter what such sessions were called. The ketchup container made a plopping sound as it repeatedly struck the table-top. It was nothing short of ridiculous, the woman snappishly exclaimed, to refer to sessions like that as a bit of fun on a Sunday afternoon when the truth was that films were being made for red-necked businessmen to get turned on by in a Soho cellar, twenty quid a head. 'I'm telling you straight, Ron, that girl's not performing for cameras again.'

It was a bit of luck hearing about dirty films. Tomorrow the whole conversation could be repeated, everything the couple said, all the stuff about a Soho cellar. Eventually it would get to Clicky Hines's ears and he'd give his excited screech, throwing his head back the way he did. The making of sex films would fascinate Clicky.

The man and the woman rose, spots of red in the woman's cheeks, the man looking truculent. Without speaking again they left the Rialto Café and Joy watched them walking, still without speaking, past the window. She'd perhaps embroider it a bit, she'd perhaps describe how the girl had had to be held down, like Mavis Pope that day in the toilets. She'd describe how her clothes had been torn, how four or five men had gone at her, while all the time the camera was turning.

Slowly, relishing them, Joy consumed her chips. She wished she didn't go to Tite Street Comprehensive. Several times recently, when dragging her way through the streets of Fulham in the mornings, she'd had it in mind to spend the day in a park. Increasingly there didn't seem much point in arriving in 3B classroom and sitting there, not being able to hear properly because of the noise. It broke the monotony when a fire broke out at the back of the room or when the Fulham supporters tried to get nasty, but neither was much of a consolation really, especially when you couldn't eat any of the dinner. What she actually wanted was to leave the place and go and work in the Bovril factory, where a girl called Sharon Tiles had found a job last September.

It was then, while thinking about the Bovril factory and with two chips actually on the way to her mouth, that she saw her father walking with a girl on the street outside. Her heartbeat quickened, the way it always did when she saw him. She felt warm all over, and for a moment she couldn't believe her eyes.

The heat of the day had lifted.

By the tube station people stood outside a green public house, waiting for it to open. Other people hurried home from work, some impatiently buying an evening paper from a man at the entrance to the tube. A clock hanging above a jeweller's gave the time as twenty-five past five. 'Would you like to have a drink?' Francis suggested.

'That would be lovely.'

Susanna had told him about herself as they'd walked through the streets, about her drama school and after that a travelling seaside show that became a pantomime in winter. Being of an optimistic nature, melancholy had not persuaded her to turn her back on the theatre, nor had the emptiness of dreary towns on Sundays, nor cold, unpleasant digs. She'd played small parts in television plays she hadn't liked and then, astonishingly, there'd been this.

'Cinzano, please,' she said, sitting down in a corner, on a padded bench that ran along the green walls of the bar. She smiled as she spoke, knowing she was acting with her eyes and lips. She made her smile crooked, which was something she had practised in front of her bedroom looking-glass.

'Tell me more about yourself, Susanna,' he said when he returned with their drinks.

She told him she'd been lucky. She was the youngest of three daughters, the delicate one as a child, the one they'd all looked after. They were a happy family and always had been: there were jokes at mealtimes, and her father's easy laughter, her mother's niceness. One of her sisters worked in the British Museum, the other was a radiologist. Susanna was the only one who still lived at home, but her sisters often came at weekends and always at Christmas and Easter, towing with them various boyfriends. Everyone still made a fuss of her because she'd once been delicate and was talented, because she was so determined about the theatre, with its excesses and its dangers. What friends she brought home were carefully examined, especially if they were men. This scrutiny wasn't beady-eyed or harsh, but it did occasionally make Susanna think of herself as a protected species.

'I'm very happy really,' she said as she sipped her Cinzano. 'It's just that I sometimes think I've had too easy a life.'

Francis replied that of course that couldn't be true. He said that when he'd first noticed her in the drill-hall he'd wondered if her name was real. 'Born Pauline Boles? I wondered.'

'Boles?'

'Child of a girl on the streets of Nottingham. Born and not aborted because of the mother's love for a useless man. And then there was the orphanage.'

Susanna laughed and shook her head, but her companion spoke of a Nottingham orphanage as though it had really existed. He described paint-chipped corridors, and wash-rooms which were dank, and the institution's rusty cutlery. Stage-struck, he said, she had run away from it, hitch-hiking to London in a lorry loaded with drain-pipes, an event which would one day become a landmark in a famous theatrical saga, like Marilyn Monroe working in a paint shop. In London an aged lecher called Vassbacher, a dilettante of the theatre who'd helped girls in the past, helped her also. He it was who had changed her name to Susanna Music.

Drawn into the surprising fantasy, Susanna could not help seeing this figure as he was described: wizened and small, repeatedly lifting a handkerchief that smelt of peppermint to his lips, eyes running in the cold. 'Star quality is what you have,' he grunted at her as he used her body. That was, in fact, what Susanna believed she did possess: a kind of magic that crept out of hiding when she acted, something you could never mention to other people.

'Oh, yes indeed,' Francis said. 'That orphanage girl became outrageously famous.'

Susanna laughed again, but couldn't help feeling that there was a bizarreness about the speed with which an ersatz existence had been so skilfully created for her. Without any hesitation for thought the old dilettante called Vassbacher had been given life, as had the housekeeper of the orphanage in Nottingham, and the odd-job man there, a cantankerous person with a humped back. The housekeeper was a woman who'd been a missionary, whose skin had a leathery quality because of its exposure to years of African sun. Retired now, the odd-job man still came to see her, bringing vegetables from his garden. A week ago Vassbacher had been cremated – quite an occasion – in Putney Vale.

It seemed to Susanna that the talk could continue for hours, effortlessly inventing people and situations, changing her identity for her because she'd said she thought she'd had an easy time of it. 'I felt I could be Constance Kent before today,' she said, and glanced at Francis's face beside hers. She hoped he would talk about the drill-hall and Constance Kent, but he only nodded.

She'd lain awake in the early morning, she continued, and had felt herself invaded by the other girl's life: the whine of a milk trolley had not been real, nor the agile voice of the newsreader on her mother's transistor in the room beneath. 'My father's a gynaecologist,' she said, and described how it had been his rattling of tea things on the stairs that had jolted her back to the reality of her lilac bedroom.

'Make-belief is all we have,' Francis said, smiling and picking up their glasses again.

The bar had quite suddenly become lively. Girls swung their handbags as they swayed about on built-up shoes, demanding Bloody Marys or Martinis. Men in shirtsleeves or business suits crowded behind Francis at the bar, moving aside when he turned to carry through them the drinks he'd bought. As he passed the wide open doors he noticed that the sky was reddening as the sun began to set. A fiery glow softened the concrete of office buildings across the street, and lit the features of passers-by. It lit as well the features of Francis's child, the fluffy fair hair above the chapped skin of her face, her green and yellow uniform and plastic-rimmed spectacles. 'Hi,' she cried delightedly, waving a hand at him. 'Hi, Dad.'

Doris could hardly believe it. He always telephoned her at the shoe department, giving her notice, always saying how long he'd probably be in London for. Never in all the years of their love had he sprung a surprise like this.

In the bedroom she shared with Joy she lit a cigarette and then hunted for clean underclothes and an ironed blouse, for she liked to be fresh when he was in London, he being fastidious by nature. With a loping stride, she hurried between the wardrobe and the dressing-table, her thin body bent in a semi-circle. Unable to find what she sought, she rooted among the bedclothes but found nothing there either.

That it was a long time since Francis might have noted the state of her underclothing was something Doris ignored. Yet the fact was, being fastidious he was also particular: there was Joy's approaching adolescence to consider, for as he had so often quietly pointed out, you had to be careful with a growing child. The flat had only a single bedroom and when he stayed he spent the night on the sofa in the sitting-room. Even after Joy had gone to bed he was reluctant to engage in any kind of love-making, pointing out that the walls in the flat were thin. Yet on each occasion when he came to

London Doris believed that this rule he'd made would somehow be broken, that in the sitting-room he would stand in front of her and slowly take off her cardigan as once upon a time he used to, that he would kiss her eyes and then her ears, that his fingers would unzip her skirt and run about over her naked back. For all that she wished to be fresh for him.

She tidied the bedroom, having changed into clothes she'd put aside a week ago but had not yet washed. Lying idle like that often added a bit of life to clothes, making them seem fresher than those worn all day. She put away more than she normally did, making the two beds for the first time for some weeks. She collected all the used tissues she could see and rolled tights into balls. She pushed the dirty garments into drawers.

In the kitchen she washed up the dishes she and Joy had eaten their breakfast from, putting Joy's uneaten sausages in the fridge. When they'd had their meal in the Pizzaland he would come back and they'd sit together, having a drink in the kitchen while Joy watched the television in the sitting-room. She'd probably show him the last batch of the table-mats she'd made for At-Home Industries in Hammersmith, the scenes of old London. They'd sit quite close to one another at the table.

Still smoking her cigarette, Doris hurried from the kitchen to the sitting-room to gather up the exercise-books and pencils Joy should have taken to school with her but which had been lying there all day. She bundled together the materials she used to make the table-mats: cardboard she had to cut and trim, green baize, scenes of coaches travelling through the snow, Anne Hathaway's cottage. She pulled at the sofa and the armchairs, trying to tighten the creases out of the covers, deploring the stains that seemed to be everywhere, and the charred chair-leg where it had been pulled too close to the gas fire. She scraped at pieces of chewing-gum with her fingernails and drew the curtains over a bit, to keep the daylight from showing up the dust too much. When she'd finished she lit another cigarette, absent-mindedly throwing the match on to the floor and crossly picking it up again.

'He said a surprise, did he?' she inquired of Joy, who was

standing impatiently by the door, watching her. 'He definitely said a surprise, dear?'

Making a great deal of noise, Joy sighed. She repeated what she'd said already: that her father had wished to give them a surprise, that he'd intended to ring the doorbell of the flat at half past six.

'He definitely said that, Joy?'

'I told you. After I called out to him he said to keep it a surprise for you. He said to get you to come down to the Pizzaland and there he'd be. But I said you'd know immediately I mentioned the Pizzaland.'

'Like I did, dear. Of course I did.'

Doris smeared her mouth with lipstick and told Joy to go to the lavatory. She felt behind the bread-bin in the cupboard by the sink for the half bottle of vodka she'd bought at lunchtime in Value Wines. She saw no harm in giving herself a little lift, especially with the walk to the Pizzaland in front of them. She'd given herself a couple of little lifts in the Ladies' during the course of the afternoon and she felt all the better for them. 'Ciggies,' she said when Joy reappeared. 'I'll need to call in at the Bricklayer's for ciggies on the way.'

She drew on a maroon mackintosh. It made her feel excited just to think of him waiting for them in the Pizzaland. It made her even feel she had a plain golden ring on her finger because the Pizzaland was always lovely, with snow-capped mountains on the walls and the light gleaming on the carafes of red wine. Even in the old days when she hadn't had pennies to spare, any more than he had, they'd occasionally managed to eat in a restaurant because you could always find somewhere cheap. She hadn't made table-mats in the old days, but then she hadn't needed little lifts now and again, so in a way it evened out. The only trouble was the mats were getting more difficult. Recently in the evenings she hadn't felt at all like sticking down pictures of old London or cutting the corners off rectangles of cardboard. She'd had to look round for an alternative source of income, and something Frankie had said ages ago had given her the idea of going to see the dealer in Crawford Street. But none of that, of course, would she mention tonight.

They left the flat and on the way down the concrete stairs she repeated that she mustn't forget to call in at the Bricklayer's Arms for cigarettes. Joy reminded her that there was a cigarette machine outside the public house, but she explained that she didn't possess the right change. When she emerged a quarter of an hour later Joy said:

'I wonder who the bird was.'

'Bird, dear?'

'There was a bird with him on the street, and then they went into the pub. Long black hair and a blue dress on.'

'A girl you mean? With Dad?'

'Constance Kent he said her name was, something like that.'

·4·
Francis's

'Oh, dearie, lovely,' Doris cried in the Pizzaland, her lips reaching out for him. The snowy mountains were there as usual, enlivening the walls and making Doris think of ski resorts. There was music, and the carafes on the wooden tables, and the waitresses as smart as ever in their green and black get-up with their little red aprons.

He'd said at once that just for a change he'd wanted his presence in London to be a surprise, exactly as Joy had been on about. He'd stood up when they arrived. He'd said she was looking well.

'Oh, you *are* nice!' she cried. 'Oh, Frankie!' Whatever you do, she said to herself, don't refer to the girl. A man could be on a street with a girl, a man could be buying a drink for some girl he was maybe in an ad with. No harm done, for God's sake, no need to make a fuss.

'Lovely,' she said again. 'Lovely surprise, Frankie.' She helped herself to wine because it was there on the table in front of her, ordered by him already. Joy had picked up the menu, and Frankie was remarking that it wasn't an ad he was working in but some kind of telly thriller. It was hard to hear exactly what he was saying because there were other people talking at the next table and his voice was always low. It sounded gory, a body down a toilet.

Joy said she wanted a Pizzaland Special and then made a remark concerning the toilets at the Comprehensive, about what had happened to some girl there with a geography master. 'Nutty little stud he is,' Joy said, going into details and causing Doris to pretend not to hear because not hearing was always best when Joy got dirty like that. Without meaning to, she drifted into a reverie, gazing at her daughter as if seeking some clue to the complications of her personality, but the only thought that occurred to her was that Joy's hair was definitely on the skimpy side. You could see it quite clearly because of the way she was sitting; a tragedy it would be if poor Joy began to go bald.

'One Pizzaland Special,' he was saying to the waitress. 'I'll just have coffee, thanks. What about you, Dorrie?'

She reached across the table and touched his hand. She smiled at him and he smiled back. He'd got even thinner, his face especially, not that it didn't suit him. Lean bacon's best, as Irene in Handbags always said. All the girls on the floor knew what he looked like of course because of being on the television, especially since he'd become the Man with the Pipe and there were more close-ups of his features. 'Dishy,' young Maeve who brought the tea to the floor supervisor's office had said only three weeks ago. But some of the other girls, aware of how long Doris had been waiting for him, sometimes pursed their lips.

'I'll have the one with the prawns,' she said.

'And a baked potato with mine, Dad. And a Tizer?' Joy hopefully inquired of the waitress, but the waitress said there was only Coca-Cola.

Doris poured herself more wine from the carafe while Joy continued to tell him about various doings at Tite Street

Comprehensive. She didn't listen herself, preferring to think about July 2nd 1966, her favourite day. A few months previously her father had remarried and as a result of that Doris had moved out of the house she'd lived in all her life, not being able to stand the woman. She'd been feeling miserable about all that on a bus while the bus was caught in a traffic jam in Oxford Street, in the dumps because she'd taken it for granted when her mother had died that she and her father would become chummier than ever. 'Quicker to walk,' the chap beside her had said, and five minutes later they were sitting in a saloon bar in Woodstock Street. The Spread Eagle it was called, the chap was Frankie.

Joy was talking about vomiting again, going through the business of being sick over the postman's letters. She was peering at Frankie through her spectacles, waving a fork about.

'July the second,' Doris said, hoping he'd forgive the coarseness about vomit. She tried to frown at Joy, but found it difficult. 'I was a mile down Memory Lane, Frankie.'

The flash of his teeth appeared, responding as he always did.

'That day on the bus,' she said. 'I'll never forget it, Frankie. When Dad and me met,' she reminded Joy. 'A 73 it was.'

'I know,' Joy said.

'A red-letter day I call it.'

Lager and lime she used to drink then. 'Carlsberg, if they have it,' she'd said in the Spread Eagle. She'd held back a bit, not wishing to seem easy or a pick-up because when it came to the point she wasn't. She'd always rather avoided men, being so chummy with her dad, not needing them really, not interested.

'I went into the Spread Eagle the other day,' she said, 'just to see.'

He nodded agreeably, and she nodded back. She often went into the Spread Eagle as a matter of fact, since Woodstock Street was only just across Oxford Street from the store where she worked. She climbed the stairs to the upstairs bar, just as they'd done on that first Saturday afternoon, except that everything was a bit different now. There were pictures of birds on the stairs, which there hadn't been in the old days, and the upstairs bar was called the Inn People's Place. But the buttoned brown velvet was just as it had been, with the red shades on the wall-lights and the eagle over the bar, and the big fan in the centre of the ceiling, like a propeller. When she sat alone there her eye was always caught by the movement of the fan and she was reminded of an aeroplane, which made her think of faraway places, of the holidays together she knew there would one day be. 'Join you?' a man might boldly inquire, plonking a glass down beside hers, but she always looked away.

''Course nowhere's the same,' she said. 'There's this jukebox now.'

Again he nodded. The last time he'd come up from Folkestone he had definitely said the dressmaker's heart condition was worse. Doris had imagined him carrying meals on trays, pouring out medicine. Recently she'd begun to feel it in her bones that the release would be any day now.

A prawn pizza was placed in front of her, and again she reached across the table and touched one of his hands. In the Spread Eagle that day he'd made up for everything. He'd listened when she'd told him about the chumminess there'd been between her and her dad, he'd held her hand and said he understood. A few weeks later he'd brought her to a hotel near King's Cross and she'd been unable to believe she was enjoying it so much, realizing she'd never been in love before.

'All righty?' she said. 'All righty, love?'

Beneath the table she tried to find his knee with hers. She wasn't able to, but he seemed to understand her intention. A tiny smile cut into the delicacy of his face.

'Run to another carafe, shall we, Frankie?'

He raised a hand and the waitress came. He ordered the wine and more Coca-Cola for Joy, and another potato because Joy had asked for it as well.

'Lovely, the wine they have here,' Doris said. She lowered her voice. 'How's her shaking, Frankie?'

'How's what?'

'Her shaking. You were saying last time about her shaking.'

'She's taking something for the shaking.'

'But she's worse is she, Frankie?'

'They have pills for everything these days.'

He felt sorry for his wife, he'd said so that first day in the Spread Eagle. She was the cross he bore; no one could love an invalid. Consoling herself with that, Doris put her head on one side, the way he liked. She wanted to ask him about the girl, to come straight out with it, but she didn't. 'Great, it sounds,' she said instead. 'Your telly thriller.'

His entire stay in London had been ruined just because the child had noticed him on the street. He'd felt shaky, almost unwell, when he'd seen her in the doorway of the bar, peering at him through her unattractive glasses. He'd been obliged to listen to a long rigmarole about how she'd been in a café eating chips, which she'd had to finish before running after him. He should have known that bad luck was going to strike again. He should have guessed that he couldn't simply walk about the crowded streets of London without being bothered by a child. Anger crept through him in a familiar way, and he struggled to control it. While the voices of Doris and the child continued, he tried to convince himself that none of it would matter in the end. Fate had turned round: Julia Ferndale's love for him made up for everything.

But the anger wouldn't quite go away. As vividly as Doris remembered July 2nd 1966, he remembered it also: it was on the morning of that day that the dressmaker had finally told him to go. He'd gone into her workroom after breakfast, watching for a moment while she cut out a dress, waiting to ask her about the shopping. She'd been cross the evening before, and he'd been hoping the crossness would have passed. Her bouts of bad temper had become more frequent recently, and it was during one of the worst of them that she'd thrown the sewing-machine cover at him, severely damaging a wall of the workroom with it. 'Fish fingers, shall I get, dear?' he'd said on the morning of July 2nd, and in reply she had requested him to leave her house, claiming she'd repeatedly asked him to do so before. When he'd opened his mouth to speak she'd threatened him with the police.

It made Francis angrier when he thought how often in his life it had been the same, how things had gone swimmingly in the houses where he found himself, how he'd fitted in and tried to help, and had then been turned upon. Even the night before he had suddenly found the eyes of Julia Ferndale's mother on him, with suspicion in her wrinkled face.

'Maybe a bread-knife,' Doris was saying to the child. 'Was it a bread-knife the throat was cut with, Frankie?'

He said he didn't know what kind of a knife it was, and did his best to smile. It was extraordinary to think she'd once been so very pretty, so nice to be seen on a street with. Older than he was of course, by quite a year or so, but still seeming a sweet little shopgirl. The fact that she'd been forlorn about her father's remarriage had given her a wispy quality. Little girl lost, he'd thought, and had imagined her neat fingers fitting shoes on to women's feet in her shoe department and her own feet hurrying off to spend her luncheon vouchers. In the time he'd known her she'd begun to look like a skeleton, her hair gone grey, nothing forlorn about her now.

'Funny, putting a body down the toilet,' the child was musing. 'You'd think it wouldn't fit.'

'Yes, funny that,' Doris said. 'Dare say toilets were different then.'

'Bigger, were they?'

'Dare say they were, dear.'

The last time she'd forced him into a sexual encounter with her he'd wanted to commit murder himself. He'd been lying down on the sofa in her sitting-room and she'd suddenly appeared, half naked, in the middle of the night. Leaning forward to seize him, her breasts had loosely dangled, reminded him of freshly plucked chickens. Until that moment he hadn't realized just how much she rattled his nerves, and although on the point of walking out of her flat for ever he'd managed to keep calm and was afterwards glad he had: there was always the consideration that if he didn't keep her humoured she could get out a paternity order against him. It was impossible to trust women like that. It had been impossible to trust the dressmaker, and impossible to trust the doctor's wife, who had always got going with that kind of thing when her husband was conducting his afternoon surgery. There'd be the stream of patients arriving by the side entrance, and her nudging eyes when the doctor rose from the tea table to go and attend to their ailments. The doctor's wife was a woman with well-covered white thighs beneath her scented underclothes. On each occasion she turned the key in the lock of the tiny room which had been made over to him while he was staying in the house, and she always stood for a moment with her back against the door, her small eyes trying to express the naughtiness she felt, her hair fresh from its electric curlers. 'No, you must do it, darling,' she always whispered, making him undo the fastenings of her clothes, although he never wanted to. With the dressmaker, of course, the whole thing had been so repellent it made him furious even to think about it. With Doris there was always an unattractive whining.

'But I thought Constance Kent was this girl on the street,' she was saying now, looking at him.

'She's acting the part. Constance Kent was real.'

'I got the wrong end of the stick,' Joy said, and to pass the time he told them about Constance Kent. He described her and the mystery she trailed, how she'd been different until the moment of her crime, how she'd ended up in a house for the religious in Brighton.

On the ashtray in front of Doris were several half-smoked cigarettes. Without allowing his distaste to show, he pressed with his thumb one that was still smouldering. She had a forgetful habit of lighting cigarettes between mouthfuls, yet as a girl she'd been far too humble to do anything like that.

'Funny carry-on for a religious, I must say. Funny way to behave.' She emitted shrill laughter, drinking more wine. 'I'd love another glass,' she said, winking at him as if they shared some secret. 'Run along to the toilet,' she said to the child. 'Make yourself comfy.'

'I don't want the toilet.'

'Dad and I need a private word, dear.'

Because he didn't want to have a private word, he watched while the child reluctantly rose and while she knocked over a glass on a table occupied by two American tourists.

'I'm worried about her,' Doris said. 'She's twelve and she can't read.'

Francis nodded. He had yet to make it clear that he was staying in a hotel, that when this meal was over he did not intend to return to the flat in Fulham and sleep on the sofa in the sitting-room. He would have to give the name of the hotel correctly because if he didn't, if he said some place other than the Rembrandt, she would ring up and find he wasn't there, after which she might easily locate the drill-hall since the child knew the neighbourhood it was in. She began to say something else about being worried, but he smiled and interrupted. He said that the television company had booked rooms for all the actors in the production who did not live in London. He'd felt he had to accept so as not to be a nuisance, although of course he hadn't wanted to. 'The Rembrandt Hotel,' he said, speaking clearly, making certain that she heard.

Immediately she became distraught. She blinked repeatedly, her lips began to quiver. He examined the alpine scene on one of the walls. He heard her sniffing, and then blowing her nose on a tissue. In the public house he had explained to Susanna Music that the child who'd called out to him from the door had been begging. He'd quite enjoyed being with the pretty little actress, being seen with her in the public house and on the street. But she was too wrapped up in her ambitions to be a sympathetic friend. He'd guessed that quite soon.

'The other nuisance,' he said, 'is that an old uncle of mine isn't at all well.'

'Uncle, Frankie?'

'Uncle Manchester we used to call him.' He smiled and again spoke clearly. 'Because he lived there. Because he lived in Manchester.'

'I didn't know you had an uncle, Frankie.'

74

'I'm afraid I'll have to spend a bit of time in the evenings with him. As a matter of fact, I should be getting out there now. When we've finished.'

'Where, dear? Where is he?'

He'd been once to the place where his mother and his father were. He remembered the stained-glass panels of the Garden of Eden on either side of the hall door, the elephant's foot full of walking-sticks by the stairs.

'Hampton Wick,' he said. 'An old folks' home.'

'So you're staying in this hotel, Frankie? And now you're going out to Hampton Wick?' She spoke slowly, countering a slur that had developed in her speech. Her voice was mournful, her eyes lifeless.

'I'm afraid so, Dorrie.'

'But you'll be back? I mean, later tonight, Frankie? You'll come to the flat?'

'I'm afraid it'll be too late. Hampton Wick's a long way out.'

'I could slip out and come round to the hotel, dear. Easily I could. After Joy's gone to sleep. It's just it would be nice –'

'I know, Dorrie, lovely.' But he explained that it would be awkward for him to have her arriving in the Rembrandt Hotel in the middle of the night. Hotel managements objected to that kind of thing.

Joy returned and was told by her mother to stand some distance away because the conversation was private. She began to protest, getting red in the face and whispering, but in the end she obediently hovered by the table at which the American tourists were now eating spaghetti bolognese.

'It's a real disappointment,' Doris said. 'It's spoilt the surprise you made for us, Frankie.'

'I know, Dorrie. I'm sorry.'

He lit her cigarette because it was dangling from her lips, bent in the middle like all the cigarettes she smoked. As he did so he noticed that Joy was dipping a finger into the sugar bowl on the Americans' table, an activity the Americans did not appear to care for.

'She said you were out drinking with a girl, Frankie, but I knew it was all right. Actress out of an ad, I said to myself.'

'The Constance Kent girl actually.'

'I thought Constance Kent was –'

'This girl's acting the part, Dorrie. I explained to you, dear.'

Her large black handbag, usually hanging on a strap from her shoulder, was on the chair beside her. Francis reached for it in order to find the money to pay the bill. It was full of used tissues, empty cigarette packets and old shopping lists scrawled on bits of paper.

'I love you, Frankie,' she said, and for a second he was reminded of Julia Ferndale, who had said the same thing that morning at Cheltenham railway station. She'd said it again when he'd telephoned her an hour ago, and he had naturally replied that he loved her also. He had sent a message to her mother, and had asked after Mrs Spanners.

'Hey, sir,' called out the male American. 'Will you see to your kid? She's into our dinner here.'

Doris didn't hear this protest, so Francis beckoned to Joy and made a gesture of apology to the Americans. Joy said she'd be late for the ice-skating on the television.

'You'll phone me up at the shoe department, Frankie? They don't mind in the office.'

'Of course I'll keep in touch.'

On the street outside the Pizzaland she began to talk about a women she'd spoken of during their meal, an Arab woman who'd come into the shoe department that day and ordered three dozen pairs of lace-ups.

'You told us that,' Joy said.

'I know, dear, only I'm telling you again.'

She was trying to delay him. In a moment she'd be suggesting a quick drink before he set off on his journey, and then she'd say it was too late for him to go out to Hampton Wick and urge him to telephone instead.

'Poor Joy's missing her skating.'

'What skating's that, dear?'

They were blocking the pavement, but she didn't notice. A gang of youths pushed roughly by, smelling of beer. 'We were dare-devil once,' she suddenly said. 'London was a carnival, Frankie.'

Anger clawed at him again. It was degrading having to be in public with a drunken woman and a child who stuck her finger into other people's sugar. It was degrading having to hang about on a street listening to an incomprehensible conversation about carnivals.

'Be down the flat tomorrow night, Dad? Harry O tomorrow night.'

Successfully he smiled, not answering the query. His trouble was, he couldn't help forgiving people. He'd written to the Massmith sisters afterwards, saying bygones could be bygones. He'd written to the doctor's wife. Whenever he saw the dressmaker lumping her way from shop to shop in Folkestone he offered to help her carry things. The Massmith sisters hadn't even replied, and later they'd put down the receiver on him. There'd been a horrible document from Kilvert-Dunne's solicitor, which he'd thrown into the sea. And last night there'd been the suspicion in old Mrs Anstey's eyes, even though he'd weeded her garden for her. This woman he was standing with now should never have agreed to getting pregnant just because he'd had a whim. If she'd shaken her head there wouldn't be the fear of a paternity order, or tears in a Pizzaland when he explained that he had to visit a sick relation. The anger began to pound at him, reverberating in his head, affecting his ears in the way it often did.

'I really have to go,' he said, smiling again at both of them.

In the television lounge of the Sundown Home Mrs Tyte couldn't help her tears. Often they didn't tell you the truth: the reason he didn't ever come could easily be because he wasn't well.

'You're just a little confused,' Miss Purchase said cheerfully. 'You've got things upside down.'

'Is it 'flu?'

'No, of course not, dear.'

'Is he in the hall, Miss Purchase?'

'It's not visitors' time, dear. We couldn't have visitors at this hour, now could we?'

Miss Purchase went away, picking up the *TV Times*, which someone had thrown on the floor, even though there was a notice which specially requested them not to do so. It was particularly important that the *TV Times*, with its slippery pages, shouldn't be left lying on the floor to cause an unnecessary accident.

Mr Tyte, who was the guilty one, watched Miss Purchase's irritation with a glow of pleasure. Earlier that day he'd taken a couple of sticks out of the elephant's foot in the hall and hung them on the hallstand. When next he'd passed the elephant's foot he'd noticed that they'd been replaced. Later that evening, when the hall was quiet, he hoped to hang up another couple. In the end she would put up a notice, just as she had about taking the *Telegraph* into the garden. Breaking the rules was all the more enjoyable after a notice had gone up.

'What's the matter?' he said.

'He's not coming. He's caught 'flu.'

'He hasn't caught 'flu. You've got yourself into a stupid state again.' It made him tetchy when she cried. He wished she wouldn't.

'I thought he was in the hall.'

'It isn't even a Sunday afternoon. It's half past nine at night.'

'Would you look in the hall, Henry?'

'Oh, for heaven's sake don't be silly.'

She wiped at her shrunken cheeks with a handkerchief. There was nothing they could do if he had 'flu; he'd have to stay in bed and they'd just have to wait, hoping it wouldn't be too long. But she was certain he'd been in the hall.

'Mrs Tyte,' Mrs Uprichard called across the lounge. 'Here's your son.'

Mrs Tyte nodded very slowly. She smiled through the remains of her tears, she knew she'd been right. She'd felt it in her bones that he was coming tonight, half past nine or not, it was never too late. She turned her head and there he was, all in colour. He was sailing out to sea and smiling back at her, smoking the pipe he'd taken up. It was horrid of Henry to turn his back like that, to get up and go out as soon as their son appeared.

Near Piccadilly Circus groups of men stood about, outside the all-night cinemas. They were stunted men of Mediterranean appearance, with carefully arranged hair. They offered other men blue films or lesbian exhibitions, or girls, or youths. Sometimes they turned nasty if these offers were rejected. 'Filth,' one of them snarled, spitting on to the shoes of a man he'd assumed to be a customer. 'Poof,' another added. The girls these stunted men protected, who strolled about the nearby streets, were young, fifteen or sixteen mainly. Some had the walk of provincial girls, new to the city and the game. Their made-up faces were garish in the night-light and as they walked they stared fixedly ahead, afraid to make a sideways glance in case it should be called soliciting. Some bulged with fat. Others were pinched and rickety. West Indians trotted rapidly; older women wearily trudged.

Francis strolled in Wardour Street, examining the posters in the windows of various film companies. By a row of dustbins a cardboard carton was full of chickens' feet. A garbage van moved slowly; men in heavy rubber gloves smoked cigarettes as they tossed refuse into the bowels of its machinery. Bottles and tins clattered about; the chickens' feet disappeared and then the garbage van moved on, followed by a corporation sprinkler, its circular brushes sweeping the litter into the gutters and then spraying water on to it. Sodden and discoloured, the litter was less noticeable than it had been before.

'There's a garidge we can go to,' a rough-faced man said, pausing beside Francis. 'Denham Street. O.K., darling? Tenner O.K., is it?'

Francis nodded.

'Bloody fuzz everywhere,' the man complained. 'Often about, are you?'

'Sometimes.'

'Fancy I seen you before. Young bloke comes in the toilets Thursday, pissed like a pig. Thought you was him at first.'

'No.'

'Don't like it when a bloke's pissed. Can't care for the smell. You've had a couple, have you, darling?'

'Not much. A glass or two of wine.'

'No, I'm not saying you're pissed. No, I can see you hasn't been on it. Tony the name is.'

'Mine's Adrian.'

'Nice, that is. You in business, Adrian?'

'Insurance. The Eagle Star.'

'I'm a plasterer, 'smatter of fact. Don't mind going with a plasterer, do you, dear?'

'No, not at all.'

'If you see the fuzz popping up, Adrian, walk on ahead for a bit. Pity you hasn't a place, Adrian, pity about that. Where're you living, Adrian?'

'Bournemouth.'

'Naughty is it?'

Francis didn't answer the question because he had no idea if Bournemouth was naughty or not, having only been there once, a footman with the coach in *Cinderella*. 'I'm glad we met up,' he said to the rough-faced man.

'Pity it has to be a garidge.'

'I know.'

When it was over Francis walked away from the garage with the money the man had given him. Tears oozed from the corners of his eyes, leaving tiny tracks in his make-up, causing his face to seem older. He wished he didn't always cry.

Police cars prowled the streets, their occupants glancing sharply at his solitary figure. Two policemen on the beat spoke sharply to him but he insisted he was not a male prostitute. They told him to go home and he promised them he would, but instead he paused in Regent Street. He stood in an arcade, glancing at shop windows full of lightweight suits and overcoats.

'Looking for action, friend?' a youth with a wire ear-ring in the lobe of one ear inquired. He spoke in an affected voice. In his pale face a moustache sprouted among white-headed pimples, above the unpowdered lipstick that glistened on his lips.

Francis nodded, and walked behind the boy past an amusement arcade that had recently closed, past a Wimpy Bar where girls sat at red-topped tables and a woman in a tattered fur coat crouched over a cup of coffee. In Air Street and Glasshouse Street Francis followed his companion at a distance. Negotiations took place in a doorway and then the youth led the way to a car-park that contained a single car, an old metallic-coloured Cortina. He'd been in the car-park before, the same Cortina had been there. 'All right then, friend?' the youth said. 'A bloke'll be along. My, aren't we lovely?'

Ten minutes later a stout man appeared. He wore a chalk-striped blue suit with a waistcoat, across which a watch-chain hung. He had dark, well-shaven jowls and a head the colour of dripping, with black strands drawn carefully over his baldness. His shirt-cuffs were slightly frayed. 'He said fifteen,' were the first words he uttered. 'Fifteen right, is it?'

Francis nodded, accepting the money. He thought of it as a present, as he always did, the only nice part of what was happening. 'I gev him a five,' the man said. 'You never know if a chep'll be there. But you're here all right, aren't you, sailor?'

Francis nodded again. They stood by the car; the man moved closer to him. 'Officer cless, are you?' he inquired.

'I'm not in the navy actually.'

'Chep said you were. What's your name, love?'

'Adrian.'

'O.K. then, Adrian? Our chep's on the look-out.'

When it was over Francis again walked quickly away. 'Any time, friend,' the youth with the ear-ring invited, watchful at the entrance to the car-park. Francis had had dealings with him before, but naturally the boy had forgotten. He thought he might have had dealings with the man as well, but he couldn't be sure because the light was never good in the car-park. 'Hey,' the youth called after him and when Francis turned he said, 'You're on the telly, eh? You're on them ads?' He laughed, and Francis hurried away.

When he knew the boy couldn't see what he was doing he dried away the tears that had spread on to his cheeks. He felt unwell and he'd begun to shiver. It was always the same after anger had driven him in search of presents and the melancholy that followed was always the same too. It dragged into his mind images he didn't wish to see: his mother's face, and his father's, in 14 Rowena Avenue when he was still a child; most of all, the face of the debt-collector who was their lodger. In the sitting-room his mother's knitting-needles clicked, there was his father's talk of the Midland Bank, of customers spoken to that day, of changes due to come about. In the sitting-room there was Francis's affection for both of them, for their faces and their hands – his mother's very soft, his father's fingers stained with red ink, tobacco-brown. She smelt of powder and cleanness, his father of cigarettes.

He told them about school, every single bit of gossip, of marks he'd been awarded, compliments and criticism. The footsteps of their lodger sounded often on the stairs, and sometimes his mother said they couldn't have let the rooms to a pleasanter man. On Thursdays there was sago, its brown skin the nicest part. On Sundays there were their walks on Ealing Common, and Sunday teas of buttered toast and jam, with raisin scones, his father's special treat. 'Your father was happy?' the younger Massmith sister remarked years later when Francis told the Massmiths all about it in their bungalow. 'Yes, he was happy,' he replied. 'He wasn't boring, you know,' he said to the Kilvert-Dunnes while helping in their glasshouses on the Isle of Wight. His father's affection for the Midland Bank seemed touching to the Kilvert-Dunnes in the end, and to the Massmith sisters, and to the doctor and the doctor's wife. On the wireless in 14 Rowena Avenue there were comedy programmes, and the news at nine o'clock.

But then, when the secret came, all of it was different. When the secret came the silences in the sitting-room seemed shadowed with treachery. Francis explained all that to the Massmith sisters, and to the others, too: how the footsteps on the stairs were different then, how the stairs themselves, winding up to the attics, were not as they

82

had been. During meals or on the common, in the sitting-room where the clock and the knitting-needles kept time with one another, he told years afterwards how he had fought a bleakness and a despair that often made him want to smash the cosiness to pieces by screaming out the truth. But the debt-collector had said it was their secret now. 'Yours and mine, Francis,' he'd said, his fingers cold and white, like ivory. Every morning the debt-collector cycled off, a frail man in a fawn gabardine raincoat over his pin-striped suit, a wisp of moustache enlivening his face. Francis was eleven then.

In all his conversations with the Massmith sisters and the others Francis had expunged the debt-collector's name, not wishing even to think of it himself. 'I've got the Cumberland Hussars,' the man had said, pausing in the sitting-room doorway on his way to the attics, and Francis explained to the Massmith sisters that his parents would have considered it unusual if he had not eagerly agreed to mount the stairs with their lodger to inspect the newly acquired regiment of soldiers. The secret might have unfolded there and then if Francis had hesitated too long, if he hadn't done what he had done so often before. With the colourful regiments spread out on the table kept specially for the war games, the same words were always whispered, the same passion entered the debt-collector's eyes. Among the marching soldiers the deception and the treachery increased, becoming as much part of everything as the acts the debt-collector taught him. School, and the friends there might have been there, became absurd. His mother and his father seemed like two bothersome old mice, filling the sitting-room with fustiness. 'Oh, my dear,' the younger Massmith sister tearfully murmured, hearing that. He was ashamed, he explained to the doctor's wife, to stand in the same room as his parents; but all the doctor's wife had done was to take advantage of him also. In the end the debt-collector had paid him.

Francis walked along Piccadilly, hurrying away from what had taken place in the car-park. He'd have a bath in the Rembrandt Hotel, no matter what the time was when he arrived there. 'Hi, dear,' a woman with a Pekinese said and he didn't answer, knowing that the woman would demand money, not offer it. Taxis, their orange lights glowing, moved rapidly on the wide, empty street. He passed the Ritz and thought of the people sleeping there: men with girls they'd picked up, women with bar-room lovers, dreary married couples, the rich. Once upon a time he'd believed that he might stay there himself, that he and a friend might sit among the ferns and palms, drinking Tio Pepe at two pounds a glass and laughing quietly in a companionable way.

In his bedroom in Rowena Avenue he'd imagined scenes like that, escaping from the debt-collector and from his own tears, promising himself that it would never happen again. He'd thought of Kim Novak and had replaced the debt-collector's ivory hands with hers, telling himself a story that seemed like one of her films. Sun tanned his body, the wind rustled her headscarf. Their sports car sped along the roads of islands. Money meant nothing.

Even now, the stories continued. There wasn't Kim Novak any more, nor did sunshine tan his body, nor were there island roads. But for years there'd been an idyll in an English village: a post office and village stores, a little shop that sold everything, where people met and lingered. He and his friend were there – a woman or a man, it didn't matter – he attending to the grocery side of things, his friend selling stamps, or vice versa, it didn't matter either. There'd been enough for a little red MG, his friend always driving because Francis still hadn't learnt to drive himself. Now and again on an autumn evening they slipped out together to have dinner in a lakeside hotel, dressing up a bit because both of them liked to. They kept two cats, one tawny, the other black. Recently that idyll had changed again: the village setting had been tidied away, as the headscarf of Kim Novak had been. The one that replaced it was incomplete, and shadowy. It took place in a German city.

Francis walked by the railings of Green Park, not taking a taxi, still practising the frugality he had developed after his failure to appropriate the dressmaker's money. It wasn't important that the idyll had changed again; what mattered was he had no friend. He'd gone on holidays with friends, but always there'd been sulkiness and tears. 'You're a nutter, Francis,' a girl he'd thought to be sympathetic had pronounced six months ago in Cleethorpes. 'You're sick the way you cry, old boy,' a man once said in Dieppe.

His melancholy deepened as he progressed through the London night. People left a gambling club near Hyde Park Corner, young men in evening dress shouting and laughing, girls laughing also, all of them tumbling into taxis, going on to somewhere else. For a moment Francis hated them. He stopped in his walk, indulging his dislike, listening to the shrill voices, the late-night cries of people determinedly having a good time. He wouldn't have cared if all of them had been shot down dead, if gunmen had appeared from the Mayfair doorways and opened fire in the orange street light. He imagined the bodies scattered, reminding him of the bodies in the train crash, and the victims of the terrorists the director in the drill-hall had referred to, and the victim of Constance Kent. 'What a bitter world he drew you into,' the younger Massmith sister had sadly whispered, and both of them had later condemned the debt-collector as a monster.

In the Rembrandt Hotel Francis inquired of the Vietnamese night-porter if there was a typewriter he could use for five minutes. The man said there wasn't, but under pressure he led the way to a small office behind the reception area and pointed at a typewriter on a desk. Francis inserted a piece of hotel writing-paper and typed a brief message to the effect that the jewellery listed below had been freely made over to him by Julia Ferndale, now Julia Tyte, and was his property: an amber and gold dragon brooch, a necklace of seed pearls, a pair of sapphire ear-rings with a bracelet and a ring that matched them. He typed her name, leaving a space for her signature.

Francis had learnt by heart the prayers and responses in the Catholic prayer-book he had bought. He had learnt by heart as well the Gospel according to St Mark, and often pleased Julia by murmuring the verses in the Catholic voice he'd cultivated. He had pored for hours in Folkestone public library over Butler's *Lives of the Saints*, later talking at length about St Colette and St Fulgentius. He had bought a rosary and a crucifix, and had regularly attended services in the Church of Our Lady of Grace in

Folkestone, observing how holy water was taken on the fingertips and the wafer received on the tongue. He particularly enjoyed confession and delighted in the sign of the Cross, the rapid gestures, the Father, the Son, the Holy Ghost. In Our Lady of Grace he had been present at more than forty weddings.

That night Francis dreamed of being married and making again the sign of the Cross. He dreamed of the jewellery he'd typed a message about, and of the uncle he'd invented on the spur of the moment, who came quite vividly to life. The nakedness of the dressmaker and the doctor's wife repeatedly occurred in his dream, and so did the moustached face of the debt-collector. Doris and Joy were there also, with Mrs Anstey and the two men he had met in the night, and the prettiness of Susanna Music. But it was the real Constance Kent who always was closest to him, who comforted him and made him happy, like the people in his stories.

·5·
Julia's

'Well, this is nice,' Mrs Anstey declared, in her usual place beneath the tulip tree. The evening was so still that the flow of the river could scarcely be discerned. In a distant field brown and white cattle grazed.

'Nicer than London,' Katherine said, depositing a tray on the beech-wood table beside her grandmother's chair. There were glasses on the tray, and a bottle of white burgundy, the girls' weekend gift.

'The streets are dirtier when it doesn't rain,' Henrietta said. 'London's dreadful in a heatwave.'

Henrietta was the older, twenty-three to Katherine's twenty, but often they were taken to be twins. It wasn't just the similar beauty of their features, and their hair: both had a gangling look, and unlike their mother were flat-chested and narrow-hipped. Both were taller than Julia.

The wine was poured, the talk about life in London continued. They shared a flat with two other girls in Barnes. Henrietta worked for the managing director of a mail-order firm, Katherine in a china shop in South Audley Street. The names of boyfriends littered their conversation, different names each time they came to Swan House. They still looked virginal, but Mrs Anstey knew there had been nights with these different names, Friday evening drives to somewhere pleasant like Cambridge, or Southsea out of season. No doubt they were sensibly on the pill.

'And what's been happening in Stone St Martin?' Katherine inquired, laughing a little as she spoke because in the opinion of the girls nothing did tend to happen in the town. Henrietta laughed also, but Mrs Anstey said you'd be surprised.

Easy conversation was part of the household. Without making an effort, Mrs Anstey could recall scenes that were full of it: the girls in Julia's bedroom, sprawled over a patchwork counterpane, cups of tea everywhere; walks near Anstey's Mill; moments in the garden and the kitchen and the drawing-room. The girls were always talking, Julia asking questions. Returning from St Mildred's Convent, they told of changes since her time there and complained far more about the nuns than Mrs Anstey ever remembered Julia herself complaining. Yet often there were repetitions, the girls' conversation full of shadows from Julia's own so many years ago. In Anstey's Mill Julia had chattered just as the girls did in Swan House, while Mrs Anstey had asked the questions. The difference was that at Anstey's Mill there'd been a father in the family. The death of Roger Ferndale had caused the flow of conversation in Swan House to become more feminine than it might have been.

In answer to Katherine's question about what had happened in the town Mrs Anstey mentioned Mrs Spanners. She described the charwoman's appearance on the evening of the cocktail party and told of a newspaper cutting she had brought to Swan House concerning Princess Margaret. She reported that Nevil Crapp, whose identity was remembered by the girls because he'd featured so often in court cases, had become engaged to Diane of the Crowning Glory Salon. The elderly father of Mr Humphreys, on the cheese and bacon counter in Dobie's Stores, had died a few days ago.

'And then of course,' Mrs Anstey finished up, 'there have been the preparations for the wedding.'

She spoke as casually as she could. Julia had said she would join them for a glass of wine but she might well be occupied in the kitchen for another twenty minutes: this was as good a time as any to mention the uneasiness that had first been a worry on the evening of the cocktail party and which had since persisted, in spite of her efforts to be reasonable. It was Mrs Anstey who had suggested that the girls might be invited for a weekend, a last gathering of a family that would be different in the future. 'Oh, yes,' she said. 'A deal of preparation.'

The wedding cake, already made by the Martin Street Bakery, awaited the moment of icing. A package of small cardboard boxes, printed with silver ribbons, had arrived at Swan House. In these, after the wedding, Mrs Anstey was to post pieces of the cake to those who had been unable to attend the occasion.

'I dare say Mrs Spanners is in her element.' Henrietta laughed again, and Katherine did too.

'There's something actually,' Mrs Anstey began to say, before she caught sight of Julia on her way from the house. She changed the subject, and when Julia arrived they were talking again about life in London. Julia sat down and was poured a glass of wine.

'I nearly forgot to telephone Father Lavin,' she revealed. 'It's actually his birthday.'

Mrs Anstey sighed without letting it show. How on earth, Henrietta and Katherine simultaneously thought, had a fact like that been discovered? The priest would hardly have drawn attention to the day last year or the year before, and even if he had it wasn't something an adult would remember. The dates of birthdays were what children carried with them.

'He's getting on, I suppose,' Katherine said. 'Sixty-ish?'

'Fifty-five.'

'And the new chap?'

No age was attached to the new chap beyond the fact, supplied by Mrs Anstey, that he was young: Father Dawne hadn't been in Stone St Martin long enough for Henrietta or Katherine to have met him yet. He was nice, Mrs Anstey added, but the girls, who might have wondered about his niceness had he not been a priest, failed to do so since priests were not their cup of tea. Like their grandmother, they had nothing against them, or against the notion of a God who presided over all humanity. They simply did not wish to have dealings with such a figure, either directly or through earthly minions.

Tinges of red were beginning to appear in the sky, the midges weren't biting yet. The two women and the girls sipped their wine and talked of other things; Mrs Anstey's attention drifted. On Julia's unwieldy typewriter she had noticed that morning a series of long, closely typed paragraphs concerning the sale of a field, with stipulations about boundaries and rights of way and land drains originating in another field. She often read the legal typing in case there should be something of interest, but there never was. There was no need for Julia to continue with the chore now that the girls were off her hands; there hadn't been a need for years, but it was somehow typical of her that she didn't give it up. It was typical of her, too, that she should be paying for the honeymoon in Italy, for at the back of Mrs Anstey's mind there was a suspicion that that was so. She didn't know why she thought it, something that had been mentioned presumably had caught her attention without her properly realizing.

Later that evening there was a moment after dinner when she found herself alone with Henrietta, but the conversation they had wasn't satisfactory. The truth she so strongly sensed contained no details, no faces of other people, no incidents or events, no facts of any kind: it seemed to Mrs Anstey that a fog shrouded a whole landscape. Perception couldn't cope with the mystery of that and none of it was easy to explain to a young girl, whose reaction no doubt was to think her touched.

The next morning Henrietta and Katherine shopped in the town, as they had so often done on Saturdays in the past. When they were children their mother had accompanied them, with the shopping distributed on three lists, coffee and sausage-rolls in the Bay Tree Café as a reward, then the walk back to Swan House. Henrietta and Katherine had coffee in the Bay Tree this morning, though without sausage-rolls.

'Apparently,' Henrietta said, hesitating a little and then continuing, 'Mummy should make a will.'

'But surely she has?'

'Granny says she hasn't. Granny's become all worried.'

'About wills?'

'About Francis.'

When Julia had told her daughters that she'd become engaged to an actor they'd returned as soon as possible to Stone St Martin and had not been freed of their doubts until they met Francis, some weeks later. They shared with Mrs Anstey the view that their mother's lame ducks had a way of gnawing to the bone the hand that fed them. Their mother was imbued with all the complications of goodness and the introspective nature that went with it: that was what they believed, and knew their grandmother believed it too, though none of the three of them had ever said so in conversation. 'It'll come better from you,' Mrs Anstey had said to Henrietta the night before, referring to the need for a will. A week ago, she said, she'd had a dream in which Julia appeared to be no longer alive and Francis was living in Swan House. She herself had been bundled back to Anstey's Mill, to live on charity among the people who had turned it into a geography centre.

'She says it's sometimes a nuisance,' Henrietta reported, 'when there isn't a will. But there's far more to it than that.'

In the Bay Tree Café the Saturday morning shoppers gossiped, countrywomen laden with baskets and carrier-bags, countrymen uncomfortable in their town clothes. Children sipped orangeade through straws, middle-aged waitresses did their best to remember who had ordered scones. Young husbands and wives sat in shy silence, or whispered.

'I thought Granny doted on Francis,' Katherine said.

'I thought so too.'

The two girls played with their coffee spoons, bewildered by this development. It was true it hadn't occurred to either of them that after the marriage Francis would be their mother's next of kin. When Katherine thought about it now she half understood Mrs Anstey's sudden nervousness, but understood as well that the aged easily picked up obsessions.

'What else?' she inquired.

'She wants to talk to both of us together. She doesn't want the marriage to take place.'

'A bit late –'

'Well, no, it isn't too late if there's a reason.'

They sat in silence, mulling over the facts. Francis Tyte was thirty-three years of age, an actor who might well become more successful than he had been, a charming, good-looking man. All marriage had an element of chance in it. There would be no divorces, and only happiness, if no risks were taken in the first place.

'Poor Granny,' Katherine said.

'I know.'

They left the Bay Tree and went their separate ways, to different shops. Morning sunshine warmed the yellow-grey sandstone of the gaunt King's Head and the Courtesy Cleaners and the wool bank, now the co-op. It drew a mellow tinge from Lloyd's Bank and Super Cycles; already closed for the weekend, the Post Office had a forgotten look. In the hazy summeriness of Highhill Street no one bustled; patience reigned in Dobie's Stores. Content with the *Sun* and the *Daily Express*, old men sat in line in Ely's Haircutting.

Stalls had been erected in Highhill Street, as by tradition they were on Saturdays. Farm produce was for sale, and local honey, and bedding plants. Cotton dresses hung from stands, and sheepskin jackets at bargain prices because the season wasn't right for them. There were skirts and bric-à-brac and books, leather belts with brass buckles, used gramophone records and china, knives and forks, bits of brass. Pausing by these goods, Henrietta reflected that they seemed not to have changed for years. The hanging dresses had never bothered much with fashion, leaving hemline alterations to the purchaser; the secondhand books were novels by Philip Gibbs, *Bee-Keeping Days*, *My Autobiography* by Mussolini, *The Cloister and the Hearth*. She passed the books by and bought some Worcesters, not thinking about her mother's forthcoming marriage or the reassuring of her grandmother, but about a man called Colin Halifax who was taking her, on Saturday next, to Lord's.

Katherine bought Vim, Knorr cubes, caster sugar, cream and olive oil. They'd have a quiet talk with their grandmother about the will, just the three of them, and afterwards – when the old woman wasn't present – they'd raise the subject delicately with their mother, mentioning elderly obsessions and the humouring of them.

'Quite nice actually,' Henrietta said on their way back to Swan House. 'Plays cricket himself.'

It was agreed that the time to talk quietly was when Julia was at mass on Sunday morning, and as soon as Mrs Anstey heard the car drawing away from the house she made the journey through the garden to the lawn on the river bank. Her granddaughters were reading the Sunday newspapers; her own chair had been left vacant for her.

'They're talking about a drought,' she told them, 'if this heat continues.'

The lawn had already acquired a brown look, which Henrietta now examined, though without much interest. Rain would come all too soon, Katherine vaguely said; it always did.

Mrs Anstey sat down. 'It isn't just the will,' she said. 'I mean, I had a silly dream, but it's not just that.'

The Sunday papers were put aside. 'Now, tell us,' Henrietta said. 'You're worried about Mummy?'

'Well, it's more about the marriage to tell the truth. You'll have to be patient with me.'

She told them, trying to make light of it and at the same time hoping they themselves would not. She hoped they would say that everything she said made sense and then somehow prove to her that her fears were unfounded and unjustified. But when she finished speaking there only was a silence. She tried to explain how the intuition had begun, how it had come out of the blue and had then remained, against her will. An instinct was all it was of course, and instincts were often wrong.

Steadily regarding hers, their two pairs of eyes were fair. It was true that someone other than Francis might have seemed a more suitable husband for their mother, someone older, a company director perhaps, but marriage was not always a neat arrangement of two persons, and how could there be a real objection to Francis Tyte? Their mother was not a rich widow, prey to fortune-seekers. She had in common with Francis Tyte what none of the three of them, nor her first husband either, shared with her: the spiritual life of their religion, and that in middle age must mean a lot. Besides, she had fallen in love with him.

'Yes, I know,' Mrs Anstey said, even though her granddaughters had not spoken. 'I know I'm being nasty.'

'It's natural to be concerned,' Henrietta said. 'It's natural for all of us to be concerned.'

Their father had died without leaving a will, Mrs Anstey explained to them, a fact she'd remembered and which had probably played on her nerves, causing her so oddly to dream.

'Not odd at all,' Katherine corrected her.

'Of course not,' Henrietta said.

A colour supplement was open on the grass at an advertisement for windows. *Old Windows Replaced in a Day!* a headline said. *No more rattling old frames. Cold Shield Bay Windows and Sash Windows made to measure in Satin Aluminium.* Idly, Katherine read it. She'd now worked in the china shop in South Audley Street for two years and felt it was time for a change. She'd heard there was a vacancy in the Wedgwood showrooms in Regent Street, but when she'd telephoned last week she'd been told that that wasn't so. The woman had suggested that she should come along anyway, in case something arose in the future. The face in the window advertisement reminded her of the Wedgwood woman's face. 'We'll keep your details on our files, Miss Ferndale,' she'd said with a smile when Katherine had called in on Thursday.

'It's just that I feel Julia shouldn't marry him,' Mrs Anstey said. 'It's a feeling that's come into my bones.'

Katherine's hand reached out and turned a page of the colour supplement. A man in red swimming-trunks was sitting in an armchair beneath a palm tree. The armchair was ornate, like a throne, the man old and balding. Someone famous, Katherine thought, wondering what it was all about, an armchair out in the open. It was hard to know whether to wait for a vacancy to turn up in the Wedgwood place or to continue looking elsewhere. 'Give it six months,' had been Henrietta's suggestion the night before, and that was probably best.

Mrs Anstey went on talking, faltering now and again, which usually she never did. Henrietta was still as a statue, like a ballet dancer on the browning grass, her feet tucked under her as she sat. Katherine's fingers were playing with a daisy.

'You see, I think,' Mrs Anstey said, 'Julia's paying for the honeymoon.'

Neither of them replied, their silence implying that such economics were not their business. They were sorry for her, Mrs Anstey sensed, and couldn't bring herself to say that they all three knew Julia was a person who easily became the victim of other people. She didn't say she was the victim of Mrs Spanners, and of a Church which fuelled her guilt, because all that would have sounded ridiculous. Ridiculous, too, to say there were lots of people who were victims, and predators who were drawn to them.

'There just seems something wrong,' she said instead, 'about a woman paying for her honeymoon.'

'But is she?' Henrietta inquired. 'Has she told you that?'

'Something was said, something that caught in my mind –'

'But, Granny, you don't know.' Katherine spoke while staring at the old man in the armchair. Mrs Anstey couldn't see her face, and when Henrietta added something she felt again the pity of both of them. She wanted to say that the art of illusion and deception was something to be expected of an actor, but did not in case the observation should make her sound even nastier. Women did have intuitions, she said instead, and mothers especially perhaps. One couldn't explain everything, and perhaps one shouldn't try. It was she who had first invited Francis to Swan House; airily she'd scorned away Julia's doubts about the difference in their ages.

'In a way,' Katherine said, disturbing a silence, 'Mummy probably knows best herself. As people often do.'

'Yes,' Henrietta agreed, too swiftly for Mrs Anstey's liking.

'It's just,' she began again, and realized that already they had disposed of the matter, that they were telling her to keep her forebodings to herself. Their faces did not suggest that she'd become stupid in her old age but that having been so long their mother's companion she might naturally be jealous of an interloper.

'I think if we just bring up the idea of a will,' Henrietta said, in the same quick way, 'we'll be making a point.'

'The will was only in a dream because all this had got into my mind.'

'I don't think Francis would ever turn you out of Swan House,' Katherine assured her gently, 'but I do think Mummy should put her wishes about that down on paper.'

'We'd both feel happier if she did,' Henrietta added.

Mrs Anstey felt it had all become a mess. She had mentioned her dream in order to pave the way for the other; a will was neither here nor there. It sounded nastier than ever to speak about wishes put down on paper at a time like this. It sounded grasping.

'Perhaps it would be better to forget about it. Best perhaps to leave it now.'

'No, no,' Henrietta protested.

The newspapers were picked up again, and when the car

returned to the house both girls went to have the necessary conversation with their mother, who understood at once that her own mother might be feeling left out and worried. Afterwards, over lunch, Henrietta spoke of the man called Colin Halifax, who temporarily had caused her to become interested in cricket. He'd said that Gloucestershire's middle order wasn't right, and supported Kent himself; he worked in a merchant bank. Katherine announced that she had come to a conclusion. She would wait six months in the hope that a suitable vacancy might occur in the Wedgwood showrooms.

·6·
Francis's

The telephone rang in the floor supervisor's office. There was the urgent whirring sound which indicated that the person at the other end was attempting to use a coin-operated instrument. Then a man's voice said:

'I'm awfully sorry to bother you. I wonder if I could possibly speak to Doris Smith? From the shoe department.'

It was a store rule that telephone calls should not be taken during working hours, but the Indian floor supervisor recognized the voice as that of Doris's man, which was different because of Doris's personal troubles. The exception didn't cause jealousy among the other girls on the floor because all of them were concerned about Doris, while still considering her foolish to hang on to her man, who clearly was dodgy.

'One minute, please, sir,' the Indian said, and ran quickly to the shoe department. It was a large open area, its three walls lined with shoe-boxes. In neat black dresses girls and women crouched at the feet of their customers or mounted ladders to search for what was required. Shoe-horns eased the passage of heels, measurements were accurately taken. A heavily-built foreigner, whose laces Doris had just tied, was protesting that the selection at Selfridges was better.

'Phone, dear,' the floor supervisor whispered, causing Doris to suggest to her customer that she might like to walk about for a minute or two to test the comfort of the shoes she was considering.

'What's the bother, Frankie?' she asked in the office, breathless because she'd hurried so.

'I'm afraid it's the same old story. I'll have to spend the evening with him again.'

'Him?' she repeated, knowing what he meant, giving herself time to think. For ten evenings in a row he hadn't been able to see her, ten times precisely he'd telephoned.

'My old uncle's taken a turn for the worse, Dorrie.'

'Joy's looking forward to the Pizzaland, Frankie. You said yesterday, love –'

'I know, Dorrie. I'm awfully sorry.'

'Joy mentioned it at breakfast.'

'I know, I know.'

Doris stifled a sigh, not wishing to sound a drag over the telephone, not wishing to be difficult when an old man was so ill in a home. She reached into the pocket of her black skirt for a tissue. She said:

'I'm only sorry the old chappie isn't getting better.'

'Unfortunately, he's run into trouble with his water-works. On top of everything else.'

'Is it serious, Frankie?'

'I don't know that poor Uncle Manchester'll last.'

'You mean, he's dying?'

'That's why I have to sit with him.'

'Poor old chappie,' she said. She hadn't had a drink yet, and suddenly she felt the need for one. There were hours to go until she could slip into Value Wines at lunchtime. 'Poor old chappie,' she said again.

Francis nodded. He was telephoning in a room that led off the drill-hall, the room where the kettles were boiled for coffee. It contained a small gas stove, and a motor-cycle propped against a wall. There were tins of instant coffee and powdered milk, packets of lump sugar and a cardboard box full of plastic cups. While speaking, his eye slowly travelled over these objects, and over empty shelves coated with dust. The walls were dusty also, with yellowish distemper falling away. On the one in front of him numerous telephone numbers were scrawled. He read them while her voice said that as long as he kept in touch she and Joy would understand. Any night, she said, he would be welcome in the flat for a meal and a drink, no matter what time he finished with his visiting.

He shook his head, still reading the telephone numbers. As he had before, he explained that it was always extremely late when he returned from Hampton Wick, it being so far away. He began his visual circuit of the room again. The motor-cycle would belong to the caretaker. It was strange that the room had no windows.

She wanted to go on talking. She wanted just to keep him there. It couldn't be easy for him, she said, at a time like this to be in a telly thriller that had a body down a toilet. It couldn't be easy, sitting with a poor old chappie in a home.

'He's in a bit of pain,' he replied. 'They don't quite know what it is.'

In the floor supervisor's office Doris repeated that she was sorry, and did in fact feel sorry, thinking of a dying man in distress. Then she added that she didn't mind the loss of all these evenings so long as one day they could all three make up for them. The floor supervisor's typewriter clattered noisily and Doris smacked at the receiver with her lips, as she always did. It didn't embarrass her when the typing abruptly ceased and the kissing sound filled the small office. She returned to the shoe department, saying to herself that she'd look into the Spread Eagle before she went to Value Wines for the miniature. She'd sit in the upstairs bar for a little while, over a couple of Carlsbergs.

*

Constance Kent walked the white country roads, picking flowers for the child she had already chosen as her victim. An eye in her imagination observed the blade slipping through the small neck, plunging deeper in a spasm of violence. Her face remained impassive.

On the judge's head there was a handkerchief, representing the black square he would eventually place there. 'I can entertain no doubt,' he remarked, 'after having read the evidence in the depositions, and considering this is your third confession of the crime, that your plea is the plea of a guilty person. The murder was committed under circumstances of great deliberation and cruelty.'

The clergyman to whom the confession had been made kept his head bowed also. Clerks and policemen looked solemn. The father of the accused shuffled his feet.

'That you will be taken from this place,' continued the judge, 'where you now stand to the place whence you came, and that you be hanged by the neck until your body be dead.'

'Track in fast on Constance,' commanded the toylike director. 'Did anyone know she used to crucify slugs?'

Joy was standing in the kitchen of the flat picking at the label on a jar of raspberry jam. Small shreds of paper had accumulated on the kitchen table. At the draining-board Doris turned the contents of a tin of ravioli into a saucepan.

'For God's sake stop moaning,' she snapped. 'You'd think you were the Queen Mother the fuss you make. And leave that jam alone.'

'I can't eat the stuff you're cooking. I can't eat anything reminds me of vomit.'

'Joy, will you please stop talking about vomit?' She spoke quietly, determined not to lose her temper. A smile flittered wearily in her face, an effort at friendliness. 'You know it's horrid, Joy.'

Joy gazed through her spectacles at the pot of jam, as if

concerned about it. There were smears of food on her green and yellow school tie and on her matching skirt. She said she couldn't help it if something looked like vomit, and then she left the kitchen. Doris sighed, her narrow shoulders sloped over the orange mess in the saucepan. She felt tired and in the dumps. It would be lovely to be enjoying a repetition of the little outing to the Pizzaland, lovely to be with him afterwards in the sitting-room, when Joy was asleep. In the shoe department she'd planned to tell him the next time he phoned that she'd had a little cry last night, upset because he wasn't spending the night on the sofa and wouldn't allow her to come to the Rembrandt Hotel.

Leaving the ravioli to simmer on its own for a minute, she rooted behind the packets of sugar in the cupboard by the sink. She could hear the sound of the TV coming from the living-room, so that was all right. Swiftly she poured a couple of inches of vodka into a cup. If she'd known they wouldn't be going to the Pizzaland she'd have bought some eggs, which Joy always ate without comment, especially when they were fried. Then she realized that in fact she had known, that the telephone call had come at half past eleven and she could have bought the eggs at lunchtime. For a moment she wondered why she hadn't, until she remembered that she'd been too upset to buy anything. It was all right when he was there on the phone, it was afterwards that the depression began.

She had another drink and then followed her daughter into the sitting-room. Joy was looking funny, glazed about the eyes as if something had gone wrong with her spectacles. Cartoon figures were cavorting on the television screen.

'What was she like?' Doris inquired, interrupting the high-pitched quacking of the cartoon characters, the sharpness in her voice causing Joy to give a little jump. 'The girl he was with that time, what was she like?'

'She had a blue dress on –'

'You told me about the dress. I mean, what did she seem like, Joy? What kind of person, I mean.'

'She's the one puts the kid down the toilet. Small she was, long hair, black –'

'A Negro, you mean?'

'Her hair was black. The rest of her was white.'

'Listen, Joy, was she laughing? I mean, when you saw them were they walking along the street laughing?'

No, Joy said, they hadn't been laughing. They'd just been talking. In the bar she'd been sitting down and he'd been getting drinks. The girl was good-looking, she added.

Doris returned to the kitchen. The ravioli's tomato sauce had cooked away to nothing, so she added some water to the saucepan. She poured herself some more vodka, and cleared up the shreds of paper from the table before laying it for their meal.

As soon as something happened where this Uncle Manchester was concerned she and Frankie would definitely have to have a moment in private together. They'd have to talk about Joy not being able to read. They'd have to talk about the money situation and how the mat-making had become difficult. She couldn't help it if her hands shook, she couldn't help it if the gold rim on the Big Ben ones hadn't been quite right. She had attempted to explain all that to them in a letter, but they hadn't even answered, which was typical nowadays. On top of everything else the flat needed to be redecorated. Through no fault of her own the kitchen plaster was falling down, and only the other night she'd noticed the bathroom walls were as grimy as a coal-house, running with sweat due to the steam.

Doris knew he'd want her to share these troubles with him, like he'd shared with her the thing about his Uncle Manchester being on his last legs. It was he, after all, who'd suggested the mats to her in the first place, just as he'd suggested the second-hand dealer in Crawford Street. She washed the cup she'd drunk from under the tap. There was enough in the bottle to keep her going for the evening; if she could manage to, it would be nice to leave a drop for the morning but sometimes that wasn't easy. 'Supper ready, Joy,' she cried loudly, spooning the ravioli on to two plates.

There was no response from the sitting-room. The sound of quacking continued, and eventually she opened the adjoining door. 'It'll be getting dried up, dear,' she began to say cheerily, and then she noticed that something was the matter. Ignoring a drama about a frog and some kind of bird, Joy was leaning back on the sofa, apparently in a stupor.

In the Rembrandt Hotel, in the restaurant called the Carver's Table, Francis ate roast beef, and drank half a bottle of last year's Beaujolais. Every evening since the unpleasant visit to the Pizzaland he had eaten alone in the hotel, with the *Evening Standard* propped up in front of him, now and again looking around at the people. Occasionally a child or a woman would recognize him as the man from the tobacco advertisements and it was pleasant to watch whispering take place. When he was glanced at as people passed his table he always inclined his head in return.

He might go for a walk, he thought, perhaps call in somewhere for a glass of brandy before bedtime. It was pleasant to take things slowly and easily on a summer's evening in London, mingling with the tourists. But before any of that he would telephone Julia Ferndale, as he always did after dinner. 'I'll have the trifle, I think,' he said to the Vietnamese waitress, trying to make her smile at him. 'Yes, with cream, please.' He had coffee as well. He thought about having a glass of brandy now rather than later, but changed his mind.

In his bedroom, Room 408, he sat on the edge of his bed and listened while Julia told him that everything was well in Swan House; that Mrs Spanners became daily more excited about the wedding, that Mrs Anstey's arthritis had eased quite a bit due to the continuing spell of dry weather. 'I thought I'd better make my will,' her rather faint voice reported.

'Will?'

'The girls pointed out —'

'What girls, Julia?'

'Henrietta and Katherine. They suggested at the weekend that I really should, before the wedding.'

'Yes, of course, Julia.'

'So I did it at Warboys, Smith and Toogood when I was leaving in some typing. It can be rather a nuisance if there's no will. I mean, if anything happens.'

'Happens, Julia?'

'Well, we're flying to Italy after all.'

'Yes, we are.'

'Roger didn't leave a will, you see. Everything was higgledy-piggledy for quite a while.'

'Yes, of course it would be.'

'I just thought I'd tell you, darling.'

Francis listened, and then spoke himself. He answered questions about the rehearsals, embroidering a little in a mechanical way. He tried not to think about what had been said concerning the making of a will, and it was with relief that he finally replaced the receiver. Tiny beads of sweat had broken out on his forehead and his chin. He washed his face at the basin and then replaced the small amount of make-up he wore. He found it difficult to do so because his hands were shaking.

Why had she suddenly made a will? Why had she gone behind his back to a ridiculously named firm of solicitors? Her two sharp-eyed daughters had put her up to that, homing in on her like vultures. Her mother too, no doubt. He'd never trusted the daughters, or the mother either come to that. For hours he'd listened to the old woman going on about the house she'd lived in when the family had possessed more money, as though it could possibly interest anyone. He was glad her husband had gone bankrupt, he was glad she had arthritis; he hoped the two daughters would make wretched marriages. Hotly, anger gathered within him. It was all of a piece, his own voice shouted at him, thunderously exploding in his mind. It was all of a piece with the dressmaker picking over pieces of meat in Sainsbury's, telling him to get out of her sight when he wanted to forgive her.

Francis left his bedroom, took the lift to the ground floor and dropped the key of Room 408 into a slot in the hall-porter's desk. He passed through the swing-doors and out into Brompton Road. The evening was warm and mellow, but he was no longer in a mood to appreciate it. Sweat had again broken out on his forehead, and on his back and legs. The tourists he had earlier imagined he might pleasurably mingle with looked grotesque, and so did the Victoria and Albert Museum and Brompton Oratory. The anger continued to smash at his thoughts, preventing his efforts to shape them. A fortnight ago he had given up his room in Folkestone, selling off the accumulated oddments of a lifetime, retaining only a selection of his clothes. Nothing could change that now; there was no turning back, even if he'd wanted to, which of course he didn't. That Julia Ferndale had just signed a will made not the slightest difference to any of it, one way or the other: he hadn't even been thinking of a will when he'd let down the tyre of her motor-car. She'd gone to a firm of solicitors without thinking how it would hurt him, not caring. 'But you've proved untrustworthy, Francis,' the Massmith sisters had said, and the same unjust verdict had now been passed in Swan House. 'We don't have lies between friends, Francis,' the debt-collector had said, arranging the defence of Le Haye Sainte by the King's German Legion.

He walked to South Kensington tube station and took a train to Victoria. He wanted to stand in Folkestone among the ironing-boards and the dressmaking dummies, among tape-measures and thread, and patterns cut out of old newspaper. He wanted to point at the mark on the wall where the sewing-machine cover had hit it. 'The trouble with you,' he wanted to say, 'is you're sixty-five years of age and gross and white and ugly. No wonder your husband dropped dead at a race-meeting.'

On the tube he closed his eyes and seemed already to be walking from Folkestone railway station, through familiar suburban streets. He rang the doorbell of the house and when she opened the door there was the sound of a television set. Pins decorated the bodice of her dress. There was a sty in one of her eyes.

She said at once that she despised him. He was worse than the dirt on the roads. He was nothing, she said. But he only smiled. 'I've come to tell you something,' he explained, causing a West Indian on the tube to glance at him.

Francis closed his eyes again, pushing her back into the hall of the house he should have inherited years ago. Nothing had changed in the workroom: half-completed garments hung around the walls, he could almost hear the whispery gossip of her customers. 'A girl called Constance Kent,' he said. 'Extraordinary, she was.' Slowly he repeated the story of her crime, pointing out that she, too, had been driven into corners, destroyed by other people. 'You are a hideous woman,' he said in the workroom, 'eating ice cream in Folkestone. You are full of cruelty, leching after men on the sea-front because you are alone, because nobody can be bothered with you. You picked me up and I was kind to you. I forgave you, but all you wanted to do was to be alone again, not caring if you hurt a person. What kind of a life is it, trailing from room to room of this big old house, with money hoarded away? What kind of a life is it, carrying your own shopping-bags, cooking for yourself and a budgerigar?' He reached for her scissors and her blood leapt in spurts across the room, staining the garments on the walls, and the dummies and the newspaper patterns. It spattered the wall that had been damaged when she threw the sewing-machine cover. It spattered the ceiling and the windows, and the three electric irons and the white covers of the ironing-boards, and the budgerigar in its cage.

At Victoria Francis walked among the holiday crowds instead of taking a Folkestone train. He watched the foreigners, boys and girls with haversacks, Cypriots and Sicilians pulling suitcases on little castors. He reflected that it was a railway station he particularly liked, and then he began to count up the number of journeys he had made to Folkestone from it, possibly six hundred he thought. Strange really, to have stayed on in Folkestone for all these years just to persuade a dressmaker that he forgave her.

Slowly he returned to the Underground, his anger still upsetting him, though less so than it had. He would forgive Julia Ferndale for treating him badly: he felt better, thinking about that, and again he closed his eyes. At once he thought of German cities: Hamburg and Berlin and Munich. He had never been to any of them, but in whichever seemed right there would be a modern, quite luxurious flat, not unlike the one he had told the two women he occupied in Folkestone. He would learn the language. His friend would teach him German cooking. His friend might be a girl as young as Susanna Music, a boy or an older man, a sympathetic woman. It never mattered.

He got off the train at Piccadilly and walked about the Underground station. All the women who might have been sympathetic were hurrying. A girl waited by the newspaper stand, and Francis smiled a little as he glanced in her direction, but pointedly she ignored him. A woman in black went by, and for a moment he imagined he was in Germany already. 'Oh yes, I understand,' this woman said in their pleasant flat, giving him presents because she knew he liked to receive them. 'Take this, dear,' she said, offering him little trinkets she had finished with, and German coins her father had collected. The dressmaker had never understood for an instant, nor had the doctor's wife, nor any of the others. They made him ask for things, as men did too. And Julia Ferndale wouldn't understand either. She'd start on about wills, there'd be the look in her mother's eyes, her awful daughters would make life miserable. He wanted to cry when he thought of Julia Ferndale in her house in that town, how he'd hoped at first she'd be sympathetic enough to give him things without his having to be ashamed and ask.

He thought of going to the dance-hall in Leicester Square or the one near the Strand. It was lovely when a girl he was dancing with recognized him, or when interest came into a woman's face. But for some reason he didn't feel up to a dance-hall tonight, having to smile and buy vodka and lime instead of having something bought for him. In the men's lavatory he combed his hair, seeing himself reflected in a mirror attached to a white-tiled wall. He could see as well the youths who stood around behind him, some of them pretending to wash their hands and then drying them under jets of air. There were older men also, one of them with his shirt open at the neck, his grey hair greased and brushed straight back.

'Hullo,' Francis said.

'I'm sorry, caller, there's no reply.'
'Are you sure? Are you absolutely certain?'

'No reply from 408, caller. If you hold the line, please, I'll page the hotel.'

There being no telephone in her flat, Doris was making the call from the telephone-box outside the Bricklayer's Arms. Her maroon mackintosh hung open, her large black handbag was suspended from her shoulder. She had managed to wake Joy and had helped her to get into bed. She'd looked terrible, her eyes peculiar as if she'd gone blind, and all the time she'd kept giggling and talking about an elephant.

'Sorry, caller, Mr Tyte is not in the hotel.'

He'd still be at the old people's home, sitting with his uncle. She tried to remember the name of the place, and then decided that he'd never mentioned a name. In the telephone-box there were the usual crumpled, filthy telephone directories, but no Yellow Pages. She found a set in the Bricklayer's Arms and began to telephone the old people's homes in the Hampton Wick area, repeatedly returning to the bar for change and drinks. It was almost ten o'clock before there was a response that wasn't entirely negative.

'Sundown Home,' Miss Purchase said.

'Excuse me, I'm looking for a Mr Tyte. He's sitting with his uncle somewhere out in the Hampton Wick area –'

'I'm sorry, madam, the residents are not permitted to take telephone calls in the evenings.'

'It's not a resident. It's a Mr Francis Tyte who's visiting his uncle. Is this the right place I've got?'

'This is the Sundown Home, Hampton Wick. Mr Tyte resides here, but residents are not –'

'It's the younger Mr Tyte I want. He's sitting with his uncle.'

Miss Purchase tightened her lips. 'Visiting time is Sunday afternoons, two-thirty to five. No visitor is at present on the premises.'

'It's a special case because his uncle's in a bad way. All I'm asking you is to go and get Mr Francis Tyte –'

'The younger Mr Tyte has not set foot in this house for six years.'

'Look, I think you've got your wires crossed. Frankie's been out to see his uncle every night for the past fortnight. The old chappie's

107

poorly with his water-works. It's touch and go, as a matter of fact.'

'If you're referring to Mr Francis Tyte's father, there's nothing the matter with his water-works. We have Francis Tyte's father here, and his mother. We have no uncle.'

'Frankie's mum and dad were killed in a train crash, back in the fifties. I'm talking about his Uncle Manchester.'

'Manchester?'

'They called him that apparently. Because he lived there.'

'Look here, who is this? Are you family?'

'I'm a friend of Francis Tyte's. I'm ringing on a very urgent matter. I need to speak to Frankie immediately.'

'I'm sorry, I cannot help you. Mr Tyte's father is well and his mother is well. I naturally know nothing about some uncle in Manchester. If I were you, madam, I'd contact the authorities up there.'

'No, no, it's just the man's name. A pet name they had in the family.'

'I'm sorry, I can't stand here talking about people's pet names. In point of fact I can't stand here talking about anything. This is a particularly busy time of the evening for me.'

'All I'm saying is the old chap you have is Frankie's uncle, not his father at all. You've got a wire crossed there.'

'Please stop repeating that, madam. Francis Tyte is his father's son, that's all there is to it. And he is not here at this present moment.'

'Are you absolutely sure? Would you go and look? Would you just mind looking to see?'

'I most certainly would mind. Francis Tyte never visits here. It is absurd to suggest that he is here now.'

The receiver was replaced. The emptiness of a telephone between calls echoed in Doris's ear. She replaced the receiver and went to buy herself a drink. She couldn't understand any of it because it didn't make sense. Whoever the insistent woman on the phone was she certainly hadn't got her facts straight. But it did seem strange that she'd been so very emphatic, especially about Frankie not being there.

The girl was small, Joy had said. They'd been on the street together, walking along talking, and then drinking in a pub. He'd explained about the girl, he hadn't denied a thing: the girl was just a girl. But the image that slowly assembled itself in Doris's mind didn't quite agree. The blue dress and the long black hair were sinister; the laughing, pretty face was full of mockery.

Doris mulled over the image in the Bricklayer's Arms and bought half a bottle of vodka just before it closed. In the kitchen of the flat she sat over what remained of it, going through everything again. He'd been the first person she'd thought of when she'd got Joy on to the bed. Joy was his, after all. Any woman would go out and attempt to contact the father.

She went to have another look at their child, closing one eye because she kept seeing two of her. She woke her up and asked her how she felt. 'Great,' Joy said, adding that the stuff she'd taken was a tranquillizer for elephants which Clicky Hines had sold her. 'Fantastic,' she said.

The simple explanation was that the person in the old people's home must have been one of the elderly inmates who'd happened to be passing when the phone rang. The old woman had picked it up and in a state of senile confusion had simply said the first thing that came into her head. They'd smile over it when she told him. He'd say again that the girl in the blue dress was just an actress, and then he'd listen while she told him about the drug. She'd tell him how one minute poor Joy had been fiddling with a pot of jam and the next in a stupor in front of the TV, how stuff for elephants could have killed her. Afterwards they could discuss everything else, the letter she'd received from the headmaster, the bathroom sweating dirt.

At half past two she made another journey to the telephone-box outside the Bricklayer's Arms, and when the voice from the Rembrandt Hotel said there was still no reply from Room 408 the image of the blue dress and the long black hair slowly formed itself again, pushing everything else away.

*

Miss Purchase emerged from her cubbyhole in the hall, where her desk and her filing-cabinet and the telephone were. From the dining-room came the sounds of breakfast and the voices of George and Cyril, the two male nurses, as they raised them to address the hard of hearing. The morning sun livened the stained-glass panels on either side of the hall door. The long row of overcoats was complete, the elephant's foot contained what sticks were not in use. All was well in the hall, Miss Purchase's experienced eye informed her, and that at least was something.

She moved to the open door of the dining-room and surveyed the old people at their different tables, George and Cyril moving among them in their neat white coats. Mrs Tyte, she noticed, was weeping again and she wondered if she shouldn't mention this to Dr Mary. Dementia could quite easily be setting in.

'If you don't eat fast enough,' the old woman's husband was saying to her as Miss Purchase approached the table the couple shared with four others, 'you won't get enough toast.'

'Well then, and how's this little lot this lovely morning?' Miss Purchase inquired.

No one answered except Mrs Dacey, who said she couldn't manage her prunes.

'If you don't get the toast into you,' Mr Tyte warned his wife, 'you'll be hungry by eleven. You'll be moaning in the garden, complaining about the wasps.'

'All right then, Mrs Tyte dear?'

Mrs Tyte nodded, turning her head away. She didn't want Miss Purchase to see her tears. There was a photograph somewhere, taken in the back garden of Number 14 when he was eight, thin-legged in a new flannel suit, his Sunday best as they used to call it. She well remembered the day, Henry standing there with the camera, telling him not to move a muscle.

Miss Purchase was smiling down at her, teeth evenly displayed between her thin lips. She did her best to smile back. She'd been thinking about a photograph, she explained: he'd looked like a waif because the suit was too big for him.

'Oh, I'd love to see that some time, dear.'

'Gone up in a bonfire, all those photos did,' Mr Tyte said. 'No good keeping rubbish.'

'I wish you hadn't, Henry. I said at the time –'

'No good keeping rubbish, you said.'

'I didn't mean the snapshots.'

He crunched his toast. If she hadn't meant the snapshots she should have said so. No good mentioning snapshots twenty-five years later; biggest bonfire ever it had been.

'Never mind,' Miss Purchase said. 'Oh, and just a little thing, Mr Tyte. I'd particularly ask you not to leave the *TV Times* on the floor of the television lounge. It's an unhygienic habit in the first place, and then someone could quite easily have a fall. The paper of the *TV Times* is particularly slippery, as no doubt you've noticed.'

Before she passed on to the next table she nodded firmly at the old man to show she meant it. The Tytes had become a bit of a nuisance, what with all this weeping about the son not visiting, and peculiar telephone calls, and the old chap's vindictiveness. She'd mention the vindictiveness to Dr Mary as well, no reason to suppose it wasn't a sign of dementia just like the weeping was.

'Telephone, Miss Purchase,' Cyril called across the dining-room to her.

'Yes?' she said a moment later in her cubbyhole. 'Miss Purchase here.'

'Good morning,' the voice which had been a nuisance the night before replied. 'I'm inquiring after Mr Tyte.'

'Yes, what about him?'

'I'm just wondering how he is this morning.'

'There's nothing whatsoever the matter with Mr Tyte. I explained to you last night, madam.'

'We had our wires crossed last night –'

'I cannot help you, madam, and I must ask you to desist from bothering us like this.'

'It's just that I thought I was maybe talking to one of the inmates. The thing is there's an old Mr Tyte there who's in a bit of trouble with his water-works –'

'I keep telling you there's nothing the matter with the man's water-works. You appear to have been told a pack of lies.'

Miss Purchase replaced the receiver with a sharp little snap. It was scandalous that people telephoned with nonsense like this, any hour of the day or night, no consideration for anyone. Only yesterday morning Mrs Perigo's daughter had delayed her for more than half an hour with some story about her mother being allergic to cornflour.

'Two pounds ten the suit was,' Mrs Tyte said in the dining-room, and her husband coughed, not wishing to hear her.

Expertly he flicked a pat of butter on to the parquet floor. Best of all, of course, if the Purchase woman herself went down, cracking her funny-bone or something.

Joy dawdled on her way to school. She felt perfectly normal. She'd eaten two plates of cornflakes and four slices of bread and blackcurrant jam for breakfast, and what she was thinking now was that she didn't want to put in an appearance at Tite Street Comprehensive. She didn't mind taking a drug, any more than she minded starting fires. But the latest craze Clicky Hines had come up with was tattooing, which everyone said hurt.

She gazed into shop windows, wishing her mother wouldn't always leave the cornflakes packet open so that the cornflakes became limp. She wished her mother wouldn't hide her bottles of booze all over the place. She wished she was on the way to the Bovril factory, earning money instead of having to spend it on drugs and tattoos. She'd have to save in order to get a tattoo. For weeks she wouldn't be able to call in at the Rialto or the Chik 'n' Chips.

She stared at people in cars held up at a set of traffic-lights. If only he could be in the flat, listening and understanding as he did in the Pizzaland. He understood about the Comprehensive and the boredom of the place. He understood about the sex craze, even about the student teacher in the cupboard. She could have said to him about the elephant stuff. She would have thrown it away if he'd said, not caring if 3B took the mick when she told them. He never fussed. When her mother had a drink in he was always quiet and calm; when she was embarrassing, saying he'd called the tune for her heart-strings that day on the bus, he just nodded patiently.

Joy reached the railings of the school and looked through them. The playground was empty because she was late. In 3B they'd be passing round the tattoo sketches, Niagara Falls in blues and greens, Jesus on the Cross, anchors and hearts and Mrs Thatcher. She turned and walked away.

In the shoe department the Indian floor supervisor told Doris she was wanted on the telephone. His uncle had taken another turn for the worse, Francis's voice said, and it would again be necessary to spend the evening by the old man's bedside.

'Yes,' Doris said flatly, aware that the floor supervisor was standing in the doorway, politely waiting for her to finish with his telephone. 'Yes,' she said again, wanting to say instead that she'd found Joy half dead after an intake of drugs, that she'd had conversations she didn't understand with a woman in an old people's home, and had telephoned the Rembrandt Hotel eight times during the night. But the kindly supervisor, as still as a statue in the doorway, inhibited her. She could feel he was worried for her, and could see that his cheerful smile was absent from his face. 'Thanks for ringing,' she said in the same flat tones before replacing the receiver. More desperately than ever in her life she felt the need of a miniature or a refreshing glass of Carlsberg or Double Diamond. But the time was only half past ten.

In Stone St Martin the wedding-cake was iced that morning.

·7·
Doris's

When he appeared, he looked just the same. He smiled when he handed his bedroom key to a porter. He stepped out of the hotel, and Doris followed him at a distance. She knew he wouldn't take a taxi because she'd often noticed he never did. He didn't even take a bus. He walked quite slowly, not at all in a hurry, and three-quarters of an hour later he turned into a street that was partially demolished. He passed the Rialto Café and she did so too, following him through other streets until he reached the drill-hall and disappeared into it. She returned to the Rialto and asked for a cup of tea, not quite knowing what to do next. She wanted to see the actual girl, to establish for herself what she was up against. But as she drank her tea she realized she couldn't face that until she'd taken advantage of a couple of drinks.

She had them in the Turbaned Turk, several streets away, a place she didn't want to leave. She took her large black handbag from her shoulder and placed it on the bar. The Irish landlord talked about the good weather and the prospects for Ascot, advising her to watch a horse called Brainwave. Before she finally made up her mind to go she said she'd be back, and the Irishman said she'd be more than welcome any time. Some people were nice, she thought, and then she wished that none of it had happened, that after all these years he hadn't told her a lie about visits to an old persons' home. She wished she hadn't had to tell a lie herself, informing the floor supervisor that she wouldn't be in the shoe department today because of trouble with her stomach.

But on the way back to the drill-hall she said to herself it was no use wishing; her task was unpleasant and that was that. The one thing she didn't want to do was to walk into the middle of a rehearsal of the thriller. She didn't want any embarrassment for him, and what was probably best was to find a window she could look through and size the girl up. But when she arrived at the drill-hall there weren't any windows that were convenient for her purpose. It was hard to get round to the back of the place because the alleyway which might have led there came to an abrupt end. She stood by some dustbins and lit a cigarette. Then she returned to the Turbaned Turk.

'Unfortunately I've been left in the lurch,' Francis said in the drill-hall, to the actor who played the part of Constance Kent's father. 'My best man's gone and got himself ill. Wretched glandular fever.'

Preparing the ground for this statement, Francis had listened endlessly to this actor's talk about the film he hoped to be in, about computers and laser beams. He'd drunk endless cups of tea and coffee with him, and had stood with him in different bars during lunch breaks. He had mentioned his forthcoming wedding several times. 'Thing is,' he said now, 'I need a stand-in.'

The actor whose face had reminded Susanna Music of meat didn't protest that the suggestion was too bizarre for him. He said his sister-in-law had recently suffered from glandular fever. He added that he was flattered, and put a friendly arm on Francis's shoulder. Of course he'd fill in.

On the telephone to Swan House Francis had already reported that his best man had gone down with glandular fever: Brian Donsworth whom he'd spoken so much about, his closest friend at school, now in the textile world. There was the usual pleasure of invention, the careful, lengthy explanation. Julia Ferndale sympathized and sent good wishes for Brian Donsworth's recovery: glandular fever was a ghastly thing to catch. With no difficulty whatsoever, the matter slid into place, and Francis listened while he was told that Mrs Spanners had changed her mind about the dress she was to wear on the day. She had asked that this information should be relayed to him since they had had so many chats about her clothes. She'd told him that the dress was to be green, with lace at the wrists and neck. In the event she'd gone for one in an off-the-shoulder style, a shade of violet. 'Tell her it sounds lovely,' Francis said.

At the end of the day's rehearsals Susanna Music was in a hurry because she intended to wash her hair. She walked with the bearded production assistant along the street that was being demolished and parted from him outside the Rialto Café. It was the last day in the drill-hall.

'Excuse me,' a woman in a maroon mackintosh said a few minutes later, jostling her rather. 'Excuse me, miss.'

They were on the pavement outside a tobacconist's. A boy with a pouch full of evening papers mounted a bicycle and rode away, whistling.

'I'm a friend of Frankie Tyte's,' the woman said and then, to Susanna's surprise, suggested that they should have a drink together. 'I've had you described to me,' the woman said. 'I know who you are. Doris the name is, Doris Smith as a matter of fact.'

They couldn't have a drink, Susanna pointed out, because there was nowhere open at this time of day, it being only four o'clock. 'I've a couple of miniatures in my bag,' the woman replied. 'We could go to a park.'

But Susanna, still more surprised, declined. Though curious about this woman, she protested that she was in a hurry, mentioning the washing of her hair. The woman gripped her arm and said that what she wished to talk about was extremely urgent. In the end they entered a coffee-bar.

'I'm a friend of Frankie's,' Doris said again. 'Francis Tyte. Put it another way, I have his child.'

'His child?'

'Lay off Frankie, dear. That's what I want to tell you. You're going with him, aren't you?'

'No, not at all. We're in the same television production –'

'I don't care what you're in, dear. He has worries enough as it is.'

The contents of a miniature bottle of vodka were added to the woman's cup of tea. This meeting between them was a secret, she said; she didn't want Frankie put about. 'He's a married man, remember. No one wants stuff like this coming out.'

'Are you his wife?'

'His wife's down Folkestone way. She's delicate with her heart.'

'I see.'

'What's your name, dear?'

'Susanna Music.'

'Frankie's been married thirteen, fourteen years. All the time I've known him, Susie.'

Susanna nodded. 'There's nothing between Francis Tyte and myself. Nothing.'

'I've got a few drinks in,' the woman said. 'I only meant to have a look at you, if you get what I mean.' She kept lighting cigarettes and letting them get damp in the tea on her saucer. 'I caught him out in a lie,' she said.

'I can assure you neither you nor his wife has anything to worry about where I'm concerned. I hardly know Francis Tyte. I'll probably never see him again after this present production.'

'Will you promise me that, dear?'

'Yes, of course I will.'

'Frankie means everything to me, Susie.'

She worked in a shoe department, the woman said, which she'd phoned today to say she had trouble with her stomach. She'd met him on a bus, she said, in 1966. She went on talking, repeatedly referring to the wife whom she'd referred to already, and of meals in a Pizzaland and how much they meant to her and to the child. She spoke of the birth of the child, and of her labour pains. The child couldn't read or write her name properly.

With sudden sharpness Susanna recalled the details of the fantasy Francis Tyte had so effortlessly created for her on the first afternoon of the rehearsals: the odd-job man and the housekeeper of a Nottingham orphanage, an elderly lecher called Vassbacher. For a brief, strange moment she was possessed by the notion that this woman had been created by Francis Tyte also, a figment of his pretence which had somehow acquired reality. She shook the hand the woman held out to her, reassuring her again.

'Frankie.'

She was there in the lounge of the hotel, sitting down at a table, smoking. Her handbag was on the table beside her packet of filter-tipped cigarettes. She was wearing her hideous mackintosh.

'Good heavens, Dorrie!' he said.

'I had to have a word, Frankie.' She held out a pound note and asked him to get something to drink. 'A rum and blackcurrant, love,' she said.

He crossed the large, square lounge to the bar in the corner, reflecting that she was drunk already. He wondered if she was at last going to mention a paternity order, not that it mattered any more what she mentioned.

'Lovely,' she said when he returned with her sticky drink. She had discovered about rum and blackcurrant only today, she told him, the mixture suggested by an Irish barman in a lovely pub called the Turbaned Turk.

'Is something the matter, Dorrie?'

'Well yes, dear.' She said she was sorry. She'd become upset; she had to have a word.

'Of course, Dorrie. Of course.'

'I followed you on the street to the rehearsal place. I spoke to the girl, Frankie.'

'What girl is that?'

'Susie. Is Susie her name? I was worried, Frankie.'

'You don't mean Susanna Music?'

She said she did, and added that it wasn't just the girl. While watching a television cartoon Joy had consumed a drug normally given to elephants, and had gone into a coma. Joy couldn't read or write. The bathroom walls were filthy, the whole flat was in need of decoration and the landlords wouldn't listen. Everywhere she looked there seemed to be a mess; her last lot of table-mats hadn't been accepted by the At-Home Industries people because of poor craftsmanship; she was worried about making ends meet.

'You were worried about that before, Dorrie.'

'I know.'

'I never have anything to spare, I'm afraid.' He remembered suggesting the table-mats in the first place and later telling her about the dealer in Crawford Street. Now and again he'd had to go to the man himself. The man took anything, no questions asked.

'Let's have another drink, Frankie.'

He nodded, smiling a little. He spoke quietly, collecting their two glasses. 'You've always had ill fortune, Dorrie.'

'I've been lucky in some ways, dear. I was lucky that day on the bus.'

When he stood at the bar his anger didn't erupt as it might have. She had followed him through the streets, just like the child had. She had bothered a girl he hardly knew, with whom he'd once had a drink and to whom he'd have to apologize. The condition of her bathroom had nothing to do with him, in no way was he her keeper. Yet the anger didn't come.

'I'm sorry,' she said again when he returned, and added that she had been in touch with an old people's home. He didn't understand at first what she meant, and then realized that she'd telephoned every home in Hampton Wick until she'd found one with someone called Tyte in it. 'Are your parents alive, Frankie?'

Slowly he shook his head. His mother and father had been killed in a railway crash, he reminded her. His uncle had died early that morning, at a quarter to five. 'I wasn't with him,' he said. 'I came back here at one o'clock because I was exhausted. I blame myself.'

'They kept saying there was nothing the matter with him, Frankie.'

'Who's that, dear?'

'Whoever he is. The old man in that place. You had a flirt with the girl, Frankie.'

He smiled, not saying anything. For a moment he imagined taking the train to Folkestone and having the courage of Constance Kent. Excitement quickened inside him, pleasantly spreading warmth.

'As long as it's over, Frankie.'

He noticed that her eyes weren't focusing. His parents were his own affair, she said. As long as it was over, she repeated.

'Let's go back to the flat, Dorrie.'

He would never again see her or her child. She loved him, as the dressmaker had, and the doctor's wife, as Julia Ferndale did. The ill fortune in her life had been cheered by this love; the memory of it would be a comfort for her in the future.

On the street she kept saying she was sorry and he replied that he was sorry she'd misunderstood things. She stumbled and he had to hold her by the arm. It was typical of her to go ringing up institutions because she'd got everything wrong, to go getting into a panic for no reason whatsoever. But in time he would naturally forgive her, as he forgave the others.

'Hi, Dad,' the child said in the flat.

'Hullo, Joy.'

The child began to talk about a Bovril factory. He nodded at her and smiled. She disliked her school, she said – which she had repeatedly said before – and then she turned the television on. In the kitchen Doris produced half a bottle of vodka from a cupboard and poured some of it into two cups. She talked in her usual way, about the past and the future, and then returned to the matters which were on her mind at the moment: the decoration of her flat, her inability to make table-mats any more. As soon as the child went to bed they sat in the sitting-room, on the sofa. When she seized his hand her own felt clammy, but even so he allowed her to embrace him.

'It's not my business, your mum and dad,' she repeated, adding that she needed to catch the Bricklayer's before it closed because she was running out of ciggies.

'Shall I?' he offered, but she insisted that he should remain. She came back with more vodka and stood in front of him swaying, laughing in her drunkenness.

'I want to tell you, dear,' he said, and then he described the life of Constance Kent, the viciousness of her father, her stepmother's cruelty. He told her how Constance Kent had run away, cutting her red hair off and dressing herself as a boy, how she'd been locked in a cellar as a punishment. All her life she'd been let down; other people had destroyed her. She'd been battered to shreds, turned into a crazy creature who crucified slugs.

'Poor thing,' Doris said, taking more vodka.

She cuddled into him on the sofa, happier than she'd been for ages. She'd been let down herself, he said: the day her father married again, and then again by the table-mats people and the landlords, by Tite Street Comprehensive not caring tuppence if a child could read, by the dressmaker who went on living beyond her time. He'd suffered ill fortune too, he said. All three of them were the same, he and she and Constance Kent.

Joy had been roused by the banging of the flat door when Doris returned from the Bricklayer's Arms. For ages after that she lay listening to the murmur of her father's voice through the thin partition wall. Scraps of what he said slipped through the wall, and sometimes there was her mother's voice as well. They appeared to be talking about the thriller he was in. It was nice that he didn't want to go.

She dropped off to sleep and dreamed that she was back at Tite Street Comprehensive, where Clicky Hines had persuaded her to have the face of her father tattooed on her stomach. He'd even persuaded her that he could do the job himself and had brought in a lot of colours and electrical gear. She woke up with a jerk because the drill thing he was using had got out of control and was cutting her open when it should have been putting the blue in the eyes. There was silence in the sitting-room.

·8·
Julia's

The occasion slightly puzzled the actor who had played the part of Samuel Kent. The bride's daughters, as thin as table-knives, seemed to be delighted by what was happening. The bride's mother was edgy and tried to hide it. The bride herself was like a woman in her sleep. A person he'd been introduced to as Mrs Spanners was horribly painted and clad, with bangles jangling on her arms. Francis Tyte might well have been on a stage.

With an actor's curiosity, the man who had been Samuel Kent wondered just what was going on. The fact that the bride was so in love appeared to have cast a sheen over everyone's sensibilities. No one questioned her love and because of that no one questioned anything else, no one except her mother.

The older priest murmured, the younger one stood with his head bowed. Summer dresses and hats lent a festive air, bright afternoon sunshine glittered through the stained-glass windows. There was a pleasant scent of candle-grease and incense, the organist played Bach. Yet as the proceedings advanced the acquired best man felt increasingly disconcerted. So clamorously in the end did his professional instinct protest that he even began to feel a little unwell, and shivered when he stepped out into the warm June sunshine.

The weather in England suddenly turned showery, which annoyed Mrs Anstey. It meant she was unable to sit reading under the tulip tree, well out of reach of Mrs Spanners. To pursue her to this position the cleaning woman needed a reasonable excuse, whereas no excuse of any kind was necessary for hoovering her way into the drawing-room or the dining-room, or anywhere else where Mrs Anstey might have established herself with her book. It often seemed that there was nothing Mrs Spanners liked better than winkling her out and proceeding to talk.

On the second morning of her daughter's absence in Italy she was wakened with a tray of early-morning tea. She preferred not to be roused at a quarter to seven and had said so to Mrs Spanners, only to receive the reply that none of it was any trouble. The green and brown curtains of her bedroom were pulled back briskly, noisy on their metal rails. A blast of sunshine made her blink.

'Still unsettled it said on the half-six,' Mrs Spanners informed her. 'And petrol going short again.'

'Good morning, Mrs Spanners.' Mrs Anstey began to sit up. For long periods during every night she found it difficult to sleep. She read then and usually dropped off again at about five o'clock.

'All right then, dear?' Mrs Spanners inquired. 'Garbage men out, apparently.'

Mrs Spanners began Mrs Anstey's day for her at this early hour because she liked to see that all was well before she made the journey back to her council house in order to give her husband, Charle, his breakfast. While he ate it she put together his two packets of sandwiches, one for consumption at ten o'clock and the other at one. She didn't make them the evening before because he said they got stale overnight. Many times she had explained all this to Mrs Anstey.

'O.K. then, dear?'

'Yes, I'm quite all right thank you, Mrs Spanners.'

'Fancy the garbage out again! Never think of no one but theirselves.'

She wore an overall with prancing shepherdesses on it, and was heavily scented with Love-in-a-Mist. Her face had already been made up, fingernails shaped and painted. Her tangerine hair was fresh from its curlers.

'Another thing,' she said. 'Pig products is up. Immediate from midnight.'

With that she departed. At nine o'clock, bringing breakfast into the dining-room – although Mrs Anstey would have preferred it between showers on the lawn – she would have further information to impart. There'd possibly be a tit-bit concerning Princess Margaret and information about the contents of Charle's sandwiches, and what local gossip Charle had picked up in the Three Swallows the night before. She'd stand there with her empty tray, watching to see that the scrambled eggs she'd cooked were eaten, talking about the beer-drinkers and skittles players of the Three Swallows, none of whom Mrs Anstey had ever met or even seen. Yesterday she'd protested to Mrs Spanners that she couldn't manage a cooked breakfast every morning, after which there'd been the sudden presence of Dr Tameguard in the house, asking her what the matter was.

Mrs Anstey sighed. So that there would be a residue in the cup when the tray was collected, she poured out some of the strong tea without which, in Mrs Spanners's opinion, no day could properly begin. The greater part of the tea-pot's contents would later be emptied down the lavatory.

She placed the tray on her bedside table, reflecting that Mrs Spanners's transistor information was probably correct: the sun, so early in the day, was too bright to augur well. Brilliant shafts of it penetrated the room, sharpening the outline of hair-brushes and stoppered bottles on the dressing-table. Sitting up in bed, Mrs Anstey saw herself reflected in a sunny looking-glass and hastily looked away. The premonition that had tormented her no longer nagged. The wedding ceremony had rendered it irrelevant, nothing could now be done.

She reached for *Martin Chuzzlewit*, which she had almost finished. As she did so she heard the telephone ringing, a distant sound, coming from the hall. She listened, wondering if Mrs Spanners had already left to get Charle's breakfast, and assuming she had when the ringing continued. She could never herself get to a telephone in time these days.

*

In the priests' house Father Lavin drew on his clerical trousers and arranged black braces on his shoulders. He remembered reading a detective story in which the dénouement had hinged on the corpse's twisted braces. No one, some sharp investigator had argued, would walk about like that all day. The body's clothes had clearly been re-arranged after death.

He washed at the hand-basin in his plain, cream-coloured room and then lathered his face for shaving. After breakfast, when he had read his letters and dealt with those which required an immediate answer, he planned to drive to Cheltenham to see a builder who had volunteered to repaint the guttering of the church for nothing. A Catholic apparently, a Mr Spurgeon. Father Lavin had never heard of him until someone had mentioned the name a couple of Sundays ago, and then a letter had arrived with the rather surprising offer. Drawing the blade of his safety razor through the lather of soap on his neat, small chin, Father Lavin wondered what sin this retribution followed. Would he guess it, he wondered, when he handed Mr Spurgeon the paint-card on which, the night before, Father Dawne had marked a colour called Gull Grey? The sins that popped up in the confessional sometimes seemed quite unsuitable for those who claimed them. Avarice and envy besmirched the nicest minds, dishonesty and the sexual urge were good at finding cover.

'Are you up, Father?' the voice of Father Dawne called out. 'You're wanted on the telephone.'

'I'll be there in a minute,' he called back, wiping the last wisps of soap from his face. And there were, of course, the sins that were not sins at all: the small daily errors, vindictiveness in anger, untidy gossip, petty actions. Sinners with no greater weakness to sustain them blew all these up in their repentance; being sorry brought God a little closer.

'Yes?' he said in the office, which was coloured cream also. Even the telephone he spoke into repeated the shade. A crucifix hung on the wall opposite the room's single window, the cross black but the body of Christ the same pervasive creaminess. The filing-cabinets and the metal desk were grey.

'Father Lavin,' he said.

There was a silence, then he was asked to hold the line. Voices spoke faintly. There was a crackling sound and after another silence there was Julia's voice. She said something about Francis. She said something else as well but Father Lavin couldn't hear that either, something about having tried to get Mrs Spanners at Swan House.

'It's a very bad line,' he shouted.

'Francis has left me.'

Father Lavin could make neither head nor tail of this, but he did not interrupt again. He listened while Julia seemed to tell him that something had in error been reported to the Italian police, that some reference or other had appeared in an Italian newspaper. Her voice faded away again and then returned, very clearly for a moment. Since an Englishman was involved, she feared the newspaper item might be picked up by the British press. She was thinking of her mother.

'Of course,' he said. 'But, Julia —'

'I believe he has gone to Germany.'

'Julia, what on earth's all this about?'

'I'm asking you to break it to my mother. And to tell the girls. I don't want anyone just to read it in a paper.'

'But why has Francis done this?'

There was further crackling on the line, and when he heard her voice again she was saying she would be returning as soon as she could. Other voices interrupted.

'I can't hear you, Julia.'

'Our marriage was bigamous. No more than a farce.'

The line went dead, but he listened for a moment longer before slowly replacing the receiver. As he hurried back to his bedroom, a smell of frying bacon came from the tiny kitchen, where Father Dawne was already preparing their breakfast. They took the cooking in turns, week by week.

*

Attired in his vest and trousers, having just put the kettle on and unbolted the back door to let the cat out for its morning's pursuit of wildlife, Mr Spanners was about to belch away some wind. He changed his mind when he noticed, to his astonishment, that his wife had entered the kitchen with a priest. He raised a hand to his mouth and made a coughing noise instead.

'My God,' his wife said shakily, 'there's been a terrible thing.'

'Eh?'

'Mr Tyte's gone, Charle.'

Mr Spanners stared hard at his wife, in confusion and bewilderment. 'Gone?' he said.

'She telephoned the reverend. She was trying to get me at the house so's I could keep the paper from the old lady. The reverend picked me up on the street.'

'Your wife's a little distressed, Mr Spanners.'

On the ashen whiteness of her face the cosmetic additions had acquired a brittle look. Her fingers agitated the edge of the overall with shepherdesses on it, but her husband, endeavouring to absorb the shock to his sensibilities, appeared still unaware of her distress. 'Gone?' he said again. 'Gone where?'

'Oh my God, it's terrible, Charle.' She collapsed on to a chair, shaking her head and sobbing.

'Perhaps,' suggested Father Lavin, 'your wife should have a cup of tea.' He had stopped beside her on her way from Swan House and, having broken the news and established that Mrs Anstey's *Times* was not due to be delivered for another hour, he'd given her a lift home.

'Tea?' said Mr Spanners.

'I'll make it if you tell me where everything is.'

'Kettle won't be up yet,' Mrs Spanners interjected, her face working beneath the patina of make-up. 'Oh God, I can't believe it, Charle.'

'I don't get it. Where's the man gone to?'

Father Lavin explained that the information they had was slight, but what it looked like was a rather extraordinary case of desertion.

He wondered if he should mention bigamy or not, and decided against it.

Mrs Spanners said again that she couldn't believe it. Her husband took a large brown tea-pot from a cupboard and from another a packet of Lipton's Green Label tea. He couldn't believe it himself, he confessed.

'I'm afraid it's most unpleasant,' Father Lavin said. 'Whatever it is I'm afraid it's painful.'

Mrs Spanners shook her head in further incredulity. When she spoke it was to remind her husband to heat the pot. Then she said:

'Was it a quarrel? Will they maybe get together again?'

'It didn't sound as if they would.'

Mr Spanners heaped spoons of tea into the warmed pot. 'Well, I never,' he said. 'A man like Tyte.'

Tears smudged his wife's face. She continued to sob and to shake her head, rallying a little when Father Lavin pressed a cup of tea on her.

'He was a lovely person,' she said, as if Francis Tyte no longer existed.

When Mrs Anstey descended the stairs at nine o'clock Father Lavin was standing in the hall. Seeing him, she at once recalled the early telephone call and sensed that something was the matter. *The Times* was in his hands, neatly folded.

'What's wrong?' she said.

'I'll sit with you while you have breakfast.'

'Is anything the matter?'

'I've something to tell you.'

'Is it Julia?'

'Julia's quite safe.'

She had paused on the stairs. She now continued her descent. He came towards her, as if to take her arm. He didn't, however, but walked beside her into the dining-room. 'I've been reading your *Times*,' he said on the way. It was most odd for the priest to call at this hour, and even odder that he should pretend it wasn't. It was a bit like a dream, his saying out of the blue that he'd been reading her newspaper.

As soon as she sat down, the breakfast Mrs Spanners had cooked was placed in front of her, with a Wedgewood-patterned pot of coffee and heated milk in a matching jug. Mrs Spanners was gone before she even noticed her, which added to the strangeness.

'It's Francis,' he said. 'Something has happened in Italy.'

'Happened?'

'I'm afraid it's very bad news.'

'Julia –'

'Francis appears to have deserted her.'

She stared at the pale scrambled eggs, and then raised her eyes and asked that the statement should be repeated. When it was, she still found it impossible to believe. Father Lavin was pouring coffee for her, but the last thing she wanted was a cup of coffee.

'What has happened, Father?'

'I honestly don't know.'

He told her that Julia had telephoned Swan House first, just in case something might have wormed its way into the paper. She'd been thinking of the tobacco advertisements, he imagined, which had made Francis's face quite well known. It would be news of a kind that his marriage had lasted only a single day.

'It would have shocked me more to have heard it from Mrs Spanners. *Is* it in the paper?'

'No.'

'Julia didn't deserve this.'

'I'm afraid there's something worse.'

He told her that Francis had committed bigamy, that Julia had called their marriage a farce. He stood there for a moment with *The Times* still in one hand, watching the old woman's features for any signs of weakness. When none appeared he put the paper down on the dining-table and went to the hall to telephone the office where Henrietta was employed.

Slowly Mrs Anstey lifted the cup of coffee he'd poured for her but found she could not even sip it. The smell of the scrambled eggs made her want to retch. It was typical of Mrs Spanners to cook an enormous meal for someone who had to be told such ghastly news.

'Henrietta'll pass it on to Katherine,' Father Lavin said, returning and sitting down.

'Poor Julia,' she said. 'Poor vulnerable Julia.'

'I'm afraid Francis is some kind of imposter.'

'I guessed,' she said, startling him. She told him of her conversation with Henrietta and Katherine, but did not blame them. She had known the depth of her unease and had failed to convey it because at the time it hadn't made any sense. 'I still don't know why I thought it,' she said, and added that this was the worst thing that had ever happened to her daughter.

'You mustn't feel guilty, Mrs Anstey.'

'Of course I shall feel guilty. It was I who invited him to tea.'

For another hour they sat at the dining-room table, listening to the showers of rain that came and went, spattering the window-panes. Then they walked in the damp garden, down to the river and back again, and then he said he had better go. She would be all right, she reassured him when he left her in the drawing-room, and she would telephone immediately if she wasn't. She thanked him for his help and heard him murmuring in the hall to Mrs Spanners.

She sat where he had left her, finding comfort only in her hating of the man she'd once been so happy for her daughter to marry. The familiar reflection that ever since childhood Julia had been an easy target for lame ducks was no consolation, only a source of further guilt.

Having left Swan House, Father Lavin did not return at once to the priests' house but drove into the country. He drove slowly, the windscreen-wipers rattling back and forth, rubber screeching on wet glass. Other cars passed him, he turned the radio on. A gritty voice was talking about North Sea oil, elsewhere there was clamorous music. He turned it off again.

The road narrowed, reducing the traffic to a crawl. He took a fork to the left and after a mile pulled on to a wide verge by a spinney of birch trees. It was still raining, but only slightly now and in the wood the trees were a protection. Beyond the birches was the denser foliage of conifers, a sloping, silent forest of them. Only here, among the trees, did Father Lavin ever allow himself to reflect upon his love for Julia. He had loved her for as long as he had known her, a well-mannered love from which he'd drained away the passion. Only a trace of anguish remained, and emptiness instead of jealousy; nor did there ever seem to be virtue in his sacrifice. When Mrs Anstey had first drawn his attention to the Filippo Lippi madonna he had gazed for ages at the postcard she'd held out to him, easily believing that Julia as a girl possessed the madonna's countenance that had since become her daughters'. But it was the countenance he was more familiar with which appeared now in his mind, Julia's own eyes and her lips, the pleasant roundness of her face, the few faint freckles on her forehead, the hint of red in her hair.

He walked for half a mile, dawdling slowly, and then began the unhurried journey back. One expression after another altered her features; she smiled, she frowned. Her hands placed a dish on the dining-table in Swan House, she crossed a lawn with Michaelmas daisies she had cut. Not once in his reveries did a finger of his touch one of hers, not once did he say what he might have said.

He remembered the first time he had visited Swan House, invited to dinner soon after his arrival in Stone St Martin. He'd considered the occasion alarming: the velvety dresses of the two women, the fire that blazed busily behind his chair in the dining-room, warming the small of his back. He'd felt awkward, as now and again he did in England. As a curate, he'd come to a parish in London many years before that, fresh from Co. Cork and more than a little on the raw side. It was true that in the meantime he had acquired a certain polish, but in Swan House that night he was aware of its shallowness. Julia had recently become a widow; the shadow of death hung over the house, which naturally hadn't helped his awkwardness. There'd been talk of her years abroad, in East Africa and Malaya and Germany, and talk from Mrs Anstey about the house in the locality she would have liked to live in still.

The bankruptcy of one husband and the untimely death of the other had left them with a provincial Irish priest at their dinner table: he couldn't help thinking that, and already felt that in time it might be he who became the man about this house, as a source of help in difficulty. He didn't resent the role and never had since.

That night, after dinner, the three of them had sat for an hour in the drawing-room. There was a silver-framed photograph of Roger Ferndale in officer's uniform and the stern portrait of Mrs Anstey's husband over the fireplace. A small quantity of Cointreau was drunk with coffee, and it was his turn, then, to tell them about himself, to establish that nothing could have been more different from the room he sat in than the farmhouse near Clonakilty where his mother and sister still lived. His mother always wore black, belonging to a generation of women in that part of the country who had for centuries favoured the colour. His sister reared turkeys and had once hoped to marry a man called Ned Tone, a quarry worker, but Ned Tone had remained a bachelor. The farmhouse was white and gaunt, its unused rooms full of furniture that years of sunshine had patchily bleached. The yard, where the turkeys strode, was muddy in winter, the earth of its surface baked hard in summertime. Twelve children had played there in his childhood, and it was sometimes odd to return and find the farmhouse such a quiet place. When it was sunny he liked to carry two chairs from the kitchen into the yard and sit there with his mother, while they talked about the family. He was the only one of the twelve who'd become a priest and she'd been delighted when he had.

Yet what would she think if she knew he had permitted himself to love a woman? He imagined her face turning slowly away from him, her eyes intently staring at some object in the yard, the old cart in a corner, sunshine on the turkeys' feed containers. At least she would never have to suffer that; he would visit her in a few weeks' time and they would talk once more about the family.

He paused and for a moment stood still, wishing he were a child again in the farmhouse, the family crowded around the kitchen table. What had happened in Italy? In what manner had Francis Tyte deserted his wife? It was easy now to think of him as he had not seemed, a man who for reasons of his own had led a widow on. In newspapers you read of it all the time, except that usually the widow was rich.

He told himself that had he recognized Francis as an imposter he could not have saved her from him. Women in love go their own way; he might have protested and argued, but none of it would have been any good. Even so, it seemed to Father Lavin that he need not have so unquestioningly accepted the illusion that had been presented to all of them. Without admitting it to himself, had he hoped that the marriage would knock the heart out of his own tormenting passion? As he continued to walk slowly through the trees, he knew that that was the truth, and felt selfish as well as desiccated. His well-mannered love, his sacrifice and his priestly discipline, seemed like a mess of failure. On the crackling telephone there had been in her voice such pain as he had rarely heard in the voice of any human being.

He started the engine of his car and began the journey back to the priests' house, to the lunch Father Dawne would have cooked. He prayed, since it was all he could do.

At the pavement café the white stick of a blind man touched the back of Julia's chair, but Julia didn't turn her head to see what it was. *Haiti*, it said on her coffee cup; *Controllate il vostro peso* on a blue weighing-machine at the edge of the pavement. Not far from that a traffic signal kept changing from red to green and back again: *Alt, Avanti, Alt, Avanti*. The table she sat at was round, with a pink table-cloth held in place by a shiny metal band around the table's rim. She hadn't drunk her coffee, the foam of milk on its surface had collapsed.

'Yes, I thought you were English,' the man at the next table said, a bronzed American, in early middle age. His cameras were spread out in front of him, with postcards and a guidebook. 'You can always tell an English woman,' he said, affecting a little bow to indicate that he was paying a compliment. With a swish of air-brakes a yellow and white bus halted at the lights. The lights changed, the bus crawled on. A woman weighed herself on the weighing-machine.

'Stopping long in Pisa?' the American inquired.

'No, not long.'

She wore a white linen dress and a white, brimmed hat. Around her neck were amber-coloured beads.

'Galileo's city,' the American said. 'I really appreciate it.'

She placed some coins beside her saucer and picked up her sun-glasses. The man called some kind of farewell after her but she didn't reply. Almost four more hours had to pass before her flight back to England.

She walked in the Via Maria, dragging with her the jungle of her nightmare. Through it tourists drove their cars, charabancs endlessly disgorged their loads. Guides held coloured umbrellas high above their heads, stall-holders sold replicas of the leaning tower. The sun hung like a furnace, but Julia's dark glasses transformed it into a harmless disc, laid out against a pastel sky.

She turned into the Piazza Dante. On her honeymoon in Wales the weather had been balmy, late September. Roger had studied maps and found walks among the hills and by the sea. They'd sat one afternoon for hours, crouched in the sand dunes, watching the sea birds.

'Hullo, hullo,' a man said, walking with her. *'Bellissima*, lady. *Bellissima, signora.'* He was small and dark-faced in a linen suit. He kept pulling at the lapels of his jacket to rid them of creases. 'You like *gelati*, lady? *Fragola? Cioccolata?* Lady, you like *panforte?'*

She told him to go away, but he only nodded. She remembered telling Roger that she was pregnant, and Roger's delight, the smile that had broken all over his face, his arms around her. Henrietta had been an easy baby to bear, Katherine more difficult. *I hate to see them growing up*, she'd noted in a diary, and then had crossed it out.

'I no marry Italian woman,' the man beside her said. 'Since child I like *inglese*. I show you place, lady. We have drink, Stock, *caffè? Il signor* Guzzinati, lady.'

'Please go away,' she said.

'I love *inglese. Molto, molto.'*

'Please leave me alone.' She ceased to walk as she spoke. She faced the man. There was something the matter with one of his eyes, skin disease on the lid. 'Please,' she repeated.

'Where you go, *signora*? We have *caffè* in your hotel? *Il signor* Guzzinati. *Signor* Leonardo Guzzinati, lady. We have wine? *Vino, signora*?'

She shook her head. They'd left the Piazza Dante and were off the tourist track, in a narrow street that was empty of other people. In her distress she hadn't noticed that before. She hadn't even been aware of turning into this sunless alley.

'No, no,' she said. 'I want to be alone. Please just leave me.'

He caught her arm. 'Please lady,' he said. 'We go Tirrenia. We buy *vino, signora*.'

'No, really not. No, thank you.' She tried to smile at him. Her handbag contained a small amount of money, her traveller's cheques and her passport. He could easily snatch it, or he could bundle her into a doorway. In her weakened state she felt she would not have protested. She would not even have screamed, she would let him do what he wished to do; it was nothing that she should be assaulted or raped.

Still holding her arm, he said that Tirrenia was good. It was only a short distance from Pisa, a short trip on a bus.

'In your hotel is husband, *signora*?' The hand that was not gripping her arm reached out and touched her breast. '*Bellissima*,' he said.

She pulled herself away from him and ran over the uneven paving stones. He didn't follow her. When she reached the end of the street she looked back once and saw that he was standing where she had left him, pretending to be bewildered.

People hurried by her, women carrying shopping-bags, men in shirtsleeves and light-weight suits, children with school-books. Roger, too, had called her beautiful. Roger had said her eyes were the most beautiful of all the women's he'd ever known, and afterwards she'd looked at them in the bathroom mirror. *I'm lucky*, she'd written once, *to be quite pretty*. She didn't know why she kept thinking about Roger.

She was in the Via D'Azeglio. Noticing in the distance the grey and brown façade of the railway station, she walked towards it in the hope that there she might be left in peace. But in the waiting-room she felt that people looked at her, no doubt discerning her distress. Heavy Italian women, all dressed in black, sat in a line opposite her, a huge battered suitcase in front of each. An elderly couple, the man unshaven and bent, ate bread and salami. No one spoke.

She took her hat off and put it on the seat beside her. The eyes of the women opposite passed from her pale dress and the shoes that fashionably matched it, and then glanced over her face and hair. She had been wrong to imagine that anyone could discern her distress: her eyes were blank behind dark glasses, her face would have an empty look. A silly kind of woman, the people thought, silly to spend money on clothes, silly to be a tourist. She moved from the waiting-room and stood on a platform, watching other people climbing on to a train. No one ran after her from the waiting-room with the hat she'd left behind. On the platform a dark-faced boy slowly pushed a trolley loaded with drinks and chocolate and picnic bags. The hat didn't matter; it wasn't worth going back for.

She walked from the station. In a shop window there were polishes and brushes, and in another an array of motor-cycle components, and in another cheeses. She went on walking, out on to the Livorno road because it was the first one she came to. Lorries and cars spewed up dust, drivers blew their horns or shouted. A tourist bus slowed as it passed her by. Faces gazed at her, two or three cameras were raised. To Denmark or Munich or Atlantic City they would take back a picture of a woman on the road to Livorno, her face begrimed with dust and sweat, her hair untidy. They'd puzzle maybe over the picture of a woman, wondering why she walked through the heat of an Italian day, where she was going or who she was.

She thought of Roger again, on their honeymoon and afterwards. She thought of her father, his voice gruffly telling her a story, his bulkiness weighing down the edge of her bed when she had measles. She knew she had conjured up their faces to remind herself that they were men who had always been kind to her, who had not taken advantage of her foolishness. But the cruelty that had been practised on her could not be miraculously expunged by thoughts of kindness; the nightmare couldn't be changed into one she would wake up from.

She turned back. Huge advertisements decorated the autostrada, garish with trade names: *Olivetti, Campari, Agip, Michelin*. A girl on a swing paused in mid-air, her hair and short pink skirt caught in the wind, her mouth fixedly smiling. Typewriters tumbled about, and tyres, and *panforte*, a dragon breathing fire. Her own name yelled at her: *Julia la grappa*. Confused at a roundabout, she did the wrong thing and an open Fiat skidded to avoid her. Music came from it, with shouts of laughter, no one angry that she had almost caused an accident.

Abruptly she remembered a newspaper item she'd read before she left England: a group of missionaries of the Pentecostal Church had been assassinated in Africa. They had been made to watch the killing of their children first, and then they had been killed themselves. She didn't know why she thought of that again, something that had horrified her for a moment while she prepared for her wedding. She imagined how they'd felt, lined up on their compound, unable to believe that such a thing was happening to them. It seemed like part of the nightmare that this horror had so suddenly tumbled into her mind and for another moment haunted her.

In the open spaces of the city tourists sought relief from the sun, resting on shady steps with gangs of ageing hippies. An elderly scholar led his Swan's Tour to the Triumph of Death in the Camposanto, busily explaining that this work had been an inspiration to Liszt. 'Hullo, hullo,' a voice said. 'Hullo, lady.'

She was by the Arno, on the Lungarno Sonnino; the man with the skin disease had appeared out of nowhere. '*Bellissima*,' he said, and she realized he didn't recognize her without her floppy hat and because she'd become dishevelled. 'You like *gelati*, lady? *Fragola*? *Cioccolata*? *Il signor* Guzzinati, lady.'

She moved away from him, trying to hurry. A car drew up beside them and a woman held out a piece of paper with a drawing of the leaning tower on it. Julia gestured, indicating that the tower was on the other side of the river. In excited Italian Signor Guzzinati began to explain the city's one-way traffic system. The bridge to cross was the Ponte de Mezzo, he insisted, and again she hastened to escape him.

Boys played football on the hard clay of a park. The walls of a church were drenched with crimson signs and admonitions, with slogans and counter-slogans, hammers and sickles, swastikas in black. *Morte! Morte!* was everywhere crudely daubed. 'Strega?' Signor Guzzinati suggested. '*Caffè*? Stock, lady?'

There were other people on the street beside them, but they didn't seem to notice that a woman was being plied with unwelcome attentions. Her mother had laughed about the ways of Italian men, and so had Henrietta and Katherine. 'We go your hotel, lady. We go now?'

They were by the café where she had earlier not drunk her coffee, near the blue weighing-machine. She sat down, not caring now when the man sat down as well. Excitedly he beckoned the waiter, ordering brandy.

'*Il signor* Guzzinati,' he said. 'Always I am here in Pisa, never I marry. I am rich man now, *signora, direttore della ditta Pieroni.*'

She felt sorry for him because of his diseased eye. She doubted that he was the director of a company; his only occupation was to follow women on the streets, tourist women who wouldn't report him to the police. Not once before, in all the tourist seasons he'd known, had a woman sat down with him.

'You are pretty lady, *signora.*'

His hand had seized one of hers and she didn't withdraw it. In less than a quarter of an hour she would have to walk away from him again, and it wouldn't matter if he followed her, even to her hotel, the Hotel la Pace. He might follow her to the airport, sitting beside her in the taxi, but still it wouldn't matter.

'I love you, *signora*,' he said, his bad eye blinking and running a bit. He raised a grimy handkerchief to it and she took her hand from his and drank some of the brandy the waiter had brought. She had come to Italy on her honeymoon, she said, but had got no farther than Pisa. She had not seen a single picture or eaten a meal. Her husband had married her for five pieces of jewellery that weren't even properly hers.

'You have husband, *signora?*' Signor Guzzinati said. 'This husband in Pisa, lady?'

She didn't answer. It seemed pointless talking to the man, and then it seemed pointless not to. She said:

'My husband has left me. I signed a piece of paper for him and then he went away.'

'This husband in Pisa, no?'

'My husband's in Germany by now. The manager of my hotel misunderstood things. He got in touch with the police –'

'Police? *Polizia?*'

As he spoke, Signor Guzzinati scuttled off into the crowds, and she found money in her handbag to pay for their drinks. He came from some poor part of the city, he was probably a thief. Instead of the beauty of Fra Angelico and chirlandaio, or the madonnas of Filippo Lippi whom she had once resembled, she would remember the skin disease on his eyelid when she thought of Italy.

·9·
Julia in Francis's

Julia was met at London Airport by her daughters, who had borrowed a Mini in order to help her on her journey. It had been arranged that Father Lavin should meet her at Cheltenham, and she was now driven to Reading, where she could catch an afternoon train. Henrietta and Katherine had wired her at the Hotel la Pace as soon as they heard the news and she'd wired back, assuring them she was all right. But she wasn't and they knew it; in the car their anger was like ice. 'We'll never mention it again,' Mrs Anstey had said to them on the telephone, referring to the intuition she had failed to convey.

Julia knew she should try to explain to her daughters. She should begin at the beginning, with the toothpaste smiles of the trim Alitalia girls on the flight to Pisa, with her surprise when Francis had not taken her arm as they crossed the tarmac. She should end by telling them how she had walked for hours in the heat. But she didn't.

'You'll be all right, Mummy?' Henrietta inquired as they said goodbye at Reading station.

'Yes, I'm perfectly all right.' She thanked them for meeting her, and apologized for being so silent. They said they understood.

It was a comfort to see the English countryside again, the upretentious hills and brick farmhouses, cool fields of grass. A single night it had taken in their room in the Hotel la Pace, eight hours to dismantle what there had seemed to be. They hadn't undressed or even attempted to lie down. They'd sat at a square table and he'd told her about his life, how once he'd wanted to be married to Kim Novak.

In the room she had wished she were no longer alive. The horror of the shock, like a gigantic weight, pressed down on her; coherent thought wouldn't come. She wept but he had appeared not to notice. His voice went on about himself, and when other people were mentioned it was because of the parts they had played in his life. 'People do terrible things,' he said. 'Like poor Constance Kent did.'

He didn't say he'd done a terrible thing himself. He had always known she would want to help him was how he put it instead, and then he spoke of the marriage service, the priest's hand raised in blessing, the smell of incense and candle-grease, Bach on the organ. For months he'd looked forward to it; for months he'd imagined them standing in the garden of Swan House, while people drank champagne. Every morning when he woke all that had come rushing into his mind; at night he'd sent himself to sleep with it. He would never forget a single detail of that whole afternoon; her voice accepting him as her husband would echo for him until the moment of his death.

He spoke as if the marriage had taken place purely for the occasion it presented, as if in some bizarre way the memory of the wedding afternoon would be enough for her also. His deceiving her and the fact that the marriage was illegal, his asking her for money and for her jewellery, seemed irrelevant and unimportant. 'Just enough to get me away somewhere,' he begged, and then he rooted among her possessions and spread the jewellery out on the table between them. 'It's everything to me,' he said, 'that we stood together in that little church.'

Even then she'd pleaded with him, drying away her tears. She loved him, he didn't have to go away. They could live together in Swan House, they could be happy because of love. But he'd shaken his head, and had begun all over again to tell her about himself.

'I'm sorry, Julia,' Father Lavin said, carrying two white suitcases from the train at Cheltenham station.

In the car she said as little as she had in the Mini her daughters had borrowed. Ever since she'd begun her journey home she'd been telling herself that it was all quite simple: she was a silly kind of person, deserving of what had happened to her. Every single word Francis Tyte had spoken she had believed; his caresses had easily enticed her; she'd longed to lie in bed with him. 'Yes, I'll give you some money too,' she had promised in their hotel bedroom, and in the morning had cashed her traveller's cheques for the amount he'd suggested. A stranger on the street had fondled her breast yet she had later sat down at a pavement café with him: her silliness was all of a piece.

'Stupid,' she said in Father Lavin's car, feeling heavy and unattractive. 'A stupid middle-aged woman.'

'No, Julia.'

It was after six o'clock; shadows were lengthening, the weather was still showery. They skirted the town, taking the road by the

Orchard Motel. Nevil Clapp was in trouble again, Father Lavin said, and for a moment she did not know who Nevil Clapp was and then remembered he was the boy who worked at the motel, the boyfriend of the girl who did her hair. 'Oh, poor Diane,' she said.

'At least it's all over, Julia.'

'Yes.'

Standing with the aid of her sticks, Mrs Anstey awaited her daughter in the hall of Swan House, and slowly moved forward to embrace her. Mrs Spanners was hovering in the background, ready to be greeted and to greet. No tears were shed, though Mrs Spanners displayed a tendency to sniff. 'Thank you for coping,' Julia said to her, and then invited Father Lavin to have a glass of sherry with them. 'No, we would like you to,' she insisted when he shook his head, for it seemed to Julia to be part of what had happened that she and her mother and the priest should drink a glass of sherry together, as they might have after a funeral.

They drank it in the drawing-room, although they might easily have taken their glasses outside, since the evening had become fine. But it seemed appropriate to stay indoors while the sun was shining. She knew she should talk about it to them also, for it was their due, just as it had been the due of her daughters. But she still found it difficult to say anything at all.

'I'm sorry,' Father Lavin murmured again, lifting his glass slowly. Her mother murmured also.

It was easier having the priest there. There was the effort imposed by a visitor, conversation shared among three. Alone with her mother, delicate pauses would have gathered, like webs between them.

'You'll stay to supper?' she said.

'No, no, I really mustn't.'

'Please do, Father.'

Mrs Spanners had gone, taking away her transistor and her night clothes in a carrier-bag. She'd left cold meat which they could have, and lettuce and tomatoes. In a suitably low voice she had explained all that.

'Francis is a psychopath,' Julia said. She added, after a silence had followed that statement, 'He wanted my jewellery. His parents are alive. They live in a home in Hampton Wick.'

Her mother asked about the jewellery and Julia said she'd given it to him. As she spoke, she saw again her dragon brooch on the table between them, and her sapphires and her pearl necklace.

'It was family jewellery,' her mother sharply pointed out. 'He stole it is what it amounts to.'

'No: I gave it to him. I signed a letter to that effect.'

'It wasn't entirely yours to give, Julia.'

'Yes, I know that.'

She explained how she had waited another day, not wanting to return to England, and how the manager of the Hotel la Pace had misunderstood her distress and had approached the police to inquire if an accident had befallen an English tourist in the city. She'd had to go to a police station herself to say that what had happened was that her husband had left her. She must have mentioned a honeymoon because it was a woman deserted on her honeymoon that had become a newspaper item. 'I'm sorry I make mistake,' the manager of the hotel had later apologized, drawing her attention to the item, apologizing for that too.

'I guessed about him,' Mrs Anstey said, and added that never in her life had she hated anyone as much as she hated Francis Tyte now. She hated his awful Leslie Howard face, his elegance and his smile, the striped grey clothes he wore. For as long as he lived, she hoped he would never be happy.

'I shan't bear his name,' Julia said. 'But I don't want any charges brought because of his bigamy, Father. I don't want him persecuted, wherever he is.'

'It's a criminal offence of course.'

'I just want it all forgotten.'

Her mother's weeping ceased. At supper Father Lavin told them about the builder in Cheltenham who had promised to paint the gutters of St Martin's for nothing. Julia was aware of his dogged hunt for this conversational topic and his determination in keeping it going. She imagined the builder arriving at the little church with his ladders on an autumn day, the trees in the graveyard losing their leaves, the smell of an autumn bonfire. Would enough time have passed, she wondered, would the pain be less by then?

In the kitchen she made coffee and carried the tray into the drawing-room. Her mother and Father Lavin were again making an effort to converse, he listening while her mother spoke of something that had happened in her youth. From above the mantelpiece Julia's father continued severely to survey all three of them. He would have seen through the deception, Julia suddenly thought, and she would have protested that he was being unjust.

Even here, at home, it still continued to feel like a nightmare, its reality still lost in the shock that had not ceased to numb her. She was just another person among the people he had told her about, people in whose houses he had stayed. Casually he had married a dressmaker in Folkestone in the hope of inheriting her money. Casually he'd caused a child to be born, just to see what it felt like to be a father. But casually or otherwise there had been no need to marry a second time, no need for all the long palaver of deceit and falsity: if he'd asked her for the jewellery she would have given it to him. As long ago as the day they met in the coffee lounge of the Queen's Hotel he must have noticed her dragon brooch and estimated its worth, and must afterwards have deduced that the household's only valuable objects were its jewellery. Was it just for them that he had charmed his way into her life, or had he married her in order to set another piece of cruelty in motion, to humiliate her with the truth? 'You're a good woman,' he'd said in Italy. 'You're a special kind of person, Julia.' It was hard to keep remembering that he said whatever suited him. It was hard to remember that he lived in fantasies and make-believe, that not for an instant did he cease to practise his actor's art, smiling nicely. Of course it was out of cruelty that he had bigamously married her, of course it was to mock her and insult her. He hated the kind of person she was; he had begun to revenge himself from the first moment he'd laid eyes on her.

'It's been very kind of you to let me stay.' Father Lavin stood up, though it was still early in the evening. 'Please just phone,' he said to Julia, 'if I can ever help.'

He shook hands with both of them, as he always did, and Julia walked through the hall with him. Outside there were still streaks of light in the sky, but the night air was chilly.

'There's nothing I can say to you, Julia. Friends are inadequate in these circumstances.'

'You haven't been inadequate, Father.'

He started the car and waved into the darkness as he drove away. She remained for a moment alone, remembering the evening of the cocktail party when she and Francis had stood where she was standing now, bidding goodbye to the guests while her mother was asleep in the garden. She'd taken his arm afterwards, as they turned back to the house.

'You should try a sleeping pill,' her mother advised in the hall, about to go upstairs.

'I think I'll sleep all right. You mustn't let it worry you. It's over now.'

Mrs Anstey nodded. With one hand on the banister, the other grasping a stick, she dragged herself from step to step. 'Malign,' she suddenly said, stopping and turning around. 'He brought malevolence to us.'

'That's what we have to live with now.'

Days crawled by, the showery weather continued. Julia had made no real explanation of Francis's absence to Mrs Spanners, and to the people of Stone St Martin it remained mysterious also, the subject of gossip and conjecture. She imagined that the interesting story of a woman deceived would be told to weekend visitors and to people when they settled in the area. New shopkeepers in Stone St Martin would inquire who she was; information would be given, with some details of the Anstey family, who had always been a bit different anyway because of their Catholic connexions. The marriage to an army officer called Roger Ferndale would be touched upon, and the birth of two daughters who'd grown to be beautiful. Held until last would be the extraordinariness: how a small-time actor had wriggled his way into this woman's affections, had married her and then had walked away, leaving her to suffer.

In the garden and the house there were tasks to be done, and shopping in the town. There was the preparation of meals, legalities to be typed out on her Remington, Sunday mass. Every evening either Katherine or Henrietta telephoned.

Days turned into weeks, and gradually the rawness of the wound grew its first skin. Mrs Spanners's chat began to lose its stilted note, Mrs Anstey became less grim. 'Honestly there's no need to,' Julia assured her daughters, and soon after that the daily telephoning ceased. She no longer dreaded the moment of waking in the morning, and for that mercy she gave thanks as often as she prayed. As if by consent, the past was encouraged to claim what belonged to it, and succeeded to such a degree that when a tendril from the days before the marriage suddenly presented itself there was no sense of alarm, only bewilderment. Returning from shopping one Monday afternoon, Julia met Mrs Spanners on her way out of the house. 'A chap called Hodge rung,' she said.

'Hodge?'

'He has a dog for you. In Cheltenham this Hodge is.'

Julia shook her head. She knew no one called Hodge, nor did she know anything about a dog.

'Spaniel,' Mrs Spanners persisted. 'Liver and white, seemingly.'

'But, Mrs Spanners, it was a mistake or a wrong number. It must have been.'

The cleaning woman, whose mood had been effervescent because of having to impart this peculiar news about a dog, became solemn. Having been searching Julia's face for reactions, her eyes were suddenly cast down. She spoke in the low voice she had perfected some weeks ago and recently abandoned.

'It was a dog Mr Tyte arranged for, seemingly.'

'Good Lord!'

'I thought you'd maybe be surprised, see. I mean, I knew you wasn't expecting nothing in the way of a dog. I mean, I said it to the man.' Mrs Spanners continued on her way, only imparting further the information that the telephone number of the man called

Hodge was written down on the pad in the kitchen.

When Julia rang it ten minutes later she discovered that a liver and white spaniel, one of a litter of eight, had indeed been ordered by Francis in advance of the birth. Mrs Spanners had explained to the man what had happened and he now said that although the pup had not been paid for he would not, in the circumstances, hold Julia to the arrangement. 'Oh, but,' Julia protested, 'we'll most certainly have it.'

'Lovely,' Mrs Anstey said when she was told, thinking of all the rooting up the animal would do in the garden, and the nuisance of house-training. The man claimed that Francis had telephoned him in answer to an advertisement in a local paper: in the circumstances Mrs Anstey found that odd, but did not say so. The next morning Julia drove to Cheltenham and brought the puppy back in a shoe-box.

'What on earth shall we call him?' she said, watching the tiny creature staggering about the lawn. He was soaking wet because he'd had to be washed, having been repeatedly sick in the car.

'Before you were born we used to have a terrier called Pekoe at Anstey's Mill,' Mrs Anstey said, but as they continued to watch the spaniel sniffing the grass they decided that the name wasn't suitable and so the dog remained without one.

Its arrival spurred Julia to action in another direction. Francis's help in the garden had been counted upon, and he himself had urged that no one should be employed to replace old Mr Pocock. But now, without either of them, it was beginning to look tatty and something had to be done about it. Eventually she thought of her hairdresser's boyfriend, remembering Father Lavin saying that the boy's job in the motel hadn't turned out successfully. 'It's terribly kind of you,' Diane said in the Crowning Glory Salon when Julia sounded her out, and Julia replied that it was of course up to Nevil himself and that it was only a day a week. 'I'll get him to come out and see you,' Diane promised, and three days later Nevil Clapp arrived on his motor-cycle.

For once Mrs Anstey agreed with Mrs Spanners: the whole idea of employing a person like this in the garden was ludicrous. As was her way, she did not say so, but Mrs Spanners repeated what Charle had remarked about Nevil Clapp, which wasn't complimentary.

Julia listened and nodded, but was not deterred. She showed Nevil Clapp around the garden, explaining the nature of the work which would be required of him. His mouse-coloured hair was cut very short. His face, flecked with pieces of grit after his motor-cycle ride, was mainly flat. He carried enormous motor-cycling gloves in one hand and a yellow crash-helmet in the other. The black nylon jacket he wore looked as if it had been pumped up.

'There are odd things in the house as well,' she said. 'Old Mr Pocock did them in winter, or on wet days.'

'What kind of things?'

'Bits of redecoration now and again. The central heating gives trouble occasionally.'

'Yeah, that's O.K., only I don't know nothing about a garden.'

'It's the rough work mainly, and keeping the lawns cut. Starting the lawnmower's sometimes difficult. Didn't you work in a garage once?'

'Yeah.'

'And you did the garden at the motel?'

'Gravel they have. Not much of a garden, you couldn't call it.'

'Well, if you want to give it a try, it's here for you. It would help us out.'

'Yeah.'

'I just thought it might help you out, too.'

He nodded, unwilling to commit himself as to whether it would help him out or not. A fly had settled among the specks of grit on his face, but he didn't wave it away.

'Yeah,' he said again. 'Say Mondays, then?'

Julia hesitated. Monday was Mrs Spanners's day and it seemed unwise that Nevil Clapp should share it with her. But for a reason he did not divulge he particularly wished to come on Mondays. 'Say change to Saturdays if I get employment?'

She nodded. She asked him how much he had been paid an hour at the motel and offered him a little more. Agreeable to that,

Nevil replaced his crash-helmet and roared away on his motorcycle.

Another lame duck, Mrs Anstey thought, more typing taken on to pay for him; and a week later Mrs Spanners drew attention to the fact that when Nevil Clapp came to the kitchen for his cups of tea he brought grass-cuttings with him, trailing from the ends of his jeans. He didn't rinse his hands under the tap as you'd expect a person to do before picking up a biscuit. He made a noise all the time, a kind of snuffling under his breath, whistling she supposed it was. As to the dog, was it stupid or something that it would never go on the sheets of newspapers that were put out for it, preferring to make its puddles by the fridge, which was not hygienic?

But four weeks after the dog's advent, and a fortnight after Nevil's, the new regime at Swan House had developed an air of permanence. The pain and embarrassment of what had happened was already part of Julia's life, as the death of her husband had become. The people to whom Mrs Anstey had posted little boxes of wedding-cake all knew by now that they should not have consumed it in celebration. The story which Julia had imagined being told about her in Stone St Martin was already current, but there was sympathy in Highhill Street and in the shops, though no word was ever spoken. Then, in the middle of one sunny afternoon, the telephone rang.

'Yes?' Julia said in the hall.

'It's Doris Smith here.'

'Who?'

'Doris Smith. Are you the woman that married –'

'Yes, I am.'

'This Mrs Ferndale? It gave your name on the paper. Julia Ferndale, Glos. I rang Directory Enquiries –'

'I didn't realize there'd been a newspaper report in England.'

'A couple of weeks ago, Julia, the *Evening Standard*. It said about Frankie going like that in Italy. There was a photo from the commercial he was in. Actor vanishes, it said. Honeymoon drama.'

'I see.' Julia paused, not wishing to continue. Then she said, 'Francis told me about you, Miss Smith. And about your child.'

'The thing was, Frankie was married to a woman in Folkestone. That's what I said to Joy – how could he marry someone else?'

'He committed bigamy.'

'My God!'

The line went dead, but ten minutes later, when Julia was making tea in the kitchen, the telephone rang again. She poured what remained of the boiling water into the tea-pot before going to the hall to answer it. Doris said:

'I'm sorry about that, dear. I couldn't continue for a moment.'

'There honestly isn't much we can say to one another.'

'I have to talk to you, Julia, I have to get it straightened. Thing is, I was in the Underground at Oxford Circus, queuing up for a ticket. I opened the paper and there was Frankie's face, tucked away in a corner. With this little snippet about a honeymoon. Hardly said a thing, and the photo wasn't much neither. But of course I'd recognize Frankie anywhere.'

'I'm sorry you should have found out like that.'

'The next thing, I'm lying on the floor in the traffic controller's office, with a crowd of West Indians staring down at me. It didn't make any kind of sense, see, a honeymoon in Italy.'

'No, I don't suppose it did.'

'I thought it was the girl, Julia. I said to myself, the girl's got him to Italy with her even though she made me a promise. I passed the remark to the West Indians but they looked like I was out of my tiny. So I went over to the Spread Eagle and kept on reading the little snippet, shaking my head over it. They've got it wrong, I said to myself, referring to a woman in Glos. Susie Music the girl's called.'

'Francis didn't mention that name to me, but then of course –'

'Julia, I sat in the upstairs bar watching the fan going round. There's this big fan like an aeroplane propeller in the middle of the ceiling. I'm not a drinker, Julia, but I had to have a couple that evening. There was this rock music going full blast, and all the time I was trying to remember what he said the last night when he was round in the flat. Bits of it came back to me, and when I woke up Joy to tell her it turns out she heard a bit herself on account of the wall being a partition.'

There was a pause. Julia was about to end the conversation but Doris interrupted her.

'I think he's maybe taken his life, Julia.'

'Good heavens, no.'

'I've got used to it in the time that's gone by. Well no, not used to it, I'll never get used to it. But I'm calmer, Julia. I'm not in a state, if you get what I mean?'

'Francis is in Germany.'

'I doubt he is, dear. The thing is Joy was lying awake that night and both of us was definitely under the impression it all had to do with this Constance Kent. He was on about a debt-collector, for instance, and I distinctly remember saying to myself, this is the bloke that drove Constance Kent to do the killing.'

'He told me too, but the debt-collector has nothing whatsoever to do with Constance Kent. I mean, he couldn't have.'

'I know what you mean, Julia. One minute it's the house Constance Kent was in and the next it's his mum's knitting-needles in this Rowena Avenue, and then again the dressmaker's place down Folkestone way. On top of that there was people he mentioned that Joy has no recollection of, maybe she fell asleep. Two old sisters he met on a train and then again some doctor and his missus, and another couple in their greenhouses. Only it's difficult unravelling it, if you get what I mean.'

'Francis has certainly not committed suicide.'

'I work in a shoe department, dear. I have loads of time to think. After the weeks that's passed I can tell that that last night in the flat poor Frankie was distributing the blame.'

'Blame?'

'He knew hell with that dressmaker, Julia, and then again he knew hell as a kiddy, his mum and dad elderly, this debt-collector a type of devil. I'd say the old parents have something to answer for, you know, else he wouldn't have said they didn't exist. Another thing is, Julia, Joy and myself didn't think you existed yourself. I kept saying to Joy it was an error in the newspaper. Dirty weekend with the girl I kept saying.'

'Well, I do exist and I'm really afraid there's not much point in continuing this conversation.'

'Joy cried when she heard, Julia. Joy cared for him in her way and there it was, bucketing out of her, poor kid. Not only that. I've just found out she's not attending school. She's gone bolshy and difficult, poor little scrap, trying to get a job in a Bovril factory. Can you hear me, Julia?'

'Yes, I can hear you.'

'All I'm saying is we should have a natter. Could I come and see you, Julia? Is there a train down? I would arrive on a Saturday morning. Every second Saturday I have off—'

'I'm afraid I'd rather you didn't. I have an elderly mother: I couldn't possibly have you coming here, upsetting her with all this.'

'I know. I do know, dear. And I wouldn't bother you only there's ends left dangling, Julia.'

'I don't consider there are. I'm sorry, but I'd rather you didn't telephone me again.'

'There's people to blame, Julia, I can hear him saying it. It's my opinion that on top of everything else he maybe picked up an infection off this actress girl. Don't get me wrong, Julia, I'm not stating it as a fact. But a lot of these young actresses is promiscuous, you see it on the papers. It's the age we live in, Julia, and all I'm saying is poor Frankie was made for suffering, like the Kent girl was. That's what he was getting across to us that last night, Julia. He kept on about Constance Kent, dear.'

Julia replaced the receiver, but almost at once the ringing began again. She didn't answer it. Instead she collected the tray of tea things from the kitchen and carried it to where her mother was sitting beneath the tulip tree. She placed the tray on the beech-wood table while the ringing continued in the house. Neither of them commented on it, but Julia was aware her mother had guessed that the conversation she'd just had had been about Francis. She was also aware that her mother did not wish to be told more, that whatever happened now she would prefer simply to happen, without introduction or preamble. Julia sipped her tea, and abruptly the distant ringing ceased.

Confident by now, as if the place belonged to him, the unnamed spaniel sniffed their feet.

·10·
Doris's

In London that same evening Doris telephoned the Sundown Home and from the conversation that ensued it was again confirmed that there were two Tytes in the home, a man and his wife. The following evening she made the journey to Hampton Wick and at the home she announced herself as a close friend of the Tytes' son. They had a grandchild, she told a male nurse, a fact that might be a comfort to the old people in their grief. The nurse was at a loss.

'Visiting's Sundays,' he said. 'Unless emergencies and close relatives.'

Doris was lighting a cigarette with a match from a box which was damp. Matches had been giving her trouble all day, and in the hall of the old people's home not even a glimmer of a spark occurred when she scraped the head of yet another on the abrasive side of the box.

'Ciggy?' she offered the male nurse, pressing a packet upon him. 'Got a light, have you?'

He shook his head, rejecting the cigarette and indicating that he didn't carry matches. It was preferred, he added, that visitors didn't smoke unless it was absolutely necessary. 'Visiting's Sundays,' he repeated. 'Unless otherwise for a reason.' He was small and dark-haired, with a dark jowl and a white cotton jacket that had the marks of a ballpoint pen around one of its pockets. 'You'd best see Miss Purchase,' he said, and went away.

Doris couldn't think what it was he reminded her of and then remembered: a black rubber ball. He looked as though he'd bounce if someone threw him. The hall was a dimly lit place, with coats hanging up and sticks in a thing that reminded her of the Zoo.

'Yes?' said a tall woman in a navy-blue twin-set, with spectacles on a chain. Doris gave her name and proffered her hand. The woman limply took it. 'Yes?' Miss Purchase said again.

'The Tytes.'

'What about the Tytes?'

'I'd like to see them for ten minutes.'

'I'm afraid that's impossible. Visiting is on Sunday afternoons.'

'This is it, dear. What I'm saying is –'

'Are you the person who kept telephoning us a while back?'

'I'm the mother of the Tytes' grandchild. I was saying to the bloke a minute ago the Tytes have a grandchild they don't know about. It's just that the news would cheer them up in their distress.'

'The Tytes are not in distress. No inmate here is in distress.'

'When a person takes his life you get distress. Naturally you do.'

'What person? What are you talking about, please?'

'Look, dear, I have Frankie's kid and I want to know why poor Frankie's gone. All I'm doing is making a few inquiries for my own peace of mind. It's all mixed up, Mrs Purchase, it needs unravelling.'

'I would be glad if you would do me the courtesy of addressing me correctly. My name is Miss Purchase.'

'Be that as it may, dear, what I'm attempting to explain is that poor Frankie had death on his mind because the telly thing set him going. He couldn't help it, dear.'

'I have no idea what you're talking about, madam. It would upset the Tytes beyond measure to hear these references to suicide. We have not been informed here of their son's death and until we are –'

'Take a look at this.'

154

Doris rooted in her bag and eventually produced a scrap of newspaper. *Honeymoon Drama*, Miss Purchase read. *British Actor Vanishes in Italy*. An actor, pictured above, who had recently become familiar to television viewers because of his role in a series of tobacco advertisements, had disappeared on his Italian honeymoon. His name was Francis Tyte and he had married Mrs Julia Ferndale of Stone St Martin, Glos. The report ended abruptly with a sentence that belonged elsewhere in the newspaper, to the effect that sugar prices were holding their own.

'There's not a word about death in this,' Miss Purchase said. 'It simply says he vanished.'

'I know, dear. Mrs Ferndale says he's in Germany. He married her when he shouldn't, you realize? The real wife's a dressmaker down Folkestone way. Elderly by now.'

'None of this in the very least concerns us at the Sundown. I must ask you to leave here, Miss Smith.'

Doris shook her head, making a fresh attempt to light the cigarette that hung from the centre of her mouth. But her matches would still not ignite.

'That last night he was saying goodbye. He was making his confessions to Joy and myself. He was on about Constance Kent, if ever you heard of her –'

'Will you kindly stop talking like that?' Miss Purchase almost shouted. 'And will you kindly stop striking those matches? You smell of drink. You cannot see the Tytes and that is that.'

Doris leaned against the hallstand, wondering just for an instant where she was and then remembering. She had cried when she'd found herself in the traffic controller's office in Oxford Circus, with the West Indians staring down at her. She had cried again in the upstairs bar of the Spread Eagle while the fan was going round, and again in the flat, when she told Joy. 'You take it easy now,' the West Indians had urged, but Joy hadn't been able to say anything because she'd been crying herself. Poor Joy hadn't had her spectacles on and the chapped skin of her face had reddened a bit more. 'He'll never come back,' she'd kept repeating between her bouts of tears. It was all very well the Ferndale woman insisting he was in Germany. Better to believe the worst because at least the worst wouldn't let you down. She made that point to the woman with the spectacles on a chain and then she added:

'What I'm saying is if that young actress is to blame there's maybe a few other people as well, his mum and dad for a start. There was a hell in that house, Mrs Purchase, and all I need is a brief word with your old people to straighten things out.'

'Well, you're not going to have it. You have no right to come barging in here with your wild talk and your drink. You will kindly leave, madam.'

'I have come here to see the Tytes. Are you the matron in charge?'

'Of course I'm the matron in charge. And I can only repeat that you cannot see the Tytes.'

'Tytes?' said a voice, and an old woman in grey paused before mounting the stairs. 'Henry's in the W.C.'

'Go away immediately,' Miss Purchase said fiercely to Doris. 'You are not to address Mrs Tyte.'

'Good evening, Mrs Tyte,' Doris said. 'I came to see you, dear.'

'George!' shouted Miss Purchase up the staircase. 'Cyril!'

'How d'you do, Mrs Tyte?' Doris said, proffering her bony hand again.

'I'm all right. Well as can be expected. We had that rhubarb again, and Henry can't come out of the W.C. That's the only thing.'

'George!' shouted Miss Purchase more agitatedly. 'To the hall, please.'

'I've come with my condolences,' Doris said in a solemn voice. 'I'm sorry Frankie's dead, Mrs Tyte.'

'Frankie?'

'I'm sorry your son took his life.'

'Please go at once,' shouted Miss Purchase, making as much noise as she could. She bustled about, opening the hall door and standing to one side of it.

'I didn't hear you,' said Mrs Tyte.

'I'm only saying I'm sorry your son's dead.'

'Dead?'

'For heaven's sake, George,' shouted Miss Purchase. 'There's a crisis in the hall.'

Other old men and women had gathered. They stood in ones and twos, staring at Doris.

'She's telling you your son's dead,' one of them said to Mrs Tyte.

'Dead?' said Mrs Tyte again.

'I'm the mother of your grandchild, dear. Joy she's called.'

The man like a ball hurriedly descended the stairs, with a bigger man in a similar white jacket. They seized Doris and proceeded to eject her.

'Whatever's happening?' an old man asked, and an old woman sat down on the bottom step of the stairs and began to cry. Mrs Tyte was staring vacantly.

'You have a grandchild, dear,' the woman who had spoken to Mrs Tyte before said. 'This lady's given birth to a grandchild.'

Doris tried to strike at the two men with her handbag, which was still attached to her shoulder by its strap. 'I'm sorry your son's committed suicide,' she shouted. 'But no one does it without a reason, Mrs Tyte.'

'Suicide?' an old man without any shoes said.

'The Tytes' son committed suicide,' someone else said.

'You made a hell for him,' Doris shouted. 'Your knitting-needles going in Rowena Avenue. You have that on your conscience, dear.'

The two men deposited her on the crazy paving in front of the house.

'If you return you'll instantly be arrested,' Miss Purchase snapped. 'You've upset that woman beyond measure.'

'Dead?' repeated Mrs Tyte in the hall.

'She's given birth to a grandchild,' said the woman who had said this already, raising her voice considerably because it seemed to her that Mrs Tyte had turned deaf. 'Joy,' she shouted. 'She's called Joy, dear.'

Doris rang the bell but no one answered it, and eventually she went away, the cigarette she'd tried to light still hanging from the centre of her mouth. In her struggle with the male nurses it had become crushed and more than usually bent.

'Vodka, dear,' she said in the Blue Feathers, which wasn't far away. 'And a spurt of soda, dear.'

It hadn't happened as she'd planned. She'd thought she'd sit quietly with the old couple and tell them about Joy, offering consolation and asking a few questions. She hadn't wanted to accuse them, even though she knew they were among the people who were to blame. It was extraordinary that she'd been seized by the arms and warned she'd be arrested if she returned.

In the public house she dropped into conversation with a man who seemed agreeable to buying her further glasses of vodka. She told him about her visit to the home, how the black-haired man had reminded her of a ball, and about the spectacles on a chain that the matron had been wearing. The man's bloodshot eyes were genial and kind, reminding her of her father's.

'I loved Frankie,' she said. 'And then he went with a girl. The next thing it's on the paper he's dead.' She talked about all of it, repeating herself because sometimes it was necessary to make the same point again. She worked in a shoe department, she said, in Oxford Street.

'Time to cork it up, madam,' a man who was not the bloodshot man said. He was leaning over her where she sat, smiling a little, his face and his smile moving glassily around, reflected in mirrors all over the place. She'd never seen so many mirrors.

'Frankie was battered,' she said. 'Like a kid would be.'

'Poor Frankie,' the man said. 'Come along now, please.'

'I'd like another drink. Just a glassful for the road.'

The man was wearing an apron with words on it, but the words whirled about like words in a kaleidoscope and she was reminded of that last night, when there'd been words going round in the sitting-room. 'Impossible, madam,' the man said. 'Time to cork it up, I'm afraid.'

He helped her to her feet, handling her more gently than the men in the institution had. He told her he had a taxi for her and then he led her out into the air. The engine of the car was running, one of its doors was open. A voice asked her where she lived and as best she could she gave the address in Fulham. She felt groggy in the legs, and the mirrors were going round again. 'Four quid'll cover it,' a voice said and her handbag was taken from her shoulder. She thought they were maybe looking for matches on account of their own matches being damp, but instead there was this reference to money. 'O.K.,' a voice said, and then the strap of her bag was replaced on her shoulder and a voice said something else.

She woke up in the darkness, lying on her bed with her clothes on, with the latchkey still in her hand. Almost immediately more bits of what Frankie had said that last night returned to her through a muzziness, as if his voice were actually in the room, as if he particularly wanted her to hear. Again he referred to Constance Kent. Again he spoke of Rowena Avenue and the dressmaker's house, and the wispy grey moustache of the debt-collector. 'Tit for tat,' he said.

·II·
Doris in Julia's

It was on a Thursday evening that Doris made her way to the Sundown Home. On the following Saturday morning, accompanied reluctantly by Joy, she set out on another journey.

'We took that train,' she said on the telephone. 'We're here, dear. At Cheltenham station.'

In the hall of Swan House Julia began to protest, to say she'd asked specifically that that shouldn't happen, but she changed her mind before she'd made her meaning clear. They could have whatever conversation was necessary at the station, she said.

'No hurry, Julia. Joy's having a nibble in the buffet.'

'I'll be about half an hour.'

But Mrs Anstey, on her way downstairs, suggested that whoever had arrived should be brought to the house in the normal way. She herself was going to do a little weeding and would not appear till lunchtime. She could keep out of the way entirely if that was preferred. Francis naturally had had friends.

'It's a woman who had his child.'

'She won't worry me, my dear, if that's what you're thinking about.'

Julia stood still, her hand on the telephone, watching her mother's slow descent of the stairs. When Mrs Anstey reached the bottom step she took a grey cardigan from the newel post. Julia said:

'I thought I had finished with it all.'

Mrs Anstey nodded. With the cardigan over her shoulders, she passed through the hall and the drawing-room and out into the garden, to the lily-of-the-valley bed. The spaniel trotted at her heels.

An hour later Mrs Anstey peered through shrubs to catch a glimpse of the visitors. Restraining the spaniel, whose intention it was to rush across the garden and jump up on them, she couldn't tell much from what she saw. The woman was attired in a maroon-coloured raincoat; the child, in a yellow and green school uniform, appeared to have glasses. They disappeared quickly into the house, and Mrs Anstey released her hold on the dog and continued to pull out dandelions and clover. She herself would have sent them packing over the telephone.

'Would you like a drink?' Julia offered in the drawing-room. 'What about Joy? There's orange juice. Or Ribena.'

'Tizer?' Joy suggested hopefully.

'Dear, they wouldn't have Tizer, place like this. Run along to the toilet, dear. If you're thirsty there'll be water in the tap.' Doris laughed, looking round the drawing-room.

'Excuse me,' Julia said. She took Joy to the hall and directed her to the lavatory. She showed her where the kitchen was and said there was a carton of orange juice in the door of the fridge. 'There's no one in the house,' she said. 'You can wander about as much as you like.' She said it because she imagined that the conversation in the drawing-room should be private.

'What would you like to drink yourself?' she offered Doris, who said she honestly could do with a vodka. Her face was even whiter and gaunter than it had seemed in the railway buffet. Her thin, loose body looked as though it could easily collapse, folding her into a heap on the carpet.

'Would gin do instead? I'm afraid we haven't any vodka.'

'Oh anything, anything. I'm not much of a drinker.'

She had been drinking in the station bar when Julia had arrived. She'd suggested that Julia should join her, and Julia had declined. The child had been eating crisps at a table.

'What would you like in this? Vermouth? Tonic?'

'Oh, anything, dear.'

Julia added Cinzano to the gin. She'd said they must stay to lunch, an invitation that had been accepted. The child looked hungry, her fair hair lifeless and neglected.

'Cheers, Julia.'

'Yes, cheers.' She did her best to smile. She dropped a slice of lemon into a glass of tonic water, hoping it would be taken for gin and tonic.

'I haven't been sleeping, Julia. I haven't had a night's rest since I read it on the paper weeks ago.' She paused in order to lift her glass to her lips. 'We met on a bus, you know, 1966. I was down in the dumps on account my dad had just married again. Poor Frankie warmed me up.'

Julia nodded.

'It's Joy the problem is now, as I was trying to explain to Frankie before he went. She's got his eyes, in point of fact.'

Julia looked into the clear tonic water in her glass, and heard a match being struck as Doris relit a cigarette which had gone out.

'Frankie and I weren't intimate, Julia, not for a long while. The flat wasn't big enough, what with Joy growing up and watching television late, and then the partition wall –'

'Let's not go into all that.'

'Sorry, dear.' She paused, sucking in smoke. 'He brought me into the Spread Eagle. Woodstock Street. D'you know the Spread Eagle, Julia?'

'No, I don't think I do.'

''Course he was married to this dressmaker even then. Dead unhappy he was.' Her voice had begun to falter. She sought about among her clothes and eventually produced a tissue with which she blew her nose. She said:

'I loved him all these years. I really loved him. No more than a boy he was.'

Julia listened to the sound of the woman's nose being blown, and her sniffing. She didn't look at her but at the scarlet roses she'd picked and arranged in the two vases on the mantelpiece. All she wished for was that the woman should quickly come to the point and not ever bother her again.

'D'you mind if I top myself up?' As she spoke, Doris was half way across the room, intent on the table of bottles in the bow of the window.

'Yes, do please help yourself.'

'I thought at first you might be to blame yourself, dear.'

Julia shook her head. From the mantelpiece came the quiet tick of the ormolu clock beneath the portrait of her father. The room smelt of the roses.

Doris lit another cigarette. 'Could I ask you a question, Julia? Did you have sex with Frankie?'

'No.'

'I thought that. When I heard your tone of voice I said to myself they won't have had sex.'

Julia nodded, not knowing what else to do. She caught a reflection of her face in the glass of a picture and saw that her features were pale above the red and black of the dress she was wearing, the freckles on her forehead standing out a bit.

'Was he going to live with you here, Julia?'

'I don't believe he ever intended to.'

'Did Frankie love you, dear?'

'No. Not ever.'

'Was it money, like with the dressmaker?'

'More or less. On our honeymoon I gave him my jewellery.'

'He ended up telling me fibs, you know. He ended up a weirdo, but it wasn't his fault. Battered he called it, like something that happens to a kid.'

'Yes, I know he called it that.'

'I get on Joy's nerves, you know. I have an evening drink in and my tongue runs off with me. The next thing is she's looking daggers, her poor old face sliding all over the place. But I'd do it again, dear. I'd have Frankie's child a million times over.'

'Yes.'

'She's not a virgin, Julia, twelve years of age. She's had this elephant stuff, she can't read or write, you know.' As she spoke, Doris slowly shook her head. Joy needed a father, she said. She sighed and blew her nose again. 'I blame that lodger,' she said. 'I blame the old parents. I blame that Susie Music. She's no taller than a baby, that Susie Music, two big eyes staring out of her hair at you. A scrubber's what the girls on the floor would call her.'

Julia watched while her visitor helped herself to another drink and relit her cigarette, dropping the match on the floor. She might have asked her to stop walking about the room, to sit down and listen for a change. She might have said that Francis Tyte had blamed other people when he should have blamed himself, that the blaming should not be continued. This woman who was the mother of his child, who had still not removed her mackintosh or the handbag slung over her shoulder, seemed unaware of the cruelty that distorted the man she spoke of, even though she had suffered from it. But Julia didn't say anything because she didn't think it would be listened to. Through the French windows she saw the child in the garden, standing beside her mother, who was still weeding the lily-of-the-valley bed.

'I took the trip to see his mum and dad Thursday night. God almighty, it's a place that is! These two pooftas in the hall, turn your stomach to look at them. I'll tell you one thing, I didn't get on with that matron one little bit.'

'What did you say to the Tytes?'

'I didn't want to accuse the poor old things, I just wanted a natter. Only the matron woman turned nasty, Julia. No better than a torture chamber these elderly places, you read it on the papers. Stench of cabbage nearly knocked me out.'

Again Julia did not say anything, guessing at what had happened, not wanting to think about it.

'Another fib that was,' Doris said. 'How he had an Uncle Manchester there, dying of his water-works.'

'Manchester?'

'I don't know why he made him up, dear. Old folks' home out Hampton way, he said.'

There was a silence, during which it seemed to Julia that the invention of this man belonged in the same grey limbo as the process of going through a marriage ceremony. There were the same elaborations of pretending, with truth and lies insidiously mixed and an outcome full of other people's pain. Again Julia didn't want to think about it.

'I'm glad we came down to see you,' Doris said, still walking about the room with her drink and her cigarette. 'We've tied up an end or two.'

'If you'll excuse me for a moment I'll see to lunch.'

'I don't take much lunchtime, dear. An hour we get on the floor and I generally just have a little drink. Not that I'm an alcoholic, you know.'

'No, I'm sure you're not.'

In the kitchen Julia took from the oven of the Rayburn the shepherd's pie she'd placed there before driving to the station. She'd made a salad to go with it, and afterwards there'd be raspberries. Joy had found the orange juice because the door of the fridge was open and the empty carton was on the draining-board.

'What's the dog called?'

'We haven't thought of anything to call him yet.'

'Rover or something?'

'Yes, I suppose so.'

The spaniel was trying to seize the strap of Joy's sandal between his teeth. He kept darting at it and yelping. Joy asked if he wanted to bite her, Mrs Anstey said she didn't think so. She had ceased to weed: crouched on her stool, an hour at a time was quite enough. She reached for her sticks and with one hand on the seat of the stool eased herself to her feet.

'What's your own name?' she asked Joy.

'Joy Smith. D'you think Harry O would be a name for that dog?'

'Well yes, it might be.'

'There's Harry O on the television.'

'There was a dog here a few weeks ago called Baloney.'

'What's that?'

'Nonsense. Peculiar name for a dog, I thought, but nobody really agreed.'

'Harry O's my favourite detective actually.'

'I'm afraid I don't watch much television.'

'Another one's Frank Cannon. And *The Streets of San Francisco*.'

Mrs Anstey nodded. She slowly shifted from one foot to the other in order to restore the circulation in her legs. Her back had begun to ache a bit, as it usually did after weeding, but the pain would lessen during the walk to the house.

'I have to give myself plenty of time,' she explained. 'I'm rather slow on the move.'

'Is there something the matter with you?'

'I have arthritis.'

The child's eyelashes were almost white behind her plastic-rimmed spectacles and her eyes blinked too often, as if from nervousness. Tiny pimples erupted around her mouth.

'Do you think you could carry the stool for me? And if that dog's a nuisance just give him a little kick.'

'I wouldn't want to hurt him.'

'He has to learn.'

'It's a very nice garden, this.'

'Yes, it is.'

The spaniel continued to snap at the sandal strap as the journey was made, past petunias gaudily in bloom, and the rosebeds.

'He's still in the pipe ads,' Joy said. 'He was in one last night.'

'Was he? I didn't know that.'

'On an oil rig.'

'Oh, yes?'

'I'm illegitimate, as a matter of fact.'

'Well, I don't suppose that worries you much.'

'I'd rather not be in a way.'

Julia called out from the house. 'Yes, she's with me,' Mrs Anstey called back. 'Lunch is ready,' she said to Joy, but they didn't hasten their pace.

'I don't think he's taken his life,' Joy said. 'I think she's got it all wrong.'

'No, I don't imagine for a second that he has.'

'She gets everything wrong.'

It was a difficult meal. Doris had again filled her glass with gin and Cinzano and had brought it to the table. Joy did not like the meat in the shepherd's pie and asked instead for cream crackers, of which there weren't any. Another kind of biscuit was found for her, and some Gentleman's Relish, which she'd never tasted before and didn't care for. 'Must pop to the loo,' Doris said, emptying her glass and taking it with her. She returned with it full, and said the house was the most beautiful she'd ever been in. She had taken her handbag from her shoulder but she hadn't removed her mackintosh.

'I think we've had our summer,' Mrs Anstey said.

'What's that, dear?'

'I said I think summer's been and gone.'

'Isn't your mother great?' Doris whispered to Julia, and Mrs Anstey thought she'd never in her life seen anyone who looked more unhealthy.

Julia asked Joy what food she liked, and Joy said a lot of food made her sick. She'd been sick all over a postman's letters once. Chips she didn't mind, and Pizzaland Special.

'Real gourmet she is.' Doris pushed away her own unfinished shepherd's pie and drank from her glass, laughing to emphasize that she was making a joke. 'Finicky as fi'pence,' she said.

A bowl of raspberries remained uneaten. Joy said Miss Upuku claimed that anything acid should be avoided if you wanted to have a glowing skin. Doris laughed again, saying you should see Miss Upuku's skin, black as your boot. When Julia went to the kitchen to make coffee she found that Joy had followed her.

'Would you like some cake?' Julia suggested.

Joy shook her head. 'It's embarrassing,' she said. 'She's drunk.'

'Your mother's naturally upset. We're all upset.' Grinding the coffee beans, she added:

'Miss Upuku's one of your teachers, is she?'

'I don't go to school any more.'

Julia nodded, not quite knowing how to comment on that.

'The latest thing was tattoos, only I don't want to get tattooed.'

Julia made the coffee, aware that every movement of her hands was being closely watched.

'He didn't take his life, d'you think?'

'No, he didn't.'

'He said he was going to come and live with us one day. I think it was just a lie.'

'No, no, I'm sure it wasn't.'

'Anyone'd prefer a place like this.'

'Look, you'll find a bowl of lump sugar in the cupboard in front of you. Would you put it on the tray with the cups?'

'I quite like that dog.'

'It was your father's, in a way. He ordered it.'

'Did he like it?'

'The dog wasn't born then.'

When they returned to the dining-room Doris was crying. 'Now, now, now,' Mrs Anstey was saying. Joy averted her eyes.

'Oh, dear, I'm sorry,' Doris sobbed. 'Excuse me,' she said, getting up and going away with her glass again.

'She suddenly caved in,' Mrs Anstey explained. 'I was telling her about lupins because she asked me the name of them.'

'She's always caving in these days,' Joy said.

A silence gathered. Julia poured her mother's coffee. Mrs Anstey said:

'Joy suggested we should call the dog Harry O, after a detective. Quite a nice name really.'

'Yes, it is. Do you drink coffee, Joy?'

'Maxwell House I never stop drinking.'

'I'm awfully sorry —'

'Doesn't matter.'

Doris returned, seeming cheerful again. She smiled her skeleton's smile and said she was a nuisance. Her glass had been refilled, she'd lit another cigarette. Her hands, Julia noticed, had begun to shake in spite of her return to composure.

'Coffee?'

'Just a tiny, dear. Joy, run along to the toilet.'

'I don't want the toilet —'

'Then go and play with that dog. He's eating a rag outside the lounge windows.'

Slowly Joy moved across the room, pausing to examine the sideboard. When she'd gone Doris said:

''Course the girls at work know all about Joy same's they know about Frankie. A few of them argued to me I should jack the whole thing in. Go out with another bloke, see. But of course I never would. I'm a bit of a loner, Julia, as I was explaining to your mum.'

Neither Julia nor her mother commented on that. Doris attempted to light another cigarette and abandoned the effort because she couldn't get it going. 'There was a bloke in Shavers', eight or nine years ago it would be, quite interested. Well, more than interested, if you get what I mean. Then again, a youngish chap in the warehouse. But you can't, can you? 'Course I never told the girls about Frankie being so particular about you know what. Harm the poor kid for life, he used to say, two people having sex the other side of a partition. I mean, I said to him a few times we could go to the bathroom but he wasn't keen. Well, you wouldn't, would you, cramped on the floor there, the walls sweating grime on top of you?'

'I think,' Mrs Anstey interrupted, 'we might talk about something else now.'

'Dear, I was only explaining.'

'Yes, I do know that.'

'Look, dear, I work in this shoe department. In the evenings I make mats for people's tables. Can you follow that, dear? I've kept up the mats for a long number of years because of the understanding between Frankie and myself, but, as Irene in Handbags says, you could get tired of making mats.'

'I'm sorry,' Julia interrupted, 'I'd like to drive you to the station now.'

'Put it this way, Julia, when Frankie and me sat in the Spread Eagle that day in '66 I've never known another human person to be as interested. I've never known another human person wanting to hear every single detail, Dad and myself and then Dad getting married again, and all about the shoes and the girls and what the fashions were, the time Gloria couldn't get the boot off the customer's leg, the time Mavis Soper hit her customer in the stomach. Put it this way, Julia, I was an eyeful in those days. I know I'm not now. I'm a bit of a weirdo myself, if you get what I mean. Oh, I'm definitely aware of that, dear.'

'The train's at five past four.'

'All these years I tried to pay him back, Julia. I made things nice for him while we were waiting for the day when we could be together. Then along comes yourself, Julia, and then this Susie Music. Susanna she calls herself, matter of fact, no better than a prostitute when you think about it –'

'Oh, will you please stop?' Julia was on her feet, two spots of red glowing in her cheeks. Her voice was shrill and unsteady. 'We're trying to forget Francis ever entered our lives. We don't want to talk about him or remember him.'

'Dear, that's hard about a person who's taken his life.'

'He's not dead, people like that never are. He's eaten up with self-pity, he damages everyone who has the misfortune to encounter him.'

'Oh, dear me no, Julia,' Doris said quietly. 'There's not a word of truth in that.'

'Of course it's true. Every single fact in his life has been twisted inside out so that it might seem to be something else. He created an illusion for a silly widow to fall in love with, and then he smashed it to pieces in order to watch her face. Your child was born just for fun. It was fun to commit bigamy on a summer's afternoon, fun to have a mockery of a honeymoon. He sent you to that home in Hampton Wick, knowing what would happen.'

'Dear, Frankie wouldn't ever have sent me.'

'Of course he did. And I wish you were right: I wish he'd committed suicide.'

Julia turned away from the table, her face still flushed with anger and emotion. Before she left the room she said she'd be waiting by the car in front of the house.

'She's distressed,' Doris observed to Mrs Anstey. 'I'm afraid I've gone and distressed her, dear.'

'Yes, I'm afraid you have.'

'It's just that I don't want Joy to be a weirdo like Frankie and myself. It's that what worries me, Mrs Anstey. It's being awake nights, thinking about poor Joy. And then I can't help seeing him lying there under a foreign sky. D'you mind me saying that, dear? The trouble is, when I get a drink in I always want another.'

Mrs Anstey replied that it didn't much matter what was said, and at the front of the house Julia and Joy waited. Joy was again talking about the difficulties she had with digestion when Father Lavin drove up, and Julia remembered he'd been invited to tea earlier in the week. 'Hullo,' he said to Joy.

'Oh dear, we should have done the washing-up,' Doris cried, emerging from the house. 'Whatever'll they think of us, Joy?'

But Joy was already in the back of the car, pressed into a corner with her eyes closed.

'She came to allocate blame,' Mrs Anstey said, clearing the table with the priest's assistance. They put the cutlery that hadn't been used back in a drawer of the sideboard. With a damp sponge-cloth she wiped mats that had a design of sunflowers on them. He brushed crumbs from the mahogany surface. The moment he'd seen them he'd guessed who the visitors were. Julia had told him about the telephone call.

'Would you like some raspberries, Father? Nobody wanted them.'

He protested that he couldn't eat raspberries and cream in the middle of the afternoon, but the old woman spooned some on to a plate for him and made him sit down. 'I think I'll have some myself,' she said.

They ate the raspberries, still talking about Francis and the woman whose sofa he had slept on when he had to be in London.

'That child hasn't much to keep her going,' Mrs Anstey said.

'Her mother doesn't appear to have much either.'

'Wasted lives they call them.'

'Francis –'

'Oh yes, of course: Francis too.'

They finished their plates of raspberries and cream, and then he carried the dishes to the kitchen. Together they washed and dried them.

'There are cherry slices we might have,' Mrs Anstey said, in a tone of voice which suggested to Father Lavin that the subject of the visitation had been aired and should not again be referred to.

He found the cherry slices and arranged them on a plate.

'I doubt we'll meet again,' Doris said at the station. 'I'm sorry about all that, Julia.'

'Goodbye. Goodbye, Joy.'

'Goodbye.'

'And goodbye from me,' said Doris, holding out her hand.

They passed through the barrier. Julia waved. She turned and walked back to the car. She had reached it when she heard shouting somewhere behind her. 'Julia! Julia!' Doris cried, hurrying out of the station. She was panting when she reached Julia, who'd walked back towards her, fearful lest the train should be missed.

'Thank you, dear. Thanks for everything, dear.'

'No, no.'

'I'm sorry I was such a nuisance, crying like that. It's just that I loved him.'

'Yes, I do know.'

'That's why I can't help hating this Susie Music.'

'She wasn't responsible for anything, you know.'

'I'm glad you didn't hurt him, like all the others did. I couldn't ever hate you, Julia.'

She went scurrying off, her loping stride only a little unsteady, her curiously held body making her noticeable among the other travellers. That image of her remained in Julia's mind as she drove through Cheltenham and out on to the Stone St Martin road, even though she did not wish to think about her. By common consent they would never have to meet again.

In the drawing-room Father Lavin had lit a fire because of the continuing cold. He and her mother were drinking tea and nibbling cherry slices. 'Come along, dear,' her mother said, in a brisk voice that belonged to the past, to the time when Julia was a child. But Julia stood by the door, looking at the two of them by the blazing fire, tea and tea-cups on a little table by her mother's armchair.

In the train there'd be the journey to the bar, and the child staring out at the passing landscape, not wanting to be tattooed. In Folkestone there was a harmless dressmaker whose misfortune it had been to meet Francis Tyte on the sea-front. In other parts of England there were other people, who shuddered when they recalled his name. In Hampton Wick the confusion was as he wished it to be.

When he had spent the money her jewellery raised, his letter with its German stamp would arrive. He would exact his self-allocated due as he always had from the people he came across, but it wasn't that that concerned Julia now. For the second time that summer a woman's intuition nagged uncomfortably in Swan House: the pattern she had once been unable to discern, not even

172

then being aware of the people it involved, spread itself chillingly through her. Connections suddenly were everywhere, an ugly sense crept out of hiding.

'Tea, dear?' her mother offered.

·12·
Julia's

I have lived too long among flowerbeds, Julia wrote, *I move from room to room of my doll's house. I type out conveyances and deeds of release, I have borne two children and seen a husband die. I pray to my childhood God, yet in this pretty town my life has been less real than other people's.*

She put away her diary and again tried to forget, though the ordinariness of everyday existence remained shadowed by the visit of the woman and her child. Leech-like, the visit clung, vivid in retrospect. It hovered over the people of the household, over Mrs Spanners on Mondays with her dusters, and Nevil Clapp on Mondays with his grass-cuttings, and Mrs Anstey finding corners to read in. A letter with a German stamp did not arrive, but another letter did:

Dear Mrs Ferndale, we have traced you through a newspaper cutting and I address you so because I have been informed that your marriage to Francis Tyte was not legal. The source of that information is a Miss Smith, who visited here and left the newspaper cutting behind her. She is an unreliable woman, but I trust that at least she was correct in her references to yourself. I write to you because of your connection with Francis Tyte, whose parents are in this home. I have no one else to turn to, and from Miss Smith's conversation I take it that you are connected with her also.

We at the Sundown would be grateful if this person did not again attempt to visit the Tytes. She has upset Mrs Tyte beyond measure with her talk of death. Miss Smith was not sober when she came here, in fact the hall smelt like a brewery and had to be air-sprayed. Mrs Tyte is now on drugs, and the staff here have made every effort to convince her that the visitor was just someone who'd seen her son in the television advertisements and hadn't known what she was talking about. I would be grateful if you would contact Miss Smith and inform her of the damage she has done, and inform her further that she will not be admitted if she returns.

Sincerely yours, Edith Purchase.

Julia replied to the letter, refraining from pointing out that Doris Smith was not her responsibility. She thought again that that might be the end of everything, but a few days later a man from the Cheltenham police arrived at the house. He was interested, he said, that she was still Mrs Ferndale; he had been informed that the marriage which had taken place might have been invalid. He wondered if that might be correct. He was a tall, bushy man with sideburns and a moustache and a brown herring-bone jacket. He walked about the garden with Julia, often stooping to examine a plant or a shrub.

'I don't know where he is,' she said. 'And I don't want him hounded.'

'It was bigamy on his part, was it, Mrs Ferndale? Tongues wag, you know. Perhaps we've got it all wrong.'

'He said it was bigamy, but then it was impossible to believe much of what he said.'

'He stole from you, Mrs Ferndale?'

'No.'

'I'm aware it's painful, but from what we know he deserted you in Italy. Again, I wonder if that's correct.'

'Yes, it is.'

'After a matter of days?'

'One day actually. I gave him my jewellery.'

'Gave?'

'Yes.'

The policeman admired the garden's hypericum, and its fuchsia and buddleia. He went in particularly for gardenias himself, he said. The spaniel sniffed at the bottom of his trousers.

'We've no intention of pursuing this man, Mrs Ferndale. But of course he has behaved in a criminal manner and no doubt will do so again. A description must naturally be issued, and there are plenty of photographs. Not that he'll look the same by now. Being an actor.'

The tall policeman gave an amused little laugh, and Julia wanted to say that the vigour and time of the police would be better employed in keeping an eye on an alcoholic woman called Doris Smith who appeared to be intent on upsetting people. But she didn't say that because the conversation would become difficult when she tried to explain that Francis had left a continuing horror behind him.

'If you hear from him, Mrs Ferndale, we'd be obliged if you'd inform us at once. Cheltenham 28282.'

Julia promised, knowing that she wouldn't inform anyone, not even her mother or Father Lavin, when the first letter arrived. She would write a cheque and put it in an envelope. 'Thank you for coming out,' she said, and the policeman said he'd come again in the spring if he might, to take a cutting of her Kerria japonica.

The spaniel ran after the police car as it drove away and then returned busily to smell the gravel where it had been parked. Julia was sorry now she'd accepted the dog, and her attitude to it had already changed. The dog mocked her, its drooping earnest eyes, the silly name which her mother insisted on addressing it as: Harry O. And it wasn't just the dog. Nevil Clapp's dourness had begun to irritate her. The painted face of Mrs Spanners, the wafting smell of Love-in-a-Mist, grated on her nerves. Her mother, creeping about with her sticks, inspired an impatience Julia had never in her life felt before.

Then, just after midnight one night, the telephone rang, and she knew before she answered it who was on the other end. She wouldn't have answered it at all except that the ringing would eventually arouse her mother and it didn't occur to her simply to lift the receiver and place it on the table. When she picked it up there was the beeping sound that indicated the call came from a public call-box. A moment later, slurred late-night accents floated into the hall.

'Is that Julia? Julia, Doris. Only I thought I'd better ring you.'

'Is something the matter?'

'Julia, dear, would you do me a favour? Would you put the receiver down and dial this number? 01 385 1001.'

'It's awfully late. I'm just on the way to bed.'

'Have you a pencil, dear? 385 1001.' While she spoke the beeping began to sound and then the line went dead, as though she'd put the receiver down herself. Julia dialled.

'That's sweet of you. Only I'm short of coins. Put it this way, Julia, I wanted to have a chat about the girl. I've been to see her, Julia. SW1, all done out modern the house is.'

'I really don't want to talk about that girl.'

'I rung her first only I didn't get any joy, in fact she put the receiver down.'

'Yes, well, it's understandable, you know.'

'So I hopped on a bus and there you are. C. H. Music, it says in the directory and he opened the door himself, big chap in a suit, medical he is, gyney as a matter of fact. Then the mother appears, dressed for an outing, and down the stairs comes her ladyship. I could see she was nervous of a chat in front of the parents, even though they were smiling all the time, off for a night at the opera from what I gathered. Anyway, she starts on about ringing her and I reply that there's no call to go plumping the receiver down.'

'I'm afraid I'm going to have to do the same myself. I honestly can't have you telephoning me here at all hours of the day and night.'

'All I wanted was a chat with her, Julia, same's you and I had, same's I tried for with the old people. All I wanted was to make a few queries, and if she thought I was going to let the cat out of the bag in front of her mum and dad she was mistaken. Anyway, as soon as she hears the front door banging behind them she turns on me like I was a peasant. So I mention what you and me discussed, how he got confused and mixed up, marrying you for a bit of money. She didn't take a pick of notice.'

'If you don't leave that girl alone you'll get into trouble. Mrs Tyte had to be put on drugs because of what you said to her. You're upsetting everyone, can't you see that?'

'Sorry, dear?'

'No good can come of bothering this girl.'

'She's as cold as a bullet, Julia. I told her about how he couldn't give you sex on your honeymoon on account of what she passed on to him and she didn't turn a hair. I told her about that last night in the flat, how it was all Constance Kent.'

Julia wanted to replace the receiver but knew that if she did the telephone would ring again. Beads of perspiration were breaking on her forehead and her back, even though the night was cool. Affected by her agitation, the dog was making a whining noise, crouched by the drawing-room door.

'When you think of poor Frankie who never hurt a fly, Julia —'

'You know that isn't true.'

There was a pause, and then Doris said:

'Dear, Frankie got to be a bit of a weirdo on account of things that happened to him, but if you're saying he was round the twist I couldn't agree with you, dear. The dressmaker was violent for starters. She threw a sewing-machine at him. It was criminal what the debt-collector did to him. And then some fancy little tart passes on a dose of you know what. I swear to you, Julia, I could have killed her dead in that lounge we were in.'

Julia replaced the receiver. She stood in the dimness of the hall, waiting for the telephone to ring again, which it did. She picked up the receiver and placed it on the table, wishing she had thought of that ages ago. She went into the drawing-room and sat in the dark, in the bow of the window, listening to the beeping sound and then the distant, shrill voice.

Clouds obscured the moon. Nothing outside could be discerned. The voice on the telephone ceased, and she could hear the telephone going dead. She imagined the scene there had been in the house in SW1, the surprise because this visitor had come, the awful rambling conversation.

'I cannot pray,' Julia said in the cream-coloured office of the priests' house. Her eyes had an empty look. Her face was tired, her fingers restless in her lap.

'Sometimes it is hard to pray.'

'That woman is half crazy in her grief. I'm frightened for what she may do.'

'Time will heal all this unhappiness,' Father Lavin said softly. He wanted to reach across the metal desk that was between them, to take her hands in his and to hold them for a moment without saying anything. Just for that single moment he wanted her to know he loved her and then miraculously to forget it.

'I am a useless kind of person,' she said. 'I am a middle-aged woman in whom no one can be interested. Yet I can feel afraid.'

'You're not useless, Julia. And of course people are interested in you.'

She shook her head. There was a silence in the office, which eventually she broke. More quietly than before she said:

'I didn't know there was this poisonous make-believe, a picnic of illusions instead of what is real. For the rest of my life I shall remember the pretence of gentleness in Francis's eyes, and how he smiled when he gathered up those few pieces of jewellery in a hotel bedroom. He smiled again while I cashed the traveller's cheques that took him on a journey into another pathetic dream. His own illusions are the most pitiful of all.'

'Please don't dwell on him, Julia.'

'There are his father and his mother to dwell on, too. The debt-collector and the dressmaker. That woman and her child. Those people whose houses he stayed in, and I myself of course.'

'Julia –'

'What was God thinking of, for heaven's sake?'

'God moves –'

'My bearded cloudy God who saw me through my childhood and

178

my widowing. In His tropical garden He's just a wisp of nothing now.'

'You're upset, Julia, but you mustn't speak like this.'

'I must, for He has failed me in my middle years. Is He my own particular illusion, a fog of comfort to be lost in?'

'It is a sin to speak so, Julia. And you know it isn't true.'

'I don't know that. In Italy I remembered the missionaries of the Pentecostal Church. I lay awake two nights ago and when I had ceased to think about Francis and Doris Smith I remembered them again. Do you remember those missionaries, Father?'

'Yes, I do. But they are one thing and Francis Tyte another. You're making connections that are not there.'

'They were God's creatures and surely God's creatures are all connected? Isn't that the only meaning there can be?'

'Of course we all belong together, Julia, but you are simplifying complications. You can't do that, you know.'

'They stood in a row. When the sun reached a certain point in the sky they were clubbed to death. A week ago a legless man in Arizona was tormented by teenagers until he died. In Birmingham a husband killed his wife with a knife because she wouldn't cook his bacon right. Bombs explode everywhere.'

'I beg you, Julia. Please stop this.'

' "We'll go to Italy on our honeymoon," I said, because in Italy the angels of Lorenzo di Credi gossip on their way from heaven, because the lemon groves of Fiesole are there for lovers to stroll through. In Italy, Father, the body of a politician rolled out of a moving car, shot through like a colander. In Italy Signor Guzzinati pleads with tourist women because some private reality is too awful, and who can blame him? Who can blame anyone for thinking it too awful that the children of the missionaries die while their parents watch?'

'No one, actually, is attributing blame. It was Francis, apparently, who spoke of that. But Francis is unbalanced, Julia.'

'Those missionaries died on the hard earth of their compound, and Stone St Martin nestles among the lazy wolds of Gloucestershire. How can the destruction of Doris Smith belong in the same world as the contentment of the people who came that night to have drinks on our lawn? Do you remember, Father? Dr Tameguard and his fat wife, a man who bored my mother with talk of apples, a girl with a whippet called Baloney? What will be the end of Doris Smith, Father?'

Not permitting him to answer, Julia continued to speak herself. Her voice had become unsteady, her fingers were agitatedly twisting.

'Why does it always have to be the innocent?' she cried out. 'Why did that wretched woman have to be on the bus that day?'

'You should have a holiday, Julia.'

She stared at him, with what he thought was hatred in her eyes. She spoke of a nun who had taught her at school, a Sister Burkardt, whose misshapen face had caused in her nun's heart the sin of envy. She saw her clearly, she said, still selling sacred objects in the shop where the convent's rumours had placed her. She saw her at the end of her day's work, in a room containing ugly furniture, an iron bed and brown linoleum, and a gas-ring in a niche beneath the window.

'Sister Burkardt belongs in all this too, Father.'

'No, Julia. You're being extravagant and dramatic. You're finding meanings where there aren't any.'

'I'm saying that strangers pass her by as well. Strangers enter her shop and buy something and then forget her, not wishing to dwell on the memory of her misshapen face. Strangers hurry by Signor Guzzinati on the streets of Pisa, and then forget him too. How many women every day does Doris Smith kneel before, fitting shoes on to their feet? Who cares that her child is unhappy?'

'Of course people care, Julia. I care, and so do you.'

'Francis might never have made his way to this town with its weathered stone caught in the sunlight, its river flowing away to the meadows. He might never have entered Swan House, nor the lives of two women who had no idea what it was like to be missionaries lined up for death. Has Francis spread disease all round him, Father, or is it just the truth?'

'Francis was incapable of telling the truth.'

'Then why does the memory of my First Communion make no sense to me now? Why do I think of Sister Burkardt and Signor Guzzinati, and of people whose faces I cannot even visualize? Why does it suddenly seem that in the midst of the sacraments and the mass, Calvary has become remote, just another distant act of violence? It wasn't like that when I first saw Our Lord on the Cross.'

'Julia –'

'You cannot think of St Catherine without her wheel, or St Sebastian without the agony of the arrows. That little actress is another innocent, Father. That's all I'm saying to you.'

'Nothing is going to befall the little actress.'

' "Nothing is going to befall Julia." Did you say that to my mother?'

'Your mother's feelings were never discussed between us.'

'I wish you'd ask your God to intervene.'

'He's your God too, Julia.'

'I'm asking you to do something. That woman has identified herself with Constance Kent.'

'I promise you I'll pray.'

Father Dawne came in with two cups of tea and some biscuits on a plate, declaring that he was just off to St Martin's. 'The cup that cheers,' he added in his young priest's voice.

'Francis haunts me,' Julia said, more quietly, when the curate had gone. 'His whole terrible world haunts me and frightens me.'

'Please seek God's help, Julia.'

She shook her head. That would be another pretence, she said, her tone cross, as if impatient with him because he hadn't understood. A flush had spread over her pale cheeks and her neck; in places it smudged her forehead. He had never permitted himself to imagine what a life with her would be like, banishing at once the beginnings of such thoughts. Once he had dreamed that he'd been with her on a train, having dinner in the dining-car, both of them drinking brandy with their coffee.

'Whenever I see that dog,' she said, 'I shall think of Francis, since that is what he wants.'

'Someone else would have the dog, Julia.'

'I accepted it in my foolish innocence, and there it shall remain. Mockery is Francis's stock-in-trade. He guesses from a distance now, knowing what he has done to Doris Smith. Murderers don't just happen, you know.'

'You've blown all this up, Julia.'

'No.'

Father Lavin did not protest again, nor did he drink the tea that had been brought to him. Does she think of me, he wondered, as a grey old rat, an unattractive Irish priest uselessly suggesting holidays in her moment of need? He should be on a holiday himself, visiting his mother in Co. Cork, but he had postponed all that because Julia was the person he thought about with the greatest concern and affection.

'I promise you I'll pray,' he heard himself repeating, his own voice piercing his thoughts.

The telephone, as far as Mrs Anstey could determine, was never silent these days. Beginning *Bleak House* in the drawing-room, she let the latest bout of ringing wear itself out. It might of course have been a wrong number or some query about Julia's grocery order. There was really little reason to suppose that someone else was pressing a pet upon the household or that a drunk was on the line again, but equally there was no point in taking chances. *Standing on a seat at the side of the hall*, she read, *the better to peer into the curtained sanctuary, is a little mad old woman in a squeezed bonnet, who is always in court, from its sitting to its rising, and always expecting some incomprehensible judgement to be given in her favour.*

Nevil Clapp's motor-cycle clattered over the cobbles in front of the house, and then the roar of its engine abruptly ceased. His face appeared at the window, his knuckles raised to rap on the glass. Mrs Anstey indicated that one of the other windows, though closed, was unlatched. He pushed at it and informed her that he'd heard where he could get a flange.

'Flange?'

'I was passing, see. I said to Mrs Ferndale I'd let her know. No way the thing'll work the way it is.'

'The lawnmower?'

'Yeah.'

She wondered what a flange was, but did not wish to know. She'd begun to have quite longish chats with Nevil, mainly about other employers he'd worked for. While he was correcting some fault in the lawnmower or clipping a hedge, she'd stand by him and after a while he'd begin to talk.

'I'm sure it'll be all right to get it.' In spite of their new relationship she felt a little tired for conversation just now, having had to listen that morning to Mrs Spanners's method with mutton stew. She smiled at Nevil, and as she did so the telephone rang again. He began to move away, but she raised her voice and called him back.

'My daughter's out,' she said. 'I wonder if you'd mind answering that. There's a phone in the hall, and the side door will be open.'

He didn't reply, but it appeared to please him to enter the house and to make his way to the hall. The journey would have taken her several minutes.

'No, she's out,' Nevil's voice said, and then: 'Can't say, I'm sure.' There was a long pause and then he said, 'O.K.'

Mrs Anstey smiled at him again as he entered the room. 'All right?' she said.

'Doris,' he said. 'She said to say Doris rang.'

'Oh yes.'

He nodded and went away. There was the explosion of his motor-cycle starting up as she returned to her book and when Julia returned twenty minutes later she passed the message on.

'What on earth did you let Nevil answer the phone for?'

'Because it takes me ages to get there.'

'I wish you hadn't.'

It astonished Mrs Anstey that her daughter should say that. If she had still been a child she'd have asked her quite sharply if she'd got out of bed on the wrong side that morning. Nothing more was said on the subject but later, when they were having supper, the telephone rang again. Mrs Anstey wanted to suggest that it should be ignored, but thought it wiser not to say so. She went on eating salad and risotto while Julia went to answer it.

'I have asked you to leave me alone,' she heard her daughter saying. 'I don't wish to receive telephone calls from you.'

When Julia returned to the dining-room they continued their meal in silence. Mrs Anstey had earlier tried to have a conversation about a programme she had heard on the wireless, but her efforts had met with no response. And then, just as they were finishing their meal, the ringing began again.

'My God!' Julia cried, unable to control herself.

But it wasn't Doris. 'I thought I'd better contact you,' a terse voice began. 'I can't think who else there is, I'm sure. It's Miss Purchase here. The Sundown Home, you know.'

'Is something the matter, Miss Purchase?'

'Mrs Tyte is being a nuisance about this grandchild she's supposed to have.'

Julia closed her eyes. She wanted to shout into the telephone, she wanted to say that none of it was her business, that all she asked for was to be left in peace. She calmed herself. 'She has a grandchild, yes.'

'She wants it to be brought to see her.'

'The child's a girl, Miss Purchase.'

'It doesn't concern me what it is. Mrs Tyte's got herself into a state is what I'm saying to you.'

'I suppose she might naturally want to meet the child.'

'She wouldn't even know about it if that dreadful woman hadn't poked her way in here, breaking the rules. This isn't a comedy show, you know. We're not holding a party at the Sundown, you know.'

'Yes, I do know that, Miss Purchase.'

'We cannot admit that woman again. The way she behaved you'd think the residents are here to be laughed at. And now Mrs Tyte insists that every word she said was true. I may add that for all her years here Mrs Tyte has had the most high-flown notion of her son. The old man has pulled his shutters down completely.'

184

'Perhaps the child could visit her grandmother on her own.'

'It is not permitted for any under-aged person to visit a resident unless accompanied by an adult or adults.'

'Then what do you suggest, Miss Purchase?'

'I know no one else to ring except yourself. If the child has to come here I will have to ask you to accompany her.'

'I'm sorry. I cannot possibly do that.'

'We are adamant that the woman shall in no circumstances be admitted through the hall door.'

'I'm not even related to the child. I've only met her once.'

'The old woman wishes to see this child once also. It isn't much to request of you, Mrs Ferndale, I would have thought.'

'I live miles from London, and I've never met Mrs Tyte in my life. I'd be a stranger to her.'

'If that is how you feel, madam.'

'Miss Purchase, there are considerable complications. I don't want to go into them. Mrs Tyte's son married me under false pretences. The marriage lasted no time at all, I am trying to recover from the unhappiness of it. I'm sorry but I cannot involve myself with Francis Tyte's parents.'

'I'll tell the old lady how you feel, Mrs Ferndale. It's simply that because of the fuss she's making her husband won't sit with her. And the other residents are quite rightly complaining. I doubt she'll last through this, you know.'

Julia hesitated, about to say with even greater firmness that she could not accept responsibility for a problem that was not hers.

'Very well, Miss Purchase,' she said instead, 'I will arrange to come to see Mrs Tyte and bring her grandchild with me.'

'Yes, all right,' Miss Purchase ungraciously replied, replacing the receiver.

In the dining-room Julia told her mother of this latest development and noticed, for the second time that day, that there appeared to be defiance in her voice. Mrs Anstey, deeming it wise only to nod, did so. She didn't comment on Miss Purchase's telephone call, but privately thought that by the sound of her Miss

Purchase was one of those middle-aged women whom she most disliked, patronizing and unpleasant, like Mrs Spanners.

At midnight in the kitchen Julia finished typing a contract that had had to be drawn up between a newsagent in Old Street and the brewery which owned the public house next door to his premises. It concerned the use of, and liability relating to, a common passageway. It had taken her several hours, but she always found the occupation relaxing, which was something that was difficult to explain to her mother. She lifted the typewriter from the table and placed it in one of the wall cupboards, on a shelf beside sheafs of carbon and typing paper. She put the dog out for its run and tidied a few things on the dresser. She might have telephoned Henrietta and Katherine, asking to be put up for a night while she arranged the ordeal of taking the child to see an old woman in a home. But instead she had telephoned the Rembrandt Hotel, remembering its number because she had dialled it so often when Francis had stayed there. She didn't know Doris Smith's address, but tomorrow she would go to the shoe department about which she'd been told so much and she would try to explain. She would ask permission to make the visit with the child and when the visit was over she would talk to Doris Smith. It would be a different kind of conversation from the ones that had taken place on the telephone and in Swan House. Slowly and calmly they would talk about the girl called Susanna Music, and she would patiently explain that the girl must not be harmed.

She settled the dog down in its basket by the Rayburn, forcing affection into her voice as she said good night. She was glad she had been haunted by foreboding, and glad that she had become emotional in Father Lavin's office. In her less tense mood she was even glad that Miss Purchase had made her request, for at least there was something she could now attempt to do, and doing anything was better than introspection. She'd got into a great muddle because of the drifting of her thoughts and her endeavours to come to terms with God. She'd wanted a miracle, of course: all the pain taken away, packaged explanations. She would settle now for practicalities, and an end.

The telephone rang as Julia passed through the hall on her way upstairs. For a moment she almost picked it up in the hope of making some arrangement to meet the following day. But she knew that at this hour of the night the woman would be too drunk to understand, and so she lifted the receiver and placed it on the table. A kind of screaming came from it, which continued until she put a cushion on it.

·13·
Julia in Doris's

On the day following Julia's telephone call from Miss Purchase the Indian floor supervisor greeted Doris when she arrived in the shoe department by saying he was sorry. Unusually early for him to be present, he was bustling about in his shirtsleeves, examining a sheaf of invoices. He ceased this occupation in order to address her. His manner was uncharacteristically sombre.

'We cannot but be sorry,' he said.

'Sorry?'

'Doris, this is naturally for your own good.' A faint reminder of his normal cheerfulness flitted over his face. For only a moment his very white teeth gleamed. Blankly, Doris stared back at him.

'I don't know what you're on about. What d'you mean, good?'

'Doris, you can surely not expect us to believe that all is O.K.?'

'I can't sleep, if that's what you're saying to me.' Her voice had an edge to it, reaching a shrillness it rarely acquired before evening. 'I haven't had a night's sleep since my friend went.'

'Doris, that is what we have deduced. But there is something else as well. It is that we desire to see you on an even keel again.'

There was concern all over his unhappy dark face. He was endeavouring to help her, as he had helped so many of the assistants on his floor over the years. He was endeavouring to break the bad news gently.

'You're giving me the sack,' she said.

'We desire you to sort out the problems, so that we shall let bygones be bygones. Doris, I have always understood your distress.'

She knew from the way he looked at her that they'd discovered she'd been taking bits and pieces to the secondhand place in Crawford Street. It had never been difficult if she arrived at the store early enough: when everyone was hurrying, in and out of the washrooms, all she'd had to do was to slip the things into her bag – socks, alarm clocks, ties, belts, oddments from the costume-jewellery counter, a pair of binoculars a week ago. Shoes, of course, were the easiest of all. She'd sold over fifty pairs of shoes in Crawford Street.

'It is not forgotten,' the floor supervisor reminded her, 'that you have been with us twenty years, Doris. No customer has ever complained.'

'My friend –'

'Doris, you told me that about your friend. I am sorry. But what I must say to you now is make me a promise to return to us when you're feeling better.'

'I'm not ill. There's nothing the matter with me.'

'Doris, it is not an illness. You have a new leaf to turn over, that at the most is all. When this has been completed there will again be a home for you on my floor. That I happily promise you.'

Some hours later Julia arrived in the shoe department and asked for Doris. There was a delay and then the Indian was led up to her. Miss Smith, he said, was having time off because of personal problems. He led Julia to his small office and gave her the address of Doris's flat. He said he hoped there was nothing the matter, and Julia reassured him. 'Help her if you can,' he urged, doing his best to smile.

In the sitting-room Joy turned the television off and explained that her mother wasn't in. 'Would you like some Maxwell House?' she offered, surprised that a visitor had called. Her eyes passed over Julia's coffee-coloured dress and the green silk scarf at her throat, and her shoes and her watch.

Julia declined the coffee. 'Your grandmother wants to meet you, Joy.'

Joy blinked behind her spectacles. She didn't want to meet any grandmother, she said.

'She's very old, and unhappy. It would cheer her up.'

'She's in a home.'

'Yes.'

'If I go there it'll be embarrassing.'

'Why, Joy?'

'It'll be like when we came to your place. She'll be drunk.'

'You don't have to go there with your mother. That's why I've come here: I can bring you.'

'You?'

'Yes.'

'All right then.'

'Would you like to write a note for your mother? If we set out now she'll wonder where you are.'

Joy looked at her visitor in surprise. She left the room. In a corner, on a chair, Julia saw the table-mats which Doris had referred to. There was some green baize folded over the back of the chair, and a pile of coloured reproductions of Big Ben. From the pictures with which Doris had decorated the walls, jungle beasts stared ravenously, and Negresses smiled above their hanging breasts.

Joy returned with a piece of paper torn from a cereal packet, on which she'd attempted to scrawl the words 'Gone out'. She put it on top of the television. Julia wanted to get out of the flat as quickly as she could, but nevertheless she hesitated.

'Are you sure your mother won't mind, Joy?'

'She's at the shoe department today, you know.'

'She wasn't well. They sent her home.'

'You know what that means. She won't get back all night.'

They walked to Fulham Road and took a taxi. On the way to the Sundown Home, while Joy outlined the plot of a film she'd seen the night before on television, Julia kept thinking about Doris and wondering where she was. She thought about Susanna Music as well.

There was a fuss when they arrived at the Sundown Home. Miss Purchase, who Julia had imagined would be smaller and thinner, answered the bell herself. Her whole face tightened when she saw them, a movement which began around the mouth. Visiting was on Sunday afternoons, she said.

'Miss Purchase?' Julia inquired. 'I'm Julia Ferndale. We've been talking on the phone. This is Mrs Tyte's granddaughter.'

'I can't have you here now.'

'I've come a very long way, Miss Purchase. You asked me to bring this child.'

Not speaking, Miss Purchase held the door open. Julia and Joy passed through the tinted light of the hall, by the row of coats and the walking-sticks in the elephant's foot. Miss Purchase led them into the cubbyhole under the stairs which served as her office. There was nothing to sit on.

'It is against the rules,' she said in a low voice. 'If the other residents see you with the Tytes they'll complain of unfairness. The best I can do is that you should see them in here. They won't like standing, I can tell you that, but when people come at these outlandish times there's bound to be discomfort. If the telephone rings please don't answer it.'

She left the cubbyhole, in which only a dim light burned. On top of the grey filing-cabinet there was a china representation of Peter Pan, and for the first time since Julia had met her Joy seemed inclined to giggle, unable to take her eyes off the object, although to

Julia it seemed a perfectly ordinary ornament. The telephone began to ring and after a minute or so a round, white-coated man came in and answered it, not paying the visitors any attention. 'Yes, we did try to get you, Mrs Burchell,' he said. 'Father passed this morning. Yes, I'm sorry too, madam.' He listened for a while as some instruction was given, whistling through his teeth, a hand over the mouthpiece of the telephone. 'Okey-doke, madam,' he said eventually.

Miss Purchase returned with the Tytes, and the man in the white coat said he'd told Mrs Burchell that her father had passed. There wasn't room in the cubbyhole for so many people and the elderly couple had to step back into the hall while the man in the white coat made his exit. It was a squash even without him, since Miss Purchase remained. Julia was so close to Mr Tyte that his breath, coming in sharp little puffs after the exertion of his journey from the dining-room, was warm on her cheek. Miss Purchase set the mood by speaking in a whisper. She placed her thin lips close to one of Mrs Tyte's ears and said that the child in the cubbyhole was the child the old woman had expressed a desire to meet.

'Francis's?' Mrs Tyte said.

'My name is Julia Ferndale,' Julia said, in a whisper also. 'A friend of Francis's.'

'Is this the child?' Mrs Tyte inquired, speaking normally.

'Please keep your voices down,' Miss Purchase reprimanded.

'This is Joy,' Julia whispered.

'He hasn't been to see us,' Mr Tyte said, 'for six years.'

Mrs Tyte was weeping. She'd stretched out a hand and seized one of Joy's. She murmured between sobs that she'd just wanted to see her granddaughter. She'd never known she had a grandchild. 'Joy,' she said. 'Joy.'

'Pleased to meet you,' Joy said.

Again Miss Purchase protested that the voices in the cubbyhole were too loud.

'It's nice to have a grandchild,' Mrs Tyte said while her cheeks were dabbed at by Miss Purchase. 'We just wanted to see her. Even only once, I said.'

'Your son is well, Mrs Tyte,' Julia said. 'He's abroad.'

'We were never young with him.'

'He isn't dead, you know,' Julia said to Mr Tyte.

'I know he's not dead, for God's sake.'

'Well, I think that's all now,' Miss Purchase said.

Somehow she swept Julia and Joy out of the cubbyhole, into the hall. The sound of Mrs Tyte's weeping continued as Miss Purchase moved swiftly across the brown tiles and opened the hall door. 'He's the worst of the offenders,' she vouchsafed as a form of farewell. 'A really mischievous old man.'

'Is Mrs Tyte all right? She seems very low.'

'Anyone would be low in the circumstances,' Miss Purchase retorted. 'They're more trouble than the rest of them put together, those two.'

'Excuse me,' Mr Tyte said, close behind Julia. 'I'd welcome a private word.'

'Now, now, we've had our private words,' Miss Purchase began, but Mr Tyte had already seized Julia's sleeve and had pulled her aside. 'I didn't catch your name,' he said.

'It's Mrs Ferndale. Julia Ferndale.'

His manner was different now. He spoke quietly, with a measured note in his voice. 'I want to tell you this, Mrs Ferndale,' he said.

'Of course, Mr Tyte.'

He hesitated. His face was blurred with elderly freckles, his eyes the same blue as his son's. He said:

'At first when we were here our lodger from Rowena Avenue used to visit us, Mrs Ferndale. Newberry Fruits he always brought.'

'There's no need to remember it all for me, Mr Tyte. Please don't upset yourself.'

'A man with an interest in military campaigns, you'd say, nothing much to him. But then I guessed, Mrs Ferndale, looking at him one Sunday afternoon. He knew and never came back.'

'I see.'

'He's dead now, but he hasn't taken his evil with him. Francis guessed in turn that I had added things together. That's why he doesn't come to see us.'

'I'm sorry.'

'I'm glad he doesn't. I don't want ever to know what he has become.'

'Please, Mrs Ferndale,' Miss Purchase called and that was the end of it. Julia caught a glimpse of stained-glass panels on either side of the hall door, and then she and Joy were descending steps that led to a crazy-paving path. The visit had lasted less than ten minutes.

'I'm concerned about your mother,' Julia said, looking for a taxi outside the Blue Feathers, where Doris had spent some time after her visit to the Sundown Home. 'I hope she's returned.'

But the flat in Fulham was empty.

'It's all right really,' Joy said. 'She looks after herself when she's drinking.'

'I'll come back later, Joy. I want to talk to her.'

Julia had a bath in the Rembrandt Hotel. Afterwards she sat in the huge, open lounge where Doris and Francis had sat on their last evening together. 'I'd like some whisky,' she said to the Sicilian waiter who was smiling at her. At the table next to hers a party of Japanese businessmen were drinking, and talking in English. She didn't know why she'd asked for whisky since she rarely drank it. 'Thank you,' she said when the man returned, jingling ice in a glass, still agreeably smiling at her.

She guessed that Doris had been sacked. She guessed she would not return until the public houses had closed. She wished there was a telephone in the flat in Fulham so that she could ring later on. She'd done her duty by Francis's mother, not that going to the old people's home had seemed to be anything more than a waste of everyone's time. But she'd done it, she'd made the journey from Gloucestershire, she'd stood in the flat Francis had spoken of, with its table-mats and the pictures of Negresses. There'd been the line of old overcoats and the smell of milk pudding in the Sundown Home.

She finished her whisky. People were passing through the bar on their way to dinner in the restaurant. The Japanese businessmen were calling for more lager, one of them saying that as far as he could see the British tie industry was failing. She took the lift to her room on the third floor and looked up the name *Music* in the telephone directory by her bed. There was an Albert Music and an A. M. Music. There was a C. H. Music, at an address that somehow seemed right. She wrote the number down on a piece of paper. Then she telephoned her mother, who said she was managing perfectly well. Mrs Anstey had insisted that Mrs Spanners should not move in overnight; the spaniel, she'd said, was protection and company enough.

Julia took the lift downstairs again. She went out and bought an evening paper and read it carefully, standing in the hall: no atrocity had been committed, no actress lay dead in a house in SW1. In the restaurant called the Carvers' Table she tried to eat roast beef but found she could not. Afterwards she ordered coffee in the spacious lounge and sat over it, listening to the Japanese businessmen, who were still practising their English. Eventually she took a taxi back to Fulham.

Joy was watching *The Streets of San Francisco*. 'Oh no,' she said. 'No, she'll still be boozing. She's an alcoholic, actually.'

Julia nodded bleakly. An advertisement appeared on the television screen. A woman sprayed polish on to the top of a table and said that the polish brought out the natural quality of the wood. Without the use of this polish the table was only half alive, she claimed. Joy laughed.

'I look away now when he appears,' she said. 'I've got to hate him.'

'You mustn't say that, Joy.'

'If he appeared I'd want to spit on the screen.'

But he didn't appear. There was an advertisement for margarine and one for a breakfast food that was likened to central heating. Then *The Streets of San Francisco* returned.

Julia left. She didn't know what to do. She couldn't just walk into a police station and say a woman she hardly knew had been talking wildly about killing a young actress. She returned to the Rembrandt and made another telephone call to Stone St Martin.

'I'm sorry to bother you so late,' she said. She told Father Lavin that Doris Smith had not been back to her flat. She reported that she had taken the child to the Sundown Home. 'I just wanted to know,' she said. 'Did you pray, Father?'

In the office of the priests' house he replied that he had, and when the conversation came to an end he knelt again by the metal desk.

Julia knelt also, addressing herself to the emptiness where her childhood image once had been. No reassurance consoled her, no warmth was generated, and when she rose her mind was full of the man she had allowed herself to fall in love with. She lifted her dress over her head, confessing the truth for the first time since he had taken her jewellery and gone: love couldn't so swiftly dissipate, no longer could she withhold her pity. She had called him a psychopath but that was just another word.

Slowly she took off the rest of her clothes. In the wardrobe looking-glass she examined the reflection of her nakedness, as she had on the night of the cocktail party. She was only a little plump. Men would desire her full breasts and the softness of her thighs, the bush of hair spreading towards her stomach. Signor Guzzinati had desired her; on trains and in the street men sometimes eyed her. Yet in the hotel in Pisa she'd been no more than furniture. Vividly, all that returned to her: his low voice talking about himself, the dim light in the room, the chair he sat in on one side of the shuttered window, his back half turned to her. In some moment then, still suffering from the shock, she had begun to love him for what he should have been.

She put a nightdress on, creamy white with a pattern of forget-me-nots. Her blue-green eyes stared back at her from the wardrobe looking-glass, the reddish tinge of her hair caught in the light. In the hotel in Pisa she had been bludgeoned by the shock, but within a minute of receiving it she had wanted to make the best of what there was. Even now she would have reached out towards him: he might have practised cruelty and infected Doris Smith with his own malevolence, but she wanted to caress away the pain she knew was there, to rescue him at last from his awful world. The shadow he'd dressed up in order to deceive her was nothing, what concerned her was the untouchable person.

She closed the wardrobe door and got into bed. It was different from the love she'd felt for Roger, and different totally from the love she felt for her mother and her daughters. Francis inspired such passion, and not only in herself. His mother suffered from it, as Doris did, and Joy. Escaping it, Joy hated him in the end; Doris's grief had created his death. But for as long as she lived Mrs Tyte would not be free of it.

Julia lay in the warm gloom, wondering if she'd ever become free of it herself. She closed her eyes; he gave her flowers. She walked with him in Italy, they sat in the cool of churches. In the garden of Swan House they worked together, he slowly getting better, becoming as he should have been because her sympathy was the help he'd always needed. But even while these fantasies remained she murmured into the void he'd left her with, betraying her feelings by asking for strength. She prayed that the attachment she felt, her love and her pity, might be lifted from her. She prayed that Doris might be saved from the destruction which had been wrought in her. She prayed for Joy, and that Mrs Tyte might be at peace. She got out of bed and knelt at the edge of it, distantly seeing herself in her mind's eye, head pressed on clasped hands, her bare feet, and the forget-me-nots of her nightdress. She begged again for intervention and a moment later she telephoned the number she'd written down on a piece of paper. When a voice quite cheerfully answered she replaced the receiver.

Doris followed the two men down a flight of stone steps which were slippery with moisture. The men moved slowly, one of them limping, both grasping the metal rail of the balustrade that divided the descent. On short, grimy pedestals, set in this balustrade, lights burned weakly at intervals of a dozen yards or so.

When the floor supervisor had sacked her Doris had gone

straight to Value Wines, and then she'd sat in Hyde Park waiting for the Spread Eagle to open. She'd returned to the park when it had closed in the afternoon. Hours later she'd got on to a bus when another public house, somewhere in Edgware Road, had closed. She'd sat on the bus, not caring where it went, and then she'd walked for hours. In the public house she had tried to buy half a bottle of vodka but the man had refused to sell it to her. There was none in the flat, which was why there wasn't any point in returning there.

At the bottom of the steps there was an archway, lit dimly also. Into the gloom of this the men advanced, the one with the limp pausing briefly to beckon Doris on. He wore a tattered double-breasted suit that had once been tailored for someone of greater height and girth. The other man was wrapped in a buttonless overcoat that had a naval look about it. All around them, like bundles of rags, a mass of people huddled on the ground. A cracked, old woman's voice sang dismally in the shadows.

'Con,' the man with the limp said, shaking one of the bundles.

His companion, unshaven, with rheumy eyes, nodded at Doris. This effort at communication, intended to be one of encouragement, a way of saying that the end of the journey had been reached, that all would now be well, didn't register as such with Doris. For a moment she had forgotten what she was doing with these two men or why it was she had descended a flight of steps with them. She tried to think, saying to herself it was ridiculous to forget.

She could remember the river, lights twinkling on the dark water. She could remember her father taking her on a boat trip on her birthday, but that was ages ago. 'Dorrie, I'm thinking of getting married again,' were the words her father had used on another occasion and when she'd repeated them to Frankie her hand had already been in his, the very first time.

'She'll stand a bottle, Con,' the man with the limp was saying. 'A full one for the three of us.'

The need for a drink had assailed her when she'd walked along by the embankment wall, looking down at the twinkling lights: she remembered now. She remembered the two men, how they had been poking through the contents of a waste-bin attached to a lamp-post. She remembered how the one who didn't limp had raised a bottle to his lips.

'God, I was dreaming about the wife,' said the man called Con. 'She had a broken rib.'

'This woman wants a drink, Con.'

'Ah, don't ye all want drinks? Isn't it drinks the entire long time with ye?'

His voice was like a voice there had been the day she'd taken the train to Cheltenham, with Joy. Someone had spoken like that, another man she didn't know, a small and grey-faced man in black, a clergyman of some kind, standing in front of the house in the country.

'Have you got it, Con? Have you a bottle on you?'

'Have ye two notes?'

'Two,' the man with the limp said to Doris.

'That's very cheap, missus,' his companion threw in, attempting to wag his head. 'That's good value all round.'

'You can rest yourself here, missus,' the man with the limp said. 'We'll keep an eye on you.'

'I'm not an alcoholic,' Doris said, finding the money in the bag that hung from her shoulder. 'It's just that a friend's gone.'

'It's shocking, that,' agreed the man with the limp.

Doris sat down on the ground with them and the bottle was passed from mouth to mouth. It was difficult to drink more than a sip at a time because the taste was so harsh. She leaned against the brickwork of the archway, happy at least that she'd managed to find a drink. 'Get away out of that,' one or other of her two companions kept repeating, addressing the figures that crept along the ground towards them, begging a mouthful.

Hands reached out and touched her or fingered her handbag, but when she moved or spoke they darted away. Then women arrived and dispensed soup from a huge container. They seemed distressed to see her there, and spoke sorrowfully about a new face. One of them wished to drive her somewhere in a car, to a place that sounded like an institution. She didn't take any of the soup they offered.

The women were no longer there, and in a little while the bottle was empty. The men beside her slept, the hands ceased to reach out towards her. She might have been dreaming, she didn't know; she could hear her own voice whispering. 'Oh, Frankie,' it said. 'Oh love, love. Oh Frankie darling.' Close to him on the soft brown plush of the upstairs bar she explained how she had waited on a sunny day while her father fished in the canal. She had carried home the little folding-stool, her other hand in her father's, her feet skipping to keep up. And all the time Frankie listened, his blue eyes full of happiness because of her own happiness when she was little. Always in their long love affair there had been that, the happiness when she was little, and Frankie making the happiness seem even more than it had been. A million times his presence had made up for things, a million times his smile had chased away the blues.

'You'll spare us something, missus?' the man with the limp said, and Doris realized that everyone was awake again. The silent figures were upright now, revealing the newspapers and lengths of cardboard that had been their beds. She looked for some coins to give the men but discovered that her handbag now contained no money. 'I'm sorry,' she said, and the men muttered obscenities at her. 'I think it's been stolen,' she said.

She climbed the flight of slippery steps, not caring much about the theft. Dawn was breaking as she stood again by the embankment wall which she had remembered in the night. It wasn't the money: the trouble was that Frankie was in a mess, the trouble was that Frankie was dead. His slim body was rotting away in its foreign grave, even though his voice still spoke to her, as it had on the last night in the flat. All over again it told her the story of poor little Constance Kent, who had suffered as he had and as she had herself.

*

199

When Joy awoke to find that her mother had not returned she was not surprised. Her mother was drunk more often than sober these days, and quite often did not return to the flat at night. She'd become dirty, Joy noticed, and once she'd fallen down in the kitchen and had just lain there.

She smeared blackcurrant jam on a slice of bread and took it to the sitting-room. Television hadn't started yet so she stood by the window, looking out. She was still there when the doorbell rang.

'No, she hasn't come back,' she said to Julia, nibbling at what remained of the bread.

'Excuse me, madam,' Doris said in Victoria Street.

'*Ja, so?*'

'I wonder if I could have a word with you, madam?'

'Oh, yes. *Ja,* please.'

It was good that the woman was foreign because foreigners were slow on the uptake and usually made an effort. English people just said it was disgraceful and walked away.

'Would you give me something for a cup of tea, madam?'

The woman didn't understand. She was enormous, a German Doris put her down as. She wore a leather skirt and a waistcoat that matched it, and leather boots. Her leather hat had a green feather in it.

'I've had a bit of bad luck,' Doris said. 'If you could spare me a little money, madam?'

The woman opened her handbag and took a purse from it. The handbag contained a notecase containing five- and ten-pound notes, as well as a wad of single pounds. Doris could also see traveller's cheques, a make-up compact and a pair of gloves. She wanted to reach into it and lift out the notecase, not bothering with anything else. 'Clever,' Frankie once had said. 'Clever as a card trick.' He'd told her about it, how he'd stood and watched the trick happening, and both of them had laughed in the upstairs bar. In Frankie's story it had been a woman in Wigmore Street, with her purse among the groceries in a basket, and the chap saying a bee had got into her hair.

'My own money has been stolen,' Doris explained.

The woman took ten p. from a purse and presented it to Doris, who thanked her and then suddenly cried out that a bee had landed on the woman's hat. The purse had been snapped shut, but the handbag, hanging from the woman's arm, was still open.

'A bee,' Doris cried, wafting at the hat with her fingers, astonishing herself. 'A bee,' she said again. 'A bee. You understand a bee?'

'*Ja, ja,*' the woman replied in agitation. '*Ja*, I understand a bee.'

'It's got into your hair,' Doris said.

Passers-by stopped. Doris lifted the handbag from the woman's arm and held it while the woman gingerly removed her hat. Although she had so often appropriated items in the store, she had never taken anything from an individual, foreign or otherwise. Slipping the notecase into a pocket of her mackintosh, she said to herself that it hadn't been her fault that the meths drinkers had robbed her while she sat with them. She gave the handbag to a woman who had stopped to see what was going on, asking her to return it to the German when the bee flew out of her hair. 'I'm in a hurry myself,' she said, turning into the Army and Navy Stores, where she flushed the notecase down the lavatory, having first removed the notes it contained. She was sorry that she'd had to take money from a foreigner who had given her ten p. for a cup of tea.

But none of that mattered because of the other. It didn't matter about the meths drinkers or the harsh taste of the liquid, or the clergyman who'd arrived just as she was leaving the house in the country. It wasn't the stolen money Frankie had talked about on that last long night, or the woman he'd married down Cheltenham way, or even the dealer in Crawford Street. 'Poor thing, she did what she had to do,' he'd said. 'She didn't go under.'

Doris left the Army and Navy Stores by a different set of doors, and after that the day filled up with colours. In the supermarket where she bought half a bottle of vodka the tins of soup and vegetables were startlingly vivid, as if they should be feared. She listened to a voice singing, bewildered for a moment and then remembering that it came from a machine she couldn't see. 'You've picked a fine time to leave me, Lucille,' drawled the voice. 'Four hungry children and a crop in the field.'

She sat for a while in a branch of Lloyd's Bank and when she was asked to leave she sat on a bench in a children's playground. The colours from the supermarket appeared to have accompanied her, like technicolour shadows: brightly green peas, chicken in a sauce, steam rising from kidney soup. They came and went, often making her blink. She told herself to be careful in case she fell asleep. She wondered who Lucille was, trying to remember if it was the dressmaker.

In a cinema there were different images, people and faces sliding out of focus, blurring away to nothing and then explosively returning. She sipped at the bottle she had, smoking and sipping, quite happy to be in the cinema. 'I've fallen in love with you, Dorrie,' he suddenly said, and then his face was sliding about like the others on the screen. People hurt him, his voice whispered again, telling her he only wanted to cry sometimes. In the darkness a torch was flashed and someone in a uniform said she'd have to be quiet or else leave the cinema. But Doris knew they'd got it wrong, she hadn't for a moment been shouting.

'Like tit for tat,' she said to the man in the off-licence, and the colours of the bottles behind him were like the colours in the supermarket, almost alive. All the way to the attics it was a hell, she said to the man, and all the time among the soldiers, and then again in the dressmaker's workroom. The dressmaker was old and horrible, a violent person. She'd always been horrible, grasping with her talons, greedy when he didn't want her. 'And then he caught a dose of you know what,' Doris explained. 'And then again he married this new woman just to get a bit of money so's we could be together.'

The man had a moustache which nicotine had yellowed, and pale eyes that almost matched it. He gave Doris her change, saying he was sorry to hear about her trouble. Doris stared at his moustache, wondering why she had gone into a cinema when she should be getting on with things. Going into the cinema was all part of the mix-up there sometimes was, her own fault entirely. She staggered as she hurried from the off-licence, determined that there should be no more delays, determined not to go under.

Julia mounted the stairs to the upstairs bar of the Spread Eagle. She sat there for several hours, watching the fan on the ceiling that looked like an aeroplane propeller. She sat through the lunchtime crowd and the juke-box music. At four o'clock she hovered near the shoe department just in case she had somehow misunderstood the Indian she had spoken to the day before. But Doris was not there.

She returned to the hotel and telephoned her mother to say that she might well not be returning until the morning. She again made the journey to the flat in Fulham.

'Oh no,' Joy said. 'Not a sign of her.'

A comedian was telling a joke about Irishmen drilling for oil, then four girls in glittering trouser-suits danced and sang.

'I'm worried in case she tries to hurt this actress she thinks your father was involved with,' Julia said.

'Screwing her, was he?'

Julia shook her head and again left the flat. *The number of this telephone-box is 385 1001*, a notice said, and she remembered dialling that number at Doris's instruction. She imagined Doris's cigarettes and matches on top of the grubby, dog-eared directories. Doris alone here in the middle of the night. She dialled C. H. Music's number, but there was no reply.

'Excuse me,' Doris said to a man who was wheeling a bicycle, a uniformed man, a Customs officer she put him down as. But when he paused, waiting for her question, she couldn't for the life of her remember what it was she had wanted to ask him. Her mackintosh was blown against her body by the wind, a cigarette smouldered between her fingers. The tins from the supermarket were no longer there, but the sea seemed to tumble about and she remembered being on the sand with her father, turning a sandcastle out of her red and blue bucket, and all the empty deck-chairs. 'A Saturday it was,' she said to the Customs officer. 'July 2nd 1966. He was married to that Lucille at the time.'

'Sorry?' the man said, finding it difficult to hear her above the sound of the wind.

She remembered then what it was she wanted to ask him and said to herself that she was stupid, mentioning July 2nd to a stranger when what she'd wanted to know was the way. It was all that drink, she said to herself, on an empty stomach. She laughed and ran after the man.

'Left at the traffic-lights,' he said. 'Left again at the bottom of the hill.'

'Have you looked in the Bricklayer's?' Joy asked. 'It's the nearest one. By the telephone-box?'

'Yes, I looked in there.'

'Then there's a new one she mentioned the other day. The Turbaned Turk. I don't know where that one is.'

'She could be anywhere, I suppose.'

'I wouldn't worry if I was you.'

'You haven't had a proper meal all day, Joy.'

'We could go down the Pizzaland. She's probably mentioned the Pizzaland to you.'

'Yes, I think she did.'

'We could go down while you're waiting. There's nothing much on till the film at half past ten. *The Corrupt Ones* it's called.'

'We'd better leave another note. Shall I write it this time?'

Joy had a Pizzaland Special and said she'd never before been in the restaurant with anyone except her father and her mother. It was not the kind of place she could afford to come on her own, and she told Julia about the Rialto Café and the Light of India Take-Away and the Woo Han and the Chik 'n' Chips. She told her about the disagreeable woman who'd taken over in the Rialto, and the couple who'd been there on the afternoon when she'd glanced through the window and seen her father passing by with the actress. There'd been a quarrel about blue films, she said, and told Julia all about it, easily remembering because she'd so often repeated the details in Tite Street Comprehensive. 'I took a drug,' she said, 'as she probably told you.'

'Yes, she did.'

'I wonder if the tattooing craze is over.'

'Probably.'

'You never know how long a craze'll last. Don't you like that pizza?'

'I'm afraid I'm not very hungry.'

'I think I'll maybe go back tomorrow, see if it's over. It's dead boring in the flat.'

Joy had an ice-cream, and then they returned to the flat. Doris was not there, and it wasn't time for *The Corrupt Ones*.

'I just want to make another telephone call,' Julia said, but when she rang C. H. Music's number from the box by the Bricklayer's Arms there still was no reply.

'No, with a tea-pot,' Doris said.

They made her instant coffee in the small police station, and she took an almost empty bottle of vodka from her handbag and poured what remained of it into the cup. She smiled at the three policemen who were present.

'So Frankie's gone, is he?' the desk-sergeant inquired. 'And you decided to set the matter straight? You've had a drink or two, haven't you, miss?'

'Did you ever hear of Constance Kent?'

The policemen shook their heads, and the desk-sergeant made a note of the name.

'Susie Music,' Doris said, 'played the part for the telly.'

The desk-sergeant made a note of that name also.

'Poor Frankie was a weirdo in the end. Poor Frankie was in a mess.'

'Of course, miss. Now this Susie girl. Would you remember where she lives at all?'

'C. H. Music her dad's called. sw1.'

C. H. Music, wrote the desk-sergeant, and the three policemen sighed, all of them thinking the same thing: that it was almost routine nowadays for people like this to come wandering in, weaving fantasies about the acts of violence they'd performed.

Doris drank her coffee. Quite suddenly, after the third blow, the neck had gone limp. After that she'd counted the other blows, forty-three there'd been.

'Making forty-six in all,' she said to the policeman. 'Exactly forty-six. Yes, I've had a drink or two,' she admitted.

Amusedly they listened, the desk-sergeant with his collar undone. It was half past nine, the summer dusk just giving way to darkness. They listened to her telling them about table-mats and a shoe department and how some child or other had trouble with her stomach. The desk-sergeant buttoned his collar, continuing to listen while the woman rambled on.

Julia gave the taxi-driver the address that went with C. H. Music's telephone number, not knowing what she was going to do when she arrived at wherever it was. She'd wait, she supposed, keeping an eye out for Doris Smith. She'd just look at the place, and if everything seemed all right she'd come away again.

But when she arrived there it wasn't quite like that. There were lights on in the house and she immediately rang the bell beside the hall door, without looking about her to see if Doris Smith was lurking in the shadows. It had become quite urgent, once she was actually at the house, to enter it and present her fears.

'Good evening,' a big man in a fawn suit said. He smiled at her, crunching his soft, pink face into knobs of flesh. He looked like a cherub, Julia thought, his curly white hair accentuating the aptness of this comparison. 'Good evening,' he said again.

'Mr Music?'

'Yes indeed.'

'I'm sorry to call like this. I've been trying to telephone you.'

'We've just come in.' He smiled encouragingly. 'How can I help you?'

'Are you,' she began, and hesitated and then began again. 'Are you the father of Susanna Music?'

'Yes, I am.'

'I wonder if I might see your daughter for a moment?'

He held the door open and Julia stepped into a large hall. Abstract paintings were brightly lit on the pale hessian of its walls. Somewhere music was playing: Brahms's Symphony Number 3, the end of the first movement.

'You have a visitor, Susanna,' Mr Music said, leading Julia into a room with wheat-coloured cushions on armchairs that might have come from Sweden, and long-haired rugs all over a polished wood floor. The symphony was coming from the television set; the sound ceased and the busy image of violinists was snapped from the screen.

'How d'you do,' a woman said. She smiled as Mr Music had, turning from the television set. Her hair was rinsed a shade of blue. She was much thinner and smaller than her husband.

'I'm Susanna,' another voice said, and a girl stepped out of a shadowy corner, more like her mother than her father, her eyes gazing out of long dark hair, as Doris Smith had said they did.

'I'm sorry about all this,' Julia said. 'I think you've been bothered a bit already. By a woman called Doris Smith.'

'She made a nuisance of herself to Susanna,' Mr Music said quickly, his tone rather different from what it had been a moment ago. There was a hint of suspicion in it now, and the implication that any further nonsense in this matter would not be tolerated.

'She was quite unpleasant to Susanna,' his wife supplied, speaking quickly also. No one was sitting down in the room.

'She's in rather a state. She's an alcoholic and a bit eccentric. My name is Julia Ferndale,' Julia added, realizing she hadn't revealed this yet. 'I'm the person Francis Tyte bigamously married some time ago. I don't know if you know all that.'

'She told me,' Susanna said.

'My daughter wasn't a friend of this man's. He was just another actor in a television show, Miss Ferndale.'

'It's Mrs Ferndale, actually. Yes, I know your daughter didn't know him well. It's just that I've become concerned for your daughter's safety.'

There was a pause after Julia said that. Then Mrs Music asked her to sit down. Mrs Music sat down herself and so did her husband. Mr Music turned on another light in the room, as if he wished to examine Julia more closely. He said:

'Please tell us all about this, Mrs Ferndale.'

'Yes, of course.'

Julia went through it all. She told the story of herself and Francis, and the story of Doris Smith and Francis, and the birth of the child. She mentioned the dressmaker and Francis's parents. It was a relief to tell everything to people who didn't know.

'I don't quite understand,' Mrs Music said, 'why she believes the man committed suicide.'

'Her drinking confuses her, I think.'

Susanna remembered thinking, on the afternoon when Doris had approached her on the street, that she was like someone Francis Tyte had invented. The thought had occurred to her again when Doris had come to see her and had astonishingly suggested that she had given him venereal disease.

'Yes, she's like that,' Julia said when Susanna put this theory forward. 'She has become like that. She hasn't been back to her flat for quite a time, since she left it yesterday morning in fact. I'm afraid I became alarmed. She'd been talking rather wildly.'

'It's awfully good of you,' Mrs Music said gently, as if she sought to convey with the words far more than they baldly stated. She seemed to wish to commiserate, and to applaud Julia's courage in coming to their house. 'We're grateful, Mrs Ferndale.'

'Yes, thank you,' Susanna said, and her father nodded slowly. Julia said:

'I dare say alcoholics often become like this.'

'Not quite like this, I think.' Mr Music was just beginning to expand on that in a medical way when the hall-door bell rang,

208

causing all four people in the room to share the same thought. But it wasn't Doris whom Mr Music brought back with him to the room a few minutes later. It was two uniformed policemen.

'This is my daughter,' Mr Music said. 'And this is Mrs Ferndale, who knows a lot about the matter.'

One of the policemen smiled, a long, lazy, bored smile. The other said:

'Sorry to trouble you with this, Miss Music. We had a report there might've been a spot of bother.'

'Bother?'

'Apparently there's this lady who's had a drop too much. She appeared to think she'd done you a mischief. Sorry about all that, miss.'

'Where is she?' Julia asked, and the policeman who had already spoken mentioned a police station near Victoria. He asked Julia if she happened to be a friend of the lady who was there. Julia said she knew her.

'If she's issuing threats against my daughter,' Mr Music intervened, 'I'm afraid we're going to have to do something about it.'

Susanna shook her head. She could take care of herself, she protested quite firmly.

'You can't do much, sir,' the policeman who was doing the talking pointed out, 'if the lady's on the juice. It's all just fancy stuff, you know. And it's probably gone out of her system, sir, now that she's said her bit.'

The smile began again on the other policeman's face. 'They see these things on the box,' his colleague continued. 'Guns and knives and stranglings. It was spiders sucking the blood out of people the other night.'

At that Mrs Music displayed some alarm and her husband said, laying down the law, that if the alcoholic woman visited the house again, or telephoned it even, the police would immediately be informed. He would want to see the woman arrested and calmed down. He would want to see her undergo a medical examination.

'You do that, sir,' the policeman responsible for the talking agreed, and both of them began to move out of the room. Julia rose and prepared to leave also, although she could feel that the Musics were expecting her to stay a little longer, perhaps to agree to some plan of campaign for dealing with the nuisance. In the hall the policeman said:

'If you could let us have the lady's address, madam, it would be a help. Or if you like we'll run you over to Victoria. If you'd care to have a word with her.'

Julia didn't know why she agreed, and hardly did so except just perceptibly to nod. She said good-bye to the Musics, promising she would continue to persuade Doris that she was mistaken about their daughter. 'Thank you again,' Mrs Music said. 'Thank you so very much.'

Politely a door of the police-car was held open. 'Silly, really,' the policeman who'd done all the talking said as the car began to move, and Julia felt silly herself, even though the Musics had been appreciative and nice.

'Alive and living in splendour,' the policeman reported over the car's radio system: a friend of the drunk was coming to take care of things.

The policeman who hadn't spoken was driving. 'It appears she claimed she'd done that kid,' he said now, 'with a tea-pot.' They were held up at a traffic light and he turned slightly as he spoke. Through the gloom Julia could just see the same tired smile flitting across his face. The reference to a tea-pot heightened the absurdity of everything, and Julia was glad that a tea-pot hadn't been mentioned to the Musics.

'Any idea what it's all about?' the other man inquired, turning round too.

A lot of people had been upset, Julia explained, because of someone who'd disappeared. There'd been malice and misunderstandings. In the messiness that had been created it was hard to establish just what was what.

'We got a message over the radio,' the driver said, moving the car swiftly on from the lights. 'We had our doubts, of course. Like we said to that gentleman, you always have your doubts when it's someone on the juice.'

The conversation ceased. Other messages came through on the radio system, reports of crime and distress, and of a fire somewhere. It was very kind of them to drive her all the way to Victoria, Julia said when there was a lull, but both men shook their heads, the more talkative one pronouncing that it was all in a patrolman's day.

In the police station Doris was asleep, lolling across two chairs. The policemen who were present were good-humoured and appeared to regard the incident as a joke. In the end a second police-car took Julia and Doris to the flat in Fulham and two other policemen carried Doris into the bedroom she shared with Joy. 'I go for that Nancy Kwan,' one of them said in the sitting-room, pausing for a moment to watch the action on the television screen. 'Your friend'll sleep it off,' the other one said to Julia. 'You might tell her in the morning not to cause trouble again. She's lucky not to get herself booked.'

Julia thanked them. 'I'm going to make a cup of tea,' she said to Joy, who had returned to *The Corrupt Ones*.

But in the kitchen she didn't make tea. She filled the kettle, and a moment later she heard Joy's voice saying something above the rumble of the television programme. Then Doris was in the kitchen, in her maroon mackintosh with her handbag hanging from a shoulder, just as she'd been when the policemen had deposited her on her bed. 'Julia,' she said.

'I think you should be lying down.'

'I've run out of ciggies, dear.'

'She wants me to get them for her,' Joy said, appearing in the kitchen also. She added that she'd given her mother some Maxwell House when she'd been in a similar condition last Sunday.

Doris was leaning against the door-frame, unable to focus her eyes. Joy said she didn't see why she should go down to the machine for cigarettes. She offered to make the Maxwell House instead, so Julia asked where the machine was and went herself.

When she returned Joy was watching the tail-end of the film and Doris was seated at the kitchen table. The desire for sleep had apparently left her, but she still had difficulty with her eyes and had to keep screwing them up. 'You're lovely,' she said when Julia gave her the cigarettes. She found it hard to light one and in the end Julia did it for her.

Slurred and not making sense, Doris talked for hours. The sound of the television ceased in the sitting-room, more cigarettes were smoked, cups of Maxwell House coffee refused. Every time Julia said she had to go Doris pleaded with her not to. She cried a little until Julia promised to stay, and then began again. She told of the killing of Susanna Music and of the death of Francis in Italy. She'd been walking at night, she said, just walking along, hoping for a drink. She spoke of the Indian floor supervisor in such a way that Julia for a time was under the impression that he had been with her as she walked. 'It was only bits and pieces I took,' Doris said. 'I had to keep going, dear.'

At half past one Julia made the journey to the cigarette machine for more cigarettes, and when she returned it all began again: the bits and pieces sold in Crawford Street, the meths drinkers, the German woman with the bee buzzing round her, the man in the off-licence. Sometimes Doris laughed, describing the man's tobacco-stained moustache and the feather in the German woman's hat.

'Don't you think you should go to bed now?'

'The trouble is I've had a few drinks.'

'That's why you should go to bed.'

'Will you smoke a ciggy with me, Julia? Do you never, Julia?'

'No, I don't.'

'You're good. The trouble is you're good, Julia.'

'Look, I'll help you get to bed. And then really I must go.'

'If he hadn't married Lucille I could have made him happy, Julia. Instead of which she threw the sewing-machine at him.'

'It isn't a help, you know, going over all this.'

'The food she cooked him he couldn't eat.'

'You must try and forget her.'

'You can't forget, Julia. All these years she wouldn't die.'

'You must try, Doris.'

But Doris shook her head. She began to talk about the sea, and the wind agitating its surface, and the canvas of the deck-chairs flapping about. Her dad was kindness itself, helping her with her sandcastles. She'd wanted to take his hand but unfortunately he wasn't there any more and when she looked around poor Frankie wasn't either. She dropped off to sleep while she was still speaking. Her head kept slipping sideways and then collapsed across her arms on the table. It was twenty to five.

Julia stayed. She sat in the sitting-room, hoping to doze so that the last few hours of the night would easily pass. She imagined Doris waking when Joy began to move about the flat. She imagined her terrifying the child, screaming because she had woken up sober, as such people screamed in films. But whether that happened or not, at least Susanna Music was unharmed. Her foreboding had been wrong, or perhaps indeed her prayers and Father Lavin's had been answered. 'Thank You,' she said. 'Thank You for that.' Francis's smile blinked stylishly in her mind, and when she tried to shut it away it returned and brought with it the gentleness in his eyes. For a moment it seemed absurd that she'd ever believed in what had apparently been a fantasy of her own: that Francis had left his vengeance behind him. It seemed as bizarre as Doris believing that he'd committed suicide. 'Forgive me,' she said, uncertain if she was addressing the God she'd just thanked for looking after Susanna Music, or Francis himself. Soon after that she actually slept for a while, and even vaguely dreamed. Francis had taken slips of the escallonia and wanted to replace the raspberry canes with new ones. 'It's nice he's back again,' her mother said, and Henrietta and Katherine quite agreed. 'Thank you for the dog,' she said herself, and when she woke there were shafts of light in the room. She pulled back the curtains and sunshine fell on the pictures of Negresses and jungle animals. It was five past seven.

In the kitchen Doris was still asleep. Julia boiled a kettle in order to make coffee. She rattled cups and saucers, hoping to wake Doris up and in the end succeeding.

'Good morning,' Julia said.

Doris reached out for her cigarettes. Her hands were shaking, her face the colour of paper. She didn't scream because she'd woken up sober but when she spoke she did so excessively slowly, as if pronunciation hurt her. She said she intended to have a bath. 'I'm not going to drink again,' she said, with such assurance that this appeared to be a decision she had carefully arrived at.

Joy drank Maxwell House and ate the remains of a sliced loaf. Doris returned from her bath. She was wearing a crumpled grey blouse and a grey skirt, and she'd put on some lipstick. Speaking to Joy in the same quiet way she repeated that she did not intend to drink again. She had made up her mind to get on to an even keel, as the floor supervisor had advised. She intended to try again with her table-mats. 'I'm sorry,' she said to her child, 'for all this un-pleasantness.'

Joy had been about to lift a piece of bread to her mouth when Doris had begun to speak, and the bread now crumbled between her fingers, an expression of the astonishment she was experiencing. 'Can she mean it?' she whispered as she said good-bye, and Julia replied that apparently she did. She said good-bye herself, and hoped the Comprehensive would take a turn for the better. Joy made a face.

'You've been very good to me, Julia,' Doris quietly insisted. 'I'll never bother you again. I promise you that, dear.'

'I actually came here to take Joy to see Francis's parents. His mother wanted to meet her.'

Doris nodded, as if the visit didn't surprise her. 'Straight away after I've washed the things up,' she said, 'I'm going to start in on the mats.'

Julia slept on the train. She woke up at Reading because the ticket-collector had come around and was clearing his throat beside her. She found her ticket and handed it to him. There'd been a couple sitting opposite her, but they were now gone. Faintly she remembered their getting up, the girl saying they were leaving their newspaper for her when she felt less sleepy. The newspaper was there, dark black headlines about Rhodesia, pictures of politicians and footballers, a girl in a bikini. Idly she read it, turning the pages between glances at the passing landscape. A cricketer had made a hundred and eighty-three runs. Two men disguised as house-painters had been chased and caught by the police. In the London Zoo an elephant was ill. In Folkestone an elderly dressmaker had been battered to death with a tea-pot.

·14·
Julia's

They watched Julia, unable to help themselves. Mrs Anstey watched her in Swan House, as did Mrs Spanners. Father Lavin made excuses to visit her. Her daughters came at weekends.

Julia was silent. She drove her mother through the town and through the summer lanes, to the house that meant so much to the old woman. An act of charity she thinks it is, Mrs Anstey guessed, accepting the charity for her daughter's sake. Young men in anoraks continued to go about their business in the grounds of Anstey's Mill, looking through the sights of instruments on tripods. Julia stood with her mother on the grassy path that had been the railway track, where once she'd trotted her pony, but Mrs Anstey didn't tell again about the parties there had been when she and her husband were young. Trees were being felled at Anstey's Mill, but that was irrelevant also. 'She don't say a word,' Mrs Spanners reported to her husband. 'Don't hardly open her lips.'

Nevil Clapp was struck as well by Julia's changing demeanour and said so to Diane of the Crowning Glory, with whom he was still going steady. 'Can't say I blame her,' Diane replied, which was much the same response as Mr Spanners's. Too much had happened to Julia since she'd met the unsavoury man, and the final twist of the screw had been too terrible to bear. It wasn't fair, the verdict was, though some said also that fairness was neither here nor there.

When weeks had passed Father Lavin went on his postponed holiday to Co. Cork, to see his mother. In the farmhouse near Clonakilty he listened to the news of the neighbourhood, news of children born, of deaths and illness, and high prices paid for land. His mother and his sister recalled the past, when the family had been younger in the farmhouse, but the reminiscing was blurred this year for Father Lavin, and without a life of its own. He had brought to Ireland an English tragedy and could not rid himself of it. The wolds of Gloucestershire shadowed the past there'd been in the farmhouse; the yellow-grey stone of the town he'd settled down in was all around him, and the charm of nearby Cheltenham. Julia's tears formed blots on the linen of her dress, the knuckles of her fingers tightly shone. 'Ah yes,' he said in the farmhouse. 'Ah yes, of course.'

As for Julia herself, the silence that enveloped her could not be shaken off. She did not wish to think, or ever again to lose herself in introspection. Nor did she intend to fill another diary. There'd been too much of all that in her life, too many thoughts and too much wondering, too much bothering. Her mother's and her daughters' view of her, never expressed yet clearly there, was quite correct: her compassion made a victim of her. And Father Lavin's protest that she sought connexions which didn't exist was valid also. She would continue to go to mass, for it would be too much like a gesture never again to practise her Catholic faith. But the last thing she wanted was to have to talk about herself to a priest, to listen to arguments and be assured she was prayed for. Just at the moment the very thought of prayer made her feel as cold as ice.

The first letter came, its grey German stamp tidily affixed. It did not speak of love, or any kind of reconsidering. Forgiveness was owed, one to the other, it stated inexplicably: the gift of the dog she'd paid for was a sign of this. Yet reading the letter, it seemed almost eccentric to question its sincerity: it sounded perfectly the truth that the marriage had taken place out of kindness to her, because she'd passionately wished for the formality of being joined to him. She sent the money that was required.

'My dear,' her mother said, 'I often wonder about that child, you know.'

They sat in the garden, watching the water of the river. Julia made a nodding motion and then slightly smiled, not wishing to seem entirely unreceptive. Her mother was as hard as a nut and always had been: charity begins at home, tread warily. Yet here her mother was, exchanging roles with her, her eyes implying that the child would carry with her for ever a picture of a woman killed in an alcoholic fervour, a face suddenly dead.

'We mustn't dwell on the child.' Julia made the same nodding motion again, and drifted back into her silence. She hoped she might type long pages of legalities until her very death, that her fingers would never grow too stiff or her mind too blunt. *Every notice convening a General Meeting shall comply with the provisions of Section 136 (2) of the Companies Act 1948 as to giving information to Members in regard to their right to appoint proxies* . . .

Such jargon filled her future perfectly, the antiquated Remington taken from its cupboard, the words imprecise and awkward, black on white. Her mother would die, her daughters would marry, and still the jargon would go on. Nevil Clapp would commit another theft; Mrs Spanners would no longer wish to make the journey to Swan House on Mondays; the garden would become too much, the house would acquire a grubby look. *The lien conferred by Clause 11 in Part I of Table A shall attach also to fully paid-up Shares registered in the name of any person* . . .

She didn't understand the jargon but that didn't matter either. The letters from Germany would continue to arrive, and she would continue to send money. She would live her life as best she could, still pitying a wreck of a human being who had taken everything away from her, still longing to forgive because it was her nature to.

'I'm perfectly all right, you know,' she assured her mother.

'Yes, dear, of course you are.'

The days of summer shortened. When the grass ceased to grow and the trees were brown, when suddenly it turned cold, there was the story of Constance Kent. In Gloucestershire and in London, all over England, fifteen million people were held enthralled. The people of the cocktail party were aware of a special interest. The people of the drill-hall observed their own faces with admiration or distaste. Nevil Clapp and Diane watched. So did Mr Humphreys of the cheese and bacon counter in Dobie's Stores, and so did Mrs Spanners and her husband, Charle. Father Lavin and Father Dawne watched, and Irene in Handbags and Sharon of House Beautiful, and the kindly floor supervisor. The tall policeman who had come to see Julia remarked to his wife that this was the kind of stuff that gave people ideas. Mr and Mrs Music applauded the performance of their daughter; but in their bungalow in Cheshire the elderly Massmith sisters made no comment, nor did the doctor and his wife in Lincolnshire. Henrietta was at the theatre that evening with a man called Colin Halifax who was keen on cricket. Katherine was falling in love in a restaurant with a man she'd met a fortnight before. Neither of them saw the drama, for neither of them had wanted to, and Doris didn't see it either. Long ago she had forgotten Francis Tyte and the dressmaker who had clung on to life so. That evening, as every evening now, she played with wooden pieces in the room that had been allocated to her.

Mrs Anstey didn't watch, nor did the Kilvert-Dunnes on the Isle of Wight, always put off by anything ghoulish. But the two male nurses, George and Cyril, enjoyed the production greatly; and there was silence in the television lounge while it was invaded by the figures in Victorian dress. Miss Purchase had urged an alternative programme on the residents, an account of life in Madagascar, but had met with little success. Observing her son again, and so strangely garbed, Mrs Tyte softly sobbed.

Francis spoke his few lines clearly, Julia considered; the man who'd been his best man was adequate also. The scene in the plum orchard took place, and then the scene in the breakfast-room. The

218

crippled groom held the horse's head, the dog-cart waited in front of the house, hooves pawed the gravel. An unbalanced girl revenged herself on the television screen, but it was not her story which had a point to make in the bow-windowed drawing-room of Swan House.

Julia wished her mother hadn't mentioned the child. The act of murder that was premeditated in the steamy Victorian household had been carried into the child's life, inspired by her father, perpetrated by her mother. The child was the victim of other people's worlds and other people's drama, caught up in horror because she happened to be there. There was that reality in the drawing-room while the ormolu clock quietly ticked beneath the portrait that was false, while a glossy diversion came from a machine. In subtle colours the violence was conveyed, the throat so keenly cut that the head was almost severed. It didn't mean a thing.

Forever the child would remember the flat she'd lived in, the Negresses and the jungle animals, the partition wall. The child would grow into adolescence and womanhood, pinning the fragments together: her mother and her father, victim and predator, truth and illusion. It was too late to change Francis's fate, or Doris's, or the debt-collector's or the dressmaker's. Signor Guzzinati's devotion to tourist women would continue until he was too weak to walk the streets of Pisa; the sin of envy was part of Sister Burkardt by now. The Tytes had suffered all they could, the Pentecostal missionaries were dead. It was the child's story that mattered.

The television screen emptied and was grey again. Julia sat on, trying to prevent herself from slipping further into the introspection she thought she'd finished with. Mistily, a scene gathered in her mind, seeming like a family photograph: an old woman and a child, a middle-aged priest and a middle-aged woman, a spaniel asleep in the sun. Out of all the ugliness her mother had hinted that this end should come and it was almost a miracle that she had, even if the time for miracles had passed.

Julia pulled back the curtains. She unplugged the television set and turned the lights out. Slowly she went upstairs. The end seemed like make-belief again, yet equally it wasn't: Kim Novak wasn't there, nor Doris's dream-come-true, nor Francis as he should have been. A crime of violence didn't gorgeously happen, like a dream or an advertisement. Four people sat ordinarily beneath a tree, cows grazed in the meadows beyond a river.

She washed. She brushed her teeth. She slipped her clothes from her, reflecting that company law and title deeds had failed her already. Her silenced mind would not accept the strictures she imposed; some part of her insisted that she might as well not exist if she ceased to wonder, she couldn't pack God and Francis Tyte away. All she completely knew was that the niceness of her world was not entirely without purpose, the white swan in its niche above the hall door, the roses and japonica of the garden, a plain house made the most of. Henrietta and Katherine were beautiful in their summer dresses, in winter it was pleasant to blaze a fire up.

She put her nightdress on and got into bed, gazing for a while into the darkness before she slept. The child should not have been born but the child was there, her chapped face and plastic-rimmed spectacles. She was there in the garden and the house, while time went on and the seasons unfussily changed. Leaves from the tulip tree floated away on the river, in spring there were mornings of sunshine.

READ MORE IN PENGUIN

In every corner of the world, on every subject under the sun, Penguin represents quality and variety – the very best in publishing today.

For complete information about books available from Penguin – including Puffins, Penguin Classics and Arkana – and how to order them, write to us at the appropriate address below. Please note that for copyright reasons the selection of books varies from country to country.

In the United Kingdom: Please write to *Dept. JC, Penguin Books Ltd, FREEPOST, West Drayton, Middlesex UB7 OBR*

If you have any difficulty in obtaining a title, please send your order with the correct money, plus ten per cent for postage and packaging, to *PO Box No. 11, West Drayton, Middlesex UB7 OBR*

In the United States: Please write to *Penguin USA Inc., 375 Hudson Street, New York, NY 10014*

In Canada: Please write to *Penguin Books Canada Ltd, 10 Alcorn Avenue, Suite 300, Toronto, Ontario M4V 3B2*

In Australia: Please write to *Penguin Books Australia Ltd, 487 Maroondah Highway, Ringwood, Victoria 3134*

In New Zealand: Please write to *Penguin Books (NZ) Ltd,182–190 Wairau Road, Private Bag, Takapuna, Auckland 9*

In India: Please write to *Penguin Books India Pvt Ltd, 706 Eros Apartments, 56 Nehru Place, New Delhi 110 019*

In the Netherlands: Please write to *Penguin Books Netherlands B.V., Keizersgracht 231 NL–1016 DV Amsterdam*

In Germany: Please write to *Penguin Books Deutschland GmbH, Friedrichstrasse 10–12, W–6000 Frankfurt/Main 1*

In Spain: Please write to *Penguin Books S. A., C. San Bernardo 117–6° E–28015 Madrid*

In Italy: Please write to *Penguin Italia s.r.l., Via Felice Casati 20, I–20124 Milano*

In France: Please write to *Penguin France S. A., 17 rue Lejeune, F–31000 Toulouse*

In Japan: Please write to *Penguin Books Japan, Ishikiribashi Building, 2–5–4, Suido, Tokyo 112*

In Greece: Please write to *Penguin Hellas Ltd, Dimocritou 3, GR–106 71 Athens*

In South Africa: Please write to *Longman Penguin Southern Africa (Pty) Ltd, Private Bag X08, Bertsham 2013*

BY THE SAME AUTHOR

The Collected Stories

'The finest living writer of short stories' – John Banville

Published in separate volumes as *The Day We Got Drunk on Cake*, *The Ballroom of Romance*, *Angels at the Ritz*, *Lovers of Their Time*, *Beyond the Pale*, *The News From Ireland* and *Family Sins*, this volume also contains four stories not included in these collections.

The Silence in the Garden

Winner of the *Yorkshire Post* Book of the Year Award

'Subtle, intricate and beautiful ... No-one interested in what fiction can do to illuminate and enrich life should fail to read this book' – Allan Massie in the *Scotsman*

The Boarding House

By selecting carefully, William Wagner Bird filled his boarding house with people that society would never miss – even if it noticed they were around. But then he made a fatal mistake. He died.

Fools of Fortune

Spanning sixty years, William Trevor's tender and beautiful love story has at its centre a dark and violent act which spills over into the mutilated lives of generations to come. 'To my mind William Trevor's best novel and a very fine one' – Graham Greene

Also published

Elizabeth Alone
The Love Department
Mrs Eckdorf in O'Neill's Hotel
The Old Boys
Two Lives
The Children of Dynmouth